TE SS A

COMPANION
TO
OWLS

FOX BOOKS

FOX BOOKS
Companion to Owls
Published by Fox Books
South House, The Old Factory, Bells Lane,
Glemsford, Sudbury, Suffolk CO10 7QA

British Library Cataloguing in Publication Data
A catalogue record for this book is available from
the British Library.

ISBN 978-0-9543627-2-0

Cover design by Mike Hamilton
Printed in Great Britain by
imprint**digital**.net

ACKNOWLEDGEMENTS

Firstly my thanks must go to the Thorney Society for their support. I should single out the Society's secretary Dorothy Halfhide for retaining interest in the book over a period which has turned out to be several years. The little museum in Thorney (run by the Society) has been an excellent resource for me.

When beginning to research the territory of *Companion to Owls* it was not long before I came across Trevor Bevis's booklets about the fens and their history. I would like to thank Trevor both for his encouragement and for his generosity in lending me Samuel Wells' *The History of the Drainage of the Great Level of the Fens called Bedford Level* on an overly long loan.

Thanks too are due to the staff at the Huguenot Library at University College London who helped me to find sources of facts I might not otherwise have come across.

Special thanks too to Eileen Ward and Julie and Kath Lister whose input increased my understanding of epilepsy and its impact on individuals and families.

I have also greatly valued Mike Hamilton's work on the map and family tree as well as his design of the striking cover. And thanks too to Stephen du Sautoy, John Saunders.

Finally, a big thank you to my partner Ralph whose optimism and encouragement just doesn't run out, to my brother Roger and to my children and their families. Each one of them influences my writing.

AUTHOR'S NOTE

When writing this novel I carried out a substantial amount of research into life in the fens in the 17th century. Some of the names of both people and places are ones which really existed or still exist, and I have quoted from real documents. But despite these connections with the past *Companion to Owls* is fiction.

Tessa West has lived in East Anglia all her adult life. She is the author of *The Estuary* and *The Reed Flute*.

For Florence, Bonnie and Jacob

I am the brother of dragons and a companion to owls.
Book of Job Chapter 20 Verse 29

It is a hard question, whether the Sea or the Land floods are the most potent enemies to the Fenns; but this is most certaine, that when the Sea floods and the Land floods meet, as they oftentimes doe, halfe way betwixte the high Lands and the Sea, in that very place like two powerful enemies joyning in one, they doe over-run the Levell, and drowne it from one end unto the other.

A. Burrell, 1642

The King's contract is to make these lands winter ground, that is, to free them from the overflowings of the rivers, so farr as by art can be devised.

I find it the fittest way to divide the whole level into three parts.
1. The one from Glean to Morton's Leame.
2. From Morton's Leame to Bedford River.
3. From Bedford Level southwards, being the remainder of the level.

To drain the lands between Glean and Morton's Leame, all Stowbrook, and so much of the River of Glean as the banks cannot contain, must be turned along Deeping into Welland, and all Welland into Morton's Leame, which lyeth convenient to receive Stow Brook, part of Glean, Welland and Neane, to be carried to Guyhurne, and from thence by Wisbich to the sea, and so those rivers to make but one; whereby the work will be made at lesser charges by far, and also gain a more perfect outfall, because the rivers of Wisbich and Spalding are not sufficient for want of water to keep their channels open as they should be kept, but are interrupted and subject to grow up, by reason of the sand which the sea bringeth in, whereas they ought to be kept open and have their full depths and fall, for the ground to be drayned so far upwards as into or adjoyning to the drowned grounds for the issuing of their downfall.

From A Discourse, *Cornelius Vermuyden 1642*

COMPANION TO OWLS
A novel set in East Anglia

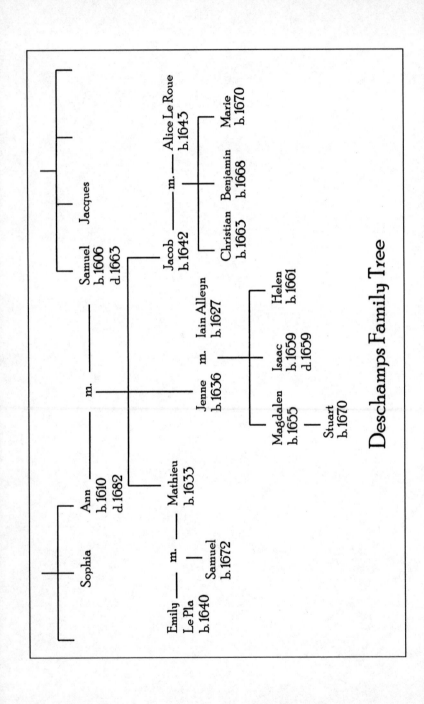

Deschamps Family Tree

PART I

1650

🦎 **September 1650, Morpeth**

The line of five thousand men wavered as it advanced but only broke when someone tried to escape. When that happened a section of it would come undone for a matter of minutes as the person was shot, and then it would re-form. Dejected by a battle they had been confident of winning, the soldiers were being forced to march in the direction they hated most: south.

They coughed and groaned but rarely spoke. They were thinking about what had gone wrong, about their fellow soldiers who had been killed, about their injuries, their homes and the way their lives were turning out. They wanted to stop and they wanted to eat.

They reached Morpeth on the second night and were herded into a walled field. In near darkness they fell on the crop of cabbages, first sucking the water caught within the leaves, then tearing them out of the ground, then devouring them even to chewing the roots.

Many died from typhoid as they marched on. In Newcastle the ailing survivors were led into a church. When morning came the bodies on the stone floor were abandoned. The ones who continued south were closer to death than to their homes in Dunbar. They cursed their own General Leslie almost as much as Cromwell.

They were given shelter in Durham Cathedral where their guards stole the water, food and coal which had been provided by the authorities for them. The prisoners resorted to setting fire to whatever was combustible: benches, the altar, vestments,

13

plaques, wooden railings. They despised England and the English and their determination to return to Scotland increased with the intensity of the conflagration.

1651

⌖ October 1651, London

A year after the Battle of Dunbar only a tenth of the original five thousand Scottish prisoners-of-war were still alive and some of these were sent to the New World as indentured servants. Already in poor shape they were shipped off to Barbados, Virginia and Massachusetts in the company of convicts, not knowing how dangerous their journey would be nor that they would face a situation little better than slavery.

The hundreds who remained in England were held in York and at Tote Hill Fields. They proved to be an inconvenience until some of the Adventurers investing in the drainage works had the pragmatic idea of using them to work in the fens. It was acknowledged that this would not be as simple as it sounded. The prisoners-of-war would have to be willing to be so employed and they would have to be paid. But the success of the drainage project was paramount to the Adventurers, so, in the autumn of 1651, enquiries were set in motion as to the viability of this plan and the following correspondence was composed:

11th Octr. 1651.

The Companie, havinge lately recd. an order from the Counsell of State for imployinge of the private Scotch prisoners in the workes of drayning, did order that a letter be written unto My Lord Chiefe Justice Saint John as followeth:

May it please yr. Lordshipp

The greatest part of all our tyme this weeke and the last hath been spent in contriving which way wee might best dispose of such of the Scotch prisoners in Totehill Fields as were able to worke, and the State should please to entrust us with, for preventing theire runninge away, or acting any thinge prejudiciall to the present Government, and keeping them at worke: To that end, wee did resolve and propose to become petitioners to his excellencye the lord generall, that hee would bee pleased to appoint some person in nature of a provost Marshall to whome the Companie would allow a reasonable salary for his service to take care of them, and prevent theire straglinge and punish the offender; and wee intend to have clothed them all in a white habite, or some other colour, with cappes of a different colour; whereby they might bee known from Englishmen; and lay a charge upon our overseers and officers in the workes, if any of them were absent from theire workes, or did oppose the established government, to give present notice to the provost Marshall, who had the charge of them, to apprehend and punish them as the state or his excellencye should please to directe. And wee did hope that they might have byn brought into so good discipline as, receiving a fitting reward from us for theire labour; they might have had just cause to blesse God for the parliamentary mercy to them.

This letter had a successful outcome. Four days later one hundred and sixty-six Scottish prisoners-of-war were allocated to *"The use and service of the Companie of Adventurers for dreyninge of the Great Levell of the Fennes"*.

1652

❧ Afternoon, 5th January 1652, Thorney

Jenne looked towards the frozen Upper Knarr Fen and the wide level beyond. An expanse of white stretched for miles until it met a wall of sky the colour of pale peat. The world seemed upside down. Usually, the earth was dark and the huge sky goose-grey, but today it was the other way round. Instead of birds making patterns against the sky, figures were moving over the ice.

She hurried down the slight slope and raced across the hard surface of the usually impassable ditches. The wind had bent the sedge and she leaped over the frozen tufts feeling as if she could take the whole of the fen in her stride. When she reached the ice she found a place to sit and tie the skates to her boots. Then she turned back for a moment towards the Abbey Church. The towers were familiar but the oaks which almost hid them were covered in snow and made the scene look different from usual. Somewhere beyond and out of sight was her home. And now Mathieu was careering down in her tracks with Jacob skidding after him.

Not wanting to waste a minute she pushed herself out on to the ice with her sticks and headed towards the ring of her friends. She wanted to skate across the whole land – as far as the Port of Lynne or even Boston – and for weeks she had been praying for a fierce frost, for the crack and creak of ice.

Last week, when she told her mother she loved skating more than anything else, Maman had said, "That's what my sister Sophia used to say. She wanted to skate all round Zeeland."

"And did she?"

"No."

"Why not?"

Maman continued stirring. "She was ill, wasn't she? My parents hardly let her out of their sight."

"Would you let me skate a long way? I'm not ill."

Her mother rested the spoon on the edge of the pot. "No, I wouldn't. What might become of you if the ice were to break?"

"Mathieu's the best skater in Thorney. He'd look after me."

"Mathieu has to study and work."

"But he can't work when everything is frozen, can he? No one works when it's like this."

Maman unhooked the meat from the spit. "Take the platters to the table, please."

"I wish it was winter all the time. Then I could skate every day."

Maman smiled. "That's what Sophia used to say."

Now she was lying on the ice, crumpled up with laughter. Mathieu came swishing up and stopped sharply beside her.

"You told me you could stay on your feet now, but you can't have managed more than a minute or two!"

"I did yesterday," said Jenne, holding out a hand. "Help me up, will you?"

Mathieu hauled her up and steadied her. Jenne started to

brush the snow off her cloak, then pulled her skirt above her ankles to inspect her feet.

"No wonder I fell – the straps have become loose. I'll have to tie them again."

She undid the skate from her left boot and hobbled to the edge of the dyke with Mathieu and Jacob skating slowly on either side of her.

"If these skates would stay put I'd be a much better skater."

"Even if you become good," Mathieu replied, "You'll never be as good as me."

The three of them sat down in a row on the bank. It felt as solid as stone.

"Mathieu, I'm going to skate to Peterborough. Do you want to come?" asked Jenne.

He turned to her in surprise. "It's miles."

She tugged at the straps. "I know. That's why I want to go."

"Père and Mère wouldn't allow it."

"They won't know. Jacob, you won't tell them, will you?"

Jacob studied his skates. Then he said, "I heard them talking about you. They don't think you should race around so much."

"What do they mean? I don't race around, not unless I'm with you two. But you mustn't tell them about me skating to Peterborough. Don't even say Mathieu might go."

Jacob went on looking at his feet.

"Come on," said Jenne, "It'll be all right. And you can come with us next year, when you're eleven. I tell you what, I'll bring in all your turves tomorrow and the next day. You won't have to do any for two days. How's that?"

Jacob nodded without looking at her.

Suddenly a pair of small boys slid towards them and into them and for a moment there was a skirmish of legs, arms and sticks.

"We've found a pike!"

"Under the ice!"

Jacob sped off with them, pushing himself along with the two thin poles he had cut from an elder tree. The three of them headed to where a larger gang was gesturing and pointing towards the ice.

"Do you think he'll tell Papa?" asked Jenne.

"No, but you shouldn't have said anything when he was here." Mathieu pushed his hands under his armpits to warm them. "And you shouldn't bribe him. You're spoiling him."

"I wanted to be sure. Papa wouldn't allow it if he found out. So, shall we go on Wednesday?"

"I haven't agreed yet, have I?"

More shouts broke out and they watched the boys in front of them turn like an untidy flock of birds and make their way over to the far side.

Jenne jabbed one of her sticks into the snow. "I've an idea. We won't go to Peterborough. I'll tell Jacob we're not going there after all." She paused. "Let's think of somewhere else, but it's got to be somewhere special."

She looked expectantly at Mathieu, but he was gazing out across the fen. Three deer were trying to run, but the snow almost reached the belly of the smallest one and they were making slow progress.

Jenne got to her feet and made ready to launch herself on to the ice again.

Mathieu remained sitting down, but suddenly he called after her, "I know. Whittlesey. I've always wanted to go to Whittlesey Meer."

ᗡ Evening, 5th January 1652, Thorney

"Seigneur, auquel gist la plénitude de tous biens, we give thanks for this meal. We beseech Thee to forgive us for our transgressions, and those transgressions committed by our brethren that cause them to suffer persecution. May our bodies be sustained by this meal as our souls are sustained by Thy spirit. Amen."

Jenne waited in silence while her father said grace, pulled out his chair and sat down, followed by her mother. When he nodded at Jenne and the boys they too scraped their chairs across the floor and settled at the table. The flames of the two lamps flickered until the air was still again. Papa took the knife and began to carve. Jenne watched him grip the leg of the goose firmly before he cut through the skin and caused the fat to flow over his fingers.

Having spent an afternoon on the ice she could hardly wait, but at last her father nodded again and they began to eat.

"Merci beaucoup, Ann."

"Merci beaucoup, Mère."

There was bread too, and Jenne dipped it in the fat and savoured it. She felt tired and content.

"So, what's the ice like?" asked Papa.

"It's thick, but not solid," replied Mathieu.

"We saw a pike underneath. It must have swum out of the dyke and into the deep flood water on the fen. We tried to chase it up one end but it kept getting away," said Jacob. "We could see it swimming through the reeds but then it dug itself into the mud."

"If you made a hole you might get it with a rod and line, but be careful. Don't go where the ice might be weak unless Mathieu's with you."

Jenne watched Jacob tip up his plate and dip his bread in the juice. For a moment she felt unkind about what she had said to him earlier. Perhaps they should take him to Whittlesey? No. She was going to suggest to Mathieu that he invite his friend Piere Roo to join them because if he agreed Mathieu would have no hesitation in going, and if Piere came, they wouldn't want Jacob. Anyway, it would be too far for him.

"Père," asked Mathieu, "When you've finished the Twenty Foot, the fresh water won't spill over into the fen in winter any more, will it?"

Jenne groaned a silent groan. Now they would get another lecture about drainage.

"That's right. That's the plan." Her father put down the bone from which he was pulling off meat. "But everything else has to work too in order for the freshwater to make its way directly into the German Ocean. If the rivers haven't been thoroughly scoured or the banks not properly constructed the floods will break through yet again." He wiped his mouth and hands with a cloth. "We are late in completing the work and tired of waiting for fields of wheat and cattle to replace eels and fish. And the money's running out."

"Samuel, there's no danger of you not being paid, is there?" asked Mère.

Père started to repeat what he'd been telling them for months.

"No. It's lucky for me I once went to Sint Maartensdijk, Vermuyden's home town. He's always remembered that, thinks of me as a Zeeland brother although I was only there for a matter of days. But even without my wages from him, the farmland I've rented will bring in a profit next year."

He stood to cut more meat making the lamplight waver again as Mathieu said, "Jenne, do you realise that when Knarr Fen is drained it won't freeze?"

Jenne sat up straight, concerned. "So where will we skate?"

Maman laughed. "There's dozens of dykes and rivers, aren't there?"

"Yes, but I don't want to go in straight lines."

She stopped herself from saying more. What she wanted was land that was almost all ice. Land where you could go anywhere and not have to take a boat, or find a bridge, or risk an unsteady plank. Life was so much better when the fens froze, even though the wind cut you and you had to bring in several loads of turves each day before you were allowed out. The thing about winter was that you could trust the land – you could place your foot anywhere on the marsh and not sink in. But, as Père was reminding them for the hundredth time, the old water courses had to be improved and new ones dug.

Then Mathieu asked, "Why is the draining taking longer than expected?"

Why did he keep asking these questions when he knew the answers? Was he trying to impress Père? He knew full well it was because there was a shortage of labour.

"Shortage of labour is the main reason, but we had all that sabotage to contend with a few years ago. That lost us the best part of a summer, and so not everything was finished when it should have been."

"Why doesn't Vermuyden hire more workers?"

Jenne gave an inward sigh. Her mother was asking her father this only because she knew he worried about work and felt better when he talked about it. Surely they could talk about something else? Surely there was more to life than drainage, or drainage and God? But her father was in full flow.

"Because there aren't any more workers. Most of us are already here. The French who remained at Sandtoft would rather put up with what they know than risk moving again. Our people have been through too much for too long. And few of the fenmen want to work for Vermuyden although he pays well. The ignorant ones hate the idea of drainage, and the few who see the sense of it never dare say so aloud."

"So when will it all be finished?"

"I don't know. There are five or six big enterprises being carried out, and our work on the Twenty Foot is one of the smaller ones. We'll get ours finished as soon as the thaw comes, but although the Hundred Foot is virtually done, the two sluices need much more work."

Jenne willed Mathieu not to ask any more questions but he immediately asked, "Could it take years?"

If it did, at least there would be plenty of winters ahead for skating across the fen.

"And couldn't workers be brought in from somewhere else?"

"They're thinking about that, but the problem is ... from where? God has helped our people to come here, and, thanks to Him, we're safe now. But who'd choose to live in this wet land where there is so much disease?" Papa pushed his chair back from the table. "I don't know where we will find more men, but God will provide them."

Jenne, though well aware of why the land needed to be drained, was dreaming again and wanting the fens to be covered with ice every winter, like today. If that happened, and if her skates were attached firmly to the bottom of her boots, she'd be able to sail across the ice like a swift across the sky.

As they cleared the table her mother reminded her to make sure her best clothes were ready for church in the morning.

She'd forgotten the next day was Sunday. Church meant no skating until the afternoon. Thinking about this made her forget to feed Hibou-Bou, but Jacob remembered and they took turns to offer him small scraps of meat which he snatched eagerly with his hooked, black beak.

On Sunday morning Jenne opened the chest and took out her favourite shift and a clean white bonnet. By quarter to ten they were setting off along the causeway.

During the night it had snowed again and it was impossible to tell where the sides of the track were. But though someone would stumble into a drift from time to time there were no complaints. In fact, as more families joined the little procession, Jenne decided that the snowy weather wakened everyone up and brought out the best in them. Maman was holding on to Papa's arm and almost giggling. Papa was laughing too and turning a blind eye to Jacob who was chasing a boy with a snowball. The sky was bright white. The usually unremarkable walk was transformed into a special occasion.

Now they turned left. The track here was easier to walk along because the English had already made a path when they attended Mass that morning.

"Look up at the towers," said Père, "Grâce à Dieu. Aren't they magnificent today?"

The towers and the stone front were covered with ice crystals and gleamed as if they were already lit by the evening sun. Jenne felt a momentary wash of dizziness from the brightness and had to close her eyes. As she entered the Abbey Church she read, as she always read, the date by the porch. She often thought about this date because her father had once told her that her life had begun in Sandtoft at the same time as the Abbey Church was being restored. He said men would have been shoving and levering slabs of stone while she was learning to walk and talk and that someone – she often wondered who – had carefully carved those four numbers: 1, 6, 3 and 8, not knowing that she, Jenne, was two years old and would one day live in Thorney and see his work.

Inside the Abbey Church families were moving to their usual places. Only last week Jacob had wondered if the family stood on exactly the same flagstones each Sunday. Perhaps he was right. She looked down at the floor and saw it was already covered in water from the snow melting off people's shoes even though they had left their pattens in the porch. She had noticed Susannah

Wantie and Isabel Guoy going to the wall for the last month or two because they were pregnant. They sat with the old people.

Jenne was looking out for the Roo family who would be late if they did not arrive soon. She thought of their farm in French Drove and realised they would face a difficult walk to reach the Abbey Church that morning. It would probably take them the best part of an hour, so perhaps they would not see Piere until the afternoon.

The murmuring lessened and people settled as the priest began to chant the first of the verses everyone knew so well: "*O Souverain pasteur et maistre...*"

Quiet voices joined in and gradually that warm feeling of being together and enclosed and safe in this huge church spread amongst them. It was like being in another sort of home: they were listening to French, praying in French, thinking in French. On Sundays they spoke only French all day. On Sundays they all felt part of this congregation, this bigger family, and it was good. Now the prayers changed to those for the people who had died or been tortured in the St Bartholomew's Day Massacre in France. Then there was a pause before the priest began his sermon. This was the long part of the service but by now Jenne had learned how to adjust her weight from one side to the other, how to shuffle her feet quietly. She looked around and started to silently name those near to her: Marie and Paul Tafin, Phillipe and Danielle Frouchart and their sleeping baby, Samuel Massingarbe whose wife died recently, the Du Quenes, the De La Noys.

She heard the church door opening and turned to see if it was the Roos. It was. There was Piere's father, leading his family in. Piere was the last to enter. She caught Mathieu's eye and he nodded a nod which confirmed he was going to ask him to go to Whittlesey. They had already talked about how they would go across Knarr Fen and down to Thorney Dyke heading south all the way until they reached the Nene.

The Nene. She had never been so far from home, except when she was little and her parents had brought her and her brothers down from Sandtoft in Yorkshire, way beyond Holland, even beyond Lincoln. But Mathieu – lucky Mathieu – had already been off in different directions. Their Uncle Jacques had taken him to Wisbech and to Chatteris, and had recently promised to take him to Ely where there was a cathedral on a hill. She could imagine its towers reaching into the clouds.

But this very week she herself would be skating on Whittlesey Meer. What could be better than that?

The hem of Jenne's shift and her boots were wet and cold, and a shiver went through her. She looked at the floor again. Strangely, instead of the water settling into the uneven dips in the stones, it was rising up in wavelets, as if wind were pushing across a pond. It shouldn't be like that but she couldn't make it lie flat. Suddenly she couldn't breathe, and she reached out to grab Papa but her back arched away from him and her hand would not do what she wanted. And now the roof and pillars were falling in and Jacob was looking down at her, his hair flopping forward round his face. She smelt blackberries as the back of her head hit the flagstones.

ᗶ 9th January 1652, Earith

The prisoners-of-war had little to do while the land and water were frozen. Some tried to escape, taking advantage of the fact that their suits – even though they were no longer white – gave some measure of camouflage in the snowy landscape. A few succeeded but more were shot by their guards who were fined for the loss of any prisoner who went beyond the Trent but not for any who died or they killed in the course of an attempted escape. Most of the Scotchmen just sat the winter out, alternately relieved and angered by their enforced idleness. They occupied themselves playing cards and trying to keep warm, and wishing away the weeks of winter still to come.

By the beginning of January they were hungry. As they waited for the thaw they cooked birds which had died from cold, breaking open and sucking the bones when they had eaten every particle of flesh. Occasionally they managed to catch fish. And some increased their contact with the guards or local people in order to gain food or warmth.

Iain Alleyn was baling snow out of a boat with a shovel scoop. He earned extra rations by ensuring the guards' boat did not freeze into the river and become damaged by the pressure of ice.

Working for his captors kept his belly full, and, if he was lucky, enabled him to pick up useful news.

That morning he had learned two things. Firstly, the Company of Adventurers was to divide the prisoners into lots and allocate them to particular places. Secondly, more shirts, suits and stockings were on their way. The information about the lots concerned him greatly for it was likely to make a significant difference to his life. And more clothing was good news for he would find a way of obtaining extra clothes to use himself or to sell.

Once he'd shovelled all the snow he got out on to the shore and carefully hacked at the ice with the tip of his spade. He grasped the gunwale and rocked it to check the boat was completely free, then carried the spade and scoop back to the guards' quarters and leaned them against the wall with other tools inside the doorway. A month ago he had cleaned and dressed a cut on the fetlock of the sergeant's horse. It healed up at once and since then he had received better treatment. The men on duty used to count out the tools as they issued them and then count them back in but now he was allowed to take what he needed when he needed it.

He trudged back in a brief squall of hailstones to the farm out-house where he lodged. He was aggrieved at the thought of moving from Earith just as he was getting to know the lie of the land and be trusted by two or three guards.

Murdo was poking the fire.

"How many times must I tell you? Don't poke at turves. A turf fire is not like a wood fire."

Murdo leaned back on his heels. He pointed into a corner.

Alleyn took a step further into the gloom and saw a good sized pike lying on the ground. "Where did you get it?"

"From the Low Lode. It's sheltered there and beginning to thaw. It was just a question of patience. That's why I'm trying to get this damned fire to produce more heat."

Alleyn grunted his approval. From under his jacket he pulled out bread and threw it to Murdo. Then he shrugged off his outer cloak and shook the moisture off it. He sat down on a pile of turves to take his boots off. He picked one up and inspected its sole. They might last another month, if he was lucky. He examined the second one. Yes, perhaps even until Easter. He put them back on.

Murdo, satisfied with the fire, stuck a stick of peeled willow through the pike and held it over the heat while cursing the smoke which made his eyes water. As the smell began to heighten their appetites Alleyn told him about how the prisoners were to be divided into lots.

By the time they had eaten the fish and bread they were warm and planning ways of finding out which were the best places to be sent to. It felt like progress.

Murdo laid a few more turves on the fire before falling asleep.

Alleyn settled himself on his pile of damp sedge weighing up who he could rely on to help him obtain and dispose of the new clothes.

He regretted boots were not going to be available for they were by far the most useful commodity. In this fenny place a pair of new boots could save a man's feet and thus perhaps his life. He went to sleep wondering what a suit would be worth. And what about shirts and stockings? Although bartering was sometimes clumsy, it certainly improved his quality of life.

✒ 10th January 1652, Thorney

Jenne was sitting up in bed.

Her mother went over to the window. "It's still snowing."

"Please let me get up. I've been here for nearly four days."

Maman came back and took her hand. "Not until tomorrow. Papa is collecting some mistletoe and this afternoon I'm going to make some medicine from it. Eva says it'll help you a great deal."

"But I'm not ill any more."

"Yes, but you've been exhausted – you've slept for hours. How's your mouth feeling now?"

Jenne ran her tongue round the inside of her left cheek. "Still sore."

"And your wrist?"

"It hurts. I'm using my left hand to brush my hair."

"Let me do that, ma petite," Maman picked up the brush and began to brush Jenne's hair.

26

"Why did it happen? Why did I fall down?"

"You're recovering now."

"Something must be wrong with me. Why can't I remember what happened?"

Maman handed Jenne the hairclips and stood up and straightened the bedcovers. "What matters is that you're almost yourself again."

Jenne traced the pattern on the blanket with her finger. Had she not been herself? Can you not be yourself? Surely if you are not yourself you are mad? Or perhaps dead.

"Might I die?"

Her mother squeezed her hand. "You're not going to die."

Quite a few people had died young: the Milleville boy, Anna's cousin, Maman's sister Sophia.

"Of course you're not going to die. The mistletoe medicine will help make you better."

What would it be like to die? To be dead? If you were dead, you might not know you were dead. You might not feel anything and just find yourself in heaven. But falling in the Abbey Church had felt different to everything. So, if you had that sort of a fall, were you dead until you woke up?

"Can someone be half-dead?"

"God will protect us. God always sends help when it is needed." Maman walked over to the window, her hands to her face.

Jenne looked at her mother and realised, guiltily, that she had made her cry. But what she had said was clearly not true, or at least, not true all the time. If God protected people why had He allowed the Massacre of St Bartholomew's Day? Or the early death of the aunt she should have had? And why would He have let those English people in Sandtoft destroy the Huguenots' dykework and burn down their homes?

Maman turned. "I can see Mathieu and Piere going down the drove. They're carrying brooms. They must be going to sweep the ice, so perhaps in a day or two you'll be able to have a little walk on the fen."

A little walk? How could anyone, *why* would anyone, 'have a little walk' on ice if they could skate? Jenne felt a sudden surge of

27

energy and pleaded, "Please let me go out tomorrow. It might thaw in a day or two, and then I'll have missed it."

"We'll see when you've had some of the medicine. You rest now, and as soon as Mathieu comes back I'll get him to come and see you. He'll cheer you up."

They had gone to Whittlesey without her. They had found, once they reached the village of Whittlesey, that they had to go still further to reach the Meer. They had kept their skates on nearly all the way, only taking them off on their way to the next frozen dyke when they had to cross the fens made featureless by snow. They were amazed by the Meer itself. It was huge, frozen as solid as Barnack stone, with people skating where the snow had been swept or blown away. They even found an island. Both well used to being on ice, Mathieu and Piere had skated and skidded and snowballed until the westerly sun turned the ice pink, and they hurried back with dusk falling and their hunger growing.

"Why didn't you wait until I could come?" complained Jenne. "It wasn't fair to go without me."

"You're ill."

"You could have waited."

"Jenne, you couldn't have come. You still keep falling asleep. What would Mère and Père have said if anything had happened?"

"But it was my idea."

"We'll go again next year."

Jenne swirled the cup of thick greenish liquid she was supposed to be drinking. Her mother had told her that though the berries of mistletoe were poisonous, the leaves were good.

"Did Piere know why I wasn't there?"

"Everybody knows. Everyone's worried about you."

Maman called from the other room, "Jenne, have you drunk that medicine yet?"

It was foul. Surely this brew must make people worse, not better. It looked as if it were something a witch would drink. She held the cup out to Mathieu while she called back, "Not quite," then whispered urgently, "Tip it away for me, will you? I'll be sick if I drink it. Please."

Mathieu refused to take the cup.

"I hate it. I'll get better without it."

28

"You ought to take it. Mère and Père are trying to help you."

"I don't need helping."

"You seem fine now, but perhaps something's wrong, badly wrong. Mère was crying this morning. No one knows why you fell like that. That's the problem, don't you see?"

Jenne looked at him. "Do *you* think it's something serious?"

"I don't know. How could I know? I've never seen anyone fall like you did, and writhe on the ground, and tighten up so tightly we couldn't prise your hand from Père's cloak so he had to take it off."

They fell into silence.

"I've got to go now. I'll tell Jacob to come and see you. He wants you to help him with his lessons."

Jenne began to spoon a little of the medicine into her mouth. She made herself take a tiny amount and then drank a couple of mouthfuls of water to take the taste away. Gradually she got through it, then, feeling exhausted, settled down in bed.

Was it possible she might die? That she, Jenne Deschamps, might die? Surely you couldn't just die suddenly, couldn't just stop being alive? There must be a reason.

Jacob put his head round the door.

"Can you help me do my arithmetic? I'm muddled up."

"Bring it over here." She pulled herself to a sitting position and looked at his slate. He sat on the side of her bed, picking up and sniffing various bottles and potions.

"These aren't sums!"

Jacob leaned over to see what Jenne was looking at. "Oh no, those are just my drawings of rabbits. The sums are on the other side."

"They're rather good. I like this one."

"Its ears are wrong. Don't you think this one's better?"

They looked at them together for a few moments until Jenne turned the slate over.

"I can see what you've done. Look, you've put these in the wrong column. Give me the chalk and I'll show you how to set it out." Jenne rubbed out part of Jacob's work. "Aie, even doing that hurts my wrist." She wrote the figures differently and showed him.

"Oh yes, that's how we're supposed to do it. I remember now. Thanks." He picked up her hairbrush and looking glass. "When are you going to get up?"

"Tomorrow, I hope."

Jacob started to brush his hair.

"Robert's not to come here any more."

"Why ever not?"

"Because you've got the falling sickness."

"The *what* sickness?"

"The falling sickness. That's what made you fall and roll about and be strange."

Jenne stared at him.

"And I heard Eleanor's mother talking to Maman. She said you must have done something wrong." He plucked at the seam of the blanket. "Have you? If you haven't, perhaps you went like that for just *thinking* about doing something wrong."

Jenne picked at the chalk with her fingernail.

"Jacob," called Papa, "Come and finish clearing the path, please. You should have done it by now."

Jacob gave his hair a final brush. "I'll come and see you after I've fed Hibou-Bou."

When he had gone Jenne picked up the looking glass and examined her face. She got out of bed and went to the window where the light was better. She searched for evidence of something different. Surely she'd be able to see something?

"Come back to bed at once, Jenne. This is no time to be thinking about new hairstyles."

Jenne turned to see her mother hurrying across the room towards her. She let herself be led back to bed and was asleep within minutes.

🦎 11th January 1652, near the Nene

The way they were walking could not be described as marching. Rather, they proceeded in twos or in single file along a line of mud which counted as a track. Land stretched out to their left and right divided by watercourses which glinted in some places like rapiers and in others like eels. The foot guards were jealous of those on horseback and joined in the prisoners' complaints about the mud, the inadequacy of their boots, the slow pace they were reduced to, the foulness of these flatlands and the certain knowledge that the place where they would sleep would be a boggy, dank hole.

The line came to an uneven halt when they reached a river where the only way across was by boat. Everyone had to be ferried with the baggage, which meant a longish wait. They were allowed to break ranks for an hour. Alleyn walked to the riverbank, bent down, cupped his hands and drank. The water looked and tasted bad. He despised this brown fenny water which smelled of rotting vegetables and tried to recall the burn near his home which wriggled in and out of the heather like a bright thread in dark fabric.

As he returned, he saw an officer studying something he thought might be a map. The officer had called a guard over and was showing him the paper and pointing into the distance.

Alleyn loitered nearby until the officer dismissed the man and rode off. Then he approached the guard but was waved away with an impatient gesture. He waited while the man turned from him, strolled to the bank, pissed in the river and ambled back towards him.

Alleyn asked, "What river is this?"

"The Nene."

"And where are we aiming for?"

The guard snorted into his hand and shook the snot off near Alleyn's feet. "The other side."

Within two hours the convoy had crossed and was on the move again.

The most substantial buildings they passed were shacks partly sunk into the ground and roofed with reed. Some were half held up by stilts. There was little evidence of agriculture but once they came across a man in a boat leading a horse almost up to its withers in water. It was a place God intended more for fish and wildfowl than people. The men and women they met did not speak to them but just stood back and let the prisoners file past. Accompanied by the suck and squelch of boots in mud these were expressionless encounters for both sides.

The land had no heart. For hour after hour they seemed to be in the same place with the same ditches, the same hovels, the same sky. Apart from the sun, direction was offered by the new waterways or the old rivers they would be straightening. It was clear to see why this work needed doing, for all around there was as much water as land. The numerous bridges, boats, planks and poles they saw were testimony to the difficulty of living in and travelling through the fens.

As the day wore on a rumour ran through the line that they would soon reach their destination. They picked up a little speed and began to scan the uninterrupted horizon for signs of a town or a village. Even a farm would do.

But when they finally reached darkness and were ordered to halt they were nowhere. They waited for their rations resenting the fact that they had to pull apart the only building – it was little more than a shack – for the guards to burn. They were told that those who lived in the fens burned either peat or dried cattle dung, but as they were not near any habitation neither of these fuels was available. Unable to make fires they fell asleep wrapped in damp blankets hoping to dream of when they were boys running free in the Lammermuir Hills.

Alleyn studied one of the widest skies he had ever seen. He thought about this life he was living and of the other lives he might have had. He thanked the stars that at least he had not been born in this place.

☙ 13th January 1652, Thorney

The doctor had entered the room reciting the prayer for the sick: *"O Seigneur, Dieu tout puissant éternel et plein de grand bénignité…"* then spent some minutes getting Jenne to describe how she had felt before she fell. All she could say was that she did not remember anything at all from that Sunday morning. He examined her right wrist which had been trodden on in church and the inside of her mouth where she had bitten her cheek. Then he went out to her parents but now they were all coming back in. She crossed her fingers beneath the covers.

They stood in a row by her bedside. The doctor announced that he had known other people to fall as she had done, and there were various reasons as to why this happened. For some, they had been like that since early childhood. For others, it seemed to be connected to their diet and digestion. In other cases there was some malady of the blood, perhaps. For still others, it was possibly the result of an injury. And he could not discount the fact that it could be a mixture of some of these causes.

He promised another medicine and said Jenne should stay in bed for three more days, and then get up but not go out of doors for a further three days. After that, he thought it likely she would be well. And if she did not have a fit in the next six months, he was sure she would never have one again.

A fit. Is that what she had had? She had never heard of a fit before.

Her mother led the way out, followed by the men. They sat down in the far room and continued to talk in low voices. Jenne got out of bed and went to the door but could not hear what was said.

It was wonderful he had not said it was the falling sickness nor that it had happened because she had done something wrong. But even a fit, whatever that was, had been frightening – it had made her fall and become unconscious and then wake up confused and having hurt herself. It seemed surprising she had become her ordinary self again after all that. But the thought of other fits lying in store was terrible. She feared she would go mad if she let herself think about that.

She walked over to the window. The snow had melted from the trees and the track leading past their house was back to its usual mud, though snow lay in the ditches. Birds had been singing all morning. To her right, the rump of the doctor's horse went in and out of view as it fidgeted where it was tied to the rail and somehow that made it feel as if things were getting back to normal.

And there came the doctor, walking towards his horse with Papa. She managed to be back in bed just before her mother came in.

"Good! Your colour is coming back. Don't you feel better now the doctor has been?"

"But did he say why it happened to *me*?"

"The good thing is he says you're getting better. You'll be up and about in a few days. Just do as he says, Jenne. You're to go on taking the mistletoe medicine as well as the one he will send us, and you must continue to rest."

Papa came in. "God is looking after us. We must give thanks for your return to good health. Let us pray now."

Jenne, still in bed, put her hands together and looked at the bent heads of her kneeling parents. She noticed the neat creases in her mother's bonnet and the place where her father's hair was thinning.

"Notre bon père tout puissant, We thank Thee for protecting our daughter Jenne. We beg forgiveness for those sins we have committed which have led Thee to be displeased with us. We recognise our unworthiness but beseech Thee to grant us Thy clemency and grace. Amen."

She had heard the words "sins" and "unworthiness" thousands of times, but had never paid them attention until today.

Her parents stood up.

"That's better. Now, Ann, didn't you tell me you had saved a treat for Jenne?"

Maman hurried out of the room and returned with a little pastry. "The boys asked me to make it for you."

"Lucky girl! If my mother had baked me a cake when I was ill, my brothers would have stolen it!"

Jenne thanked her mother and placed the pastry on the bedcover.

"Well," said Papa, "Aren't you going to eat it?"

She bit off a corner and began to eat slowly.

"Good. Now, I must be off to the meeting about the dyke-reeve election."

6th February 1652, in the fens

A thick haar was hanging in the air when the men woke. They were ordered to stay where they were and wait for bread and, to their amazement, it was produced within the hour. It was up to the leader of each gang of prisoners to divide the loaves into shares. In most groups no one questioned the leader's authority: each prisoner accepted what he was given and things seemed better as the bread filled them and the haar began to soften.

But a scuffle broke out in one gang and turned into a fight within moments. One guard clouted two prisoners with a bar and another ran at one with a sword. Immediately the men sitting nearby jumped to their feet and backed off while those who were further away closed in to see what was going on. Orders were shouted and within minutes the prisoners were again under control. The men laughed about the incident except for those who were to be punished and the one who had been slashed. No one complained that the setting off would be delayed further while a head count was carried out.

The prisoner who had been cut, Stuart Macpherson, was only just seventeen, one of the younger soldiers in General Leslie's army. Someone had hauled him into a tent and shoved a cloth against his chest to stop the bleeding. He was not expected to live.

After a count and a recount it became clear that two men were missing. It was assumed they had deliberately caused the fight to take advantage of the haar. Some prisoners considered them heroes and wished them godspeed, others cursed their own bad luck and envied them. But when guards armed with muskets were sent out to search, the common desire was for their horses to sink into the mire of the marshland.

All in all, these events livened up the morning and raised the prisoners' spirits.

By midday, Macpherson was almost unconscious and his breath had become quick and light. When the guards returned empty-handed, the captain went to have a look at him.

"The loss of two prisoners is expensive," he said to his second-in-command. "I can't afford to let this one die. Find someone who can treat these wounds."

When Alleyn was brought the captain asked why he had been sent a prisoner and not a guard.

"Because he once mended a man's arm."

The captain gestured for Alleyn to attend to Macpherson. "Do what you can."

Alleyn replied quietly, "It would have been better if he had had help earlier."

"Do what you can. If he lives, I'll see you are rewarded."

Then he left, and Alleyn bent over Macpherson and removed the cloth. He slowly undid the outer jerkin. Underneath, the shirt was torn and stuck to his chest. He gently tried to ease it from a ragged flap of skin which had been half-sliced away by the sword blade. He could see at once that though the wound was not deep it had left nearly two hand spans of flesh exposed.

He looked up at the waiting guard. "Get me some alcohol and a large blanket."

The man stared at him, angry and humiliated at being given an order by a prisoner.

"And I need water – the cleanest you can find. And a tent, or even part of a tent."

The man left and Alleyn felt for Macpherson's pulse. It was still there. Waving the mosquitoes away he began to talk to him quietly.

When the guard returned he found Alleyn murmuring in an odd up-and-down way. It took a minute for him to realise that what he was hearing was almost a song.

Alleyn used the water to soak the fabric away from where it was sticking. The surface of the open flesh was turning dark which meant the blood was coagulating. He regretted that there was hardly one green plant here at this time of year, and anyway he did not know whether the herbs he needed would grow in such wet ground. He poured a little alcohol carefully over the wound. With the guard's help he lifted Macpherson and laid him on a torn tent. Then he wrapped a blanket round him and listened again to his breathing.

"I will stay with him. You need not remain here."

The guard did not move.

"Do as you wish, but you can see he is in no state to escape, and I will watch him."

The guard took a step, hesitated, then went out.

❧ 11th March 1652, Thorney

It was more than two months since Jenne had had her fall and life was almost back to normal.

Her mother had just told her to stay at home instead of accompanying her on a visit. "You'll be bored – I might be there for two hours. It is better that you stay close by the fire."

When she had gone Jenne and Jacob decided to escape on to the fen. Even though the warmth of the sun was beginning to be felt Jenne did as her mother would have wanted and put on her thickest shift. She had been forbidden to go near the water's edge and objected to this bitterly, saying that to do so was impossible in Thorney.

"Just stay up here, on the island," her father had said. "There's no need to go down by the water."

"But I *like* going down there."

"Please do not argue. I have quite enough to think about without that. I repeat, you are not to go near any deep water or across any bridges."

"You worry about me *so much*. I won't fall in."

Then Maman said, "You remember my sister Sophia was ill? Well, she sometimes had fits – not quite like yours – but she lost consciousness and her arms and legs jerked as yours did. And one day she had a fit by some water and fell in. She drowned and died when she was only twenty years old."

Jenne froze. "You never told me that before. You only told me that she died."

"I did not want to frighten you. It's a sad tale but a true one, and it's why Père and I want you to do as we say."

Nevertheless, only two days later Jacob was leading the way to the plank across the dyke. The stream, unusually full from melt-water from the south-west, was swirling past and clouds were tearing across the highest part of the sky. The year was on the move.

Jenne stepped on to the plank and bounced it gently. The reeds were greener and the blackthorn blossom whiter than usual. They crossed the stream and made their way along the raised pathway which kept them out of the water, noting the new fronds of plants appearing at the edges of the dykes.

As they were searching for frogspawn Jacob asked, "Do you think Papa will win the election?"

"Of course he will."

Jenne had heard her parents discussing the election which was taking place that afternoon. It would be an honour for a Huguenot to become dyke-reeve. It was a position of responsibility and it looked as if their father might be voted in. She had often heard the adults talking about the difference it would make to their future if one of them were to be elected by the English as well as by the French.

"Some of the English don't want him," said Jacob. "Eleanor told me. They say he's not suitable."

Jenne was puzzled. "Why not?"

Jacob plucked at some sedge. "Because of our family."

"Our family? What about our family?"

Jacob began to tear the sedge apart. "You. They think the Devil is in you."

Immediately the day lost its edge, its brightness.

"Why?"

"Because of the falling sickness. They say if someone gets the falling sickness it means the Devil is in them."

Jenne felt nauseous. Was the Devil really inside her? Was he squirming into her heart like a worm? If he was, how had he got in? And if her father was not elected, would it be her fault?

"Let's go home. I want to go home." She hurried along the path and slithered, causing her foot to slip into the marsh and wet her boot and stocking. She felt panic until they could see the house, and then relief when she found that neither of her parents was back yet.

She changed her clothes and fetched her embroidery. She liked sewing for it was satisfying to make little patches of colour gradually expand and create the shape of a petal or a bird's wing. She sat by the fire, threaded her needle and started to stitch. The regular movement steadied her, slowed down her breathing.

Her mother returned an hour later. She hurried straight into the main room, pulling at the strings of her bonnet.

"Is your father home?"

"No."

"Mon Dieu, surely they must have finished by now?"

Jenne glanced up but continued sewing while Maman took off her coif and cloak.

"There he is now!"

Her mother went out of the room and Jenne heard her

parents greet each other but not what they said. They stayed talking in the kitchen and she stayed by the fire. She had developed a little tendril along the edge of the material, and was adding small red berries to it. She had finished four and had three more to do. She always enjoyed stitching pictures more than letters, and always did the parts she liked best first though Maman said she ought to do it the other way round. Each berry consisted of simple stitches of slightly different lengths. Starting with a brief in and out of the thread, she made the next one just a fraction longer and the next a fraction longer than that, increasing each one until she sewed the stitch which was the berry's diameter. Then she began to decrease. Only two more to go before she could start on the leaves.

That evening, Père said the after-dinner grace: *"Père éternel qui nous ordonne, grant us Thy grace for this day and this night. We beseech Thee to help us avoid displeasing Thee and to support those who have suffered for Thy sake but who, like us, have transgressed."*

Jacob and Jenne were clearing the platters away for their mother.

"Come and sit with me, Mathieu," said Père. He crossed the room and sat down heavily in his armchair.

Mathieu pulled up his stool.

"I want you to know I think Mark Le Pla is a good man who will make a fine dyke-reeve. It is right that he has been elected. People trust him and think well of him."

He paused, and gazed into the smoke.

"He will have to focus on his new tasks now which means I must focus on finishing the Twenty Foot. I have promised Vermuyden I can complete it in one month and I shall do. It will mean working from dawn till dusk every day, but the weather is right for it. And you, Mathieu, must help. You know about these men from Scotland? They will be available in a couple of days. I am going to direct twenty of them to Guyhirn where Monsieur Scribau is in charge and I want you to be his right-hand man.

"You are sensible and reliable, and it is time for you to start

39

work. I would have preferred it if you had been able to study more, but this will be excellent experience."

As Jenne and Jacob entered the room and sat down quietly he spread out a map across his knee and indicated a line. "This is where you will be working. The new channels aren't all on here yet, but this is the Twenty Foot, extending on from Bevill's Leam, turning east here and then joining up with the River Nene."

Mère set a cup of beer down beside her husband and asked, "But surely these Scotchmen are soldiers? Grown men. Will they obey Mathieu?"

"They are prisoners. Prisoners do what they are ordered to do. Anyway, they're not in good shape. They've lost a battle and they've marched for miles."

"Poor souls," murmured Mère.

Jenne looked at Mathieu. He was leaning forward, his chin in his hands, his elbows on his knees.

"Ann," said Père, "We need them to work for us and things aren't so bad for them. They're not slaves – they will be paid. Believe me, they have not suffered as we have suffered. They have been in a battle but they have not seen their babies spiked or their mothers thrown on pyres, and they were not forced to choose between losing their tongues or renouncing their faith."

He turned to Mathieu. "So tomorrow I want you to go with Monsieur Scribau to where the prisoners are lodged and help him choose twenty strong ones. If someone looks as if he can't or won't work, don't take him. Only pick the good ones."

29th March 1652, Thorney

Soon the waterways were full of boats and the sky full of birds. The rushes and reeds were thrusting up and patches of ground were beginning to dry out. In French Drove the colza seed which had been planted the previous year and lain under the snow for months was starting to germinate. Goslings and ducklings cheeped in every dyke. Willows were covered with buds whose yellow powder fell with the breeze, and behind the Abbey Church the cherry trees had already flowered.

Jenne's life regained its rhythm: lessons, jobs in the house and the village, playing outside. But it wasn't the same as before: she saw less of Mathieu, Jacob was expected to do more on the farm and two of her best friends kept talking about boys. Emily Le Pla, in particular, was always asking about Mathieu.

"But don't tell him I like him, will you? I'd be so embarrassed if he knew. He thinks I'm still a little girl."

Jenne thought this was true as she was only twelve, but all she said was, "Well, how will he know you like him then?"

Mathieu had changed. At first he was worried about what he was meant to be doing. Jenne and he knew it was no good asking their father because he was completely occupied with finishing the Twenty Foot. Every evening meal was an account of what he had done and what remained to be done. Even Maman had asked him to calm himself at home in the evenings instead of poring over maps and worrying. It was unusual for her to criticise her husband but one evening Jenne heard her say, "Samuel, you're spending so much time alone nowadays. You used to discuss things with your friends, not stay wrapped up in yourself."

In private, Mathieu complained, "What does it matter if it all takes a few days longer than a month? He's just making things difficult."

Jenne was interested in her brother's work. "Tell me about the prisoners," she said, "What are they like?"

Mathieu thought back. What were they like? On first sight he had been apprehensive when he looked at the dishevelled crowd of thin, ragged-dressed men with surly faces. But now, only a few weeks later, he was able to imagine the lanky McAllen; Murdo, who was easy-going; Anderson, sturdy and always swearing; Macpherson, whom Monsieur Scribau chose despite Mathieu's objections both because he was young ("He's your own age! Mon Dieu, have you no heart?") and because he was injured; Gunn, who reminded him of his uncle; Alleyn, quiet and intelligent.

"Watch that one," Monsieur Scribau had said, "The others respect him, and if he's not with you he'll be against you."

Mathieu answered Jenne, "They're a mixture, like any other group of men."

"Do they talk to you?"

"I can't understand most of what they say because they don't speak English the way I'm used to. But the important thing is that *they* understand *us*."

"Are you scared of them?"

"Of course not! They get on with what they are supposed to do. I've not seen anyone cause trouble but I'd deal with it if they did. And they're strong – they go at a steady pace. They ought to work faster but Monsieur Scribau doesn't try to hurry them. He says they would not be so easy to manage if we did."

"I'd like to see them."

"Jenne, I'm not taking you there."

"Will they ever come here?"

"To Thorney?"

"To anywhere near here."

"Well," said Mathieu slowly, "Morton's Leam was built years ago but it's got to be checked. The surveyor has asked for four prisoners to help him measure across the leam. He needs them to row him and hold the measuring chain."

"Morton's Leam isn't far away."

"Why do you want to see them anyway? They're just diggers and bankers, like other workers."

"They're prisoners. Prisoners are interesting. They must have done interesting things."

"Jenne, they are only prisoners-of-war. They are soldiers who were defeated by Cromwell. For God's sake, they are just damn Scotchmen who want to go home."

That was another change in Mathieu. He had begun to swear.

↷ 9th April 1652, near Thorney

Macpherson, still hardly able to dig, had found something in the mud while wandering around. He walked over to show it to Alleyn.

"Look at this stone."

"That's odd. It must be the only stone in the fens." Alleyn put down his long-handled shovel and rubbed the stone against his new but already filthy suit. "It's not an ordinary stone. Go and wash it."

Macpherson held it in a ditch until the hard mud softened and dissolved. While it was still under water he felt sharp edges, and

42

when he brought it out he saw the surface was composed of hollows, dips and ridges.

"Someone's made it like this," said Alleyn as he studied it. "Why?"

"To use as a tool. To cut and saw. Look, someone chipped out small flakes of stone carefully so this edge could cut the hide of a deer, and this point could sever sinew."

"Alleyn! You're wanted over here!"

Alleyn handed it back. "Keep it safe. It might be useful."

Macpherson hid the stone in his stocking and watched Alleyn walk over to the guard in charge. As soon as he was allowed to he went back to the lodging place resisting the desire to scratch his chest. Alleyn had said it was a good sign if the wound itched, because that meant it was healing. When he got inside he dug a small hole in the corner of the room and buried the stone.

He settled down in the doorway and undid his shirt to expose his new skin to the last sunlight of the day. It was taut and shiny and would never be as good as his old skin, but Alleyn had told him that everyone has to learn to live with the parts of themselves that become damaged.

Later he would cook a wigeon which he had caught more by luck than skill and they would eat well for once, then he dozed for an hour before beginning to build up the fire. After that he kept looking up the drove, for Alleyn should have been back soon after dusk but as the guards often re-allocated prisoners to different teams there was always the possibility that one day he might not return. The thought of losing Alleyn filled him with panic, and so did being alone in the dark here for once he had seen a light dancing over a place he knew to be a marsh and which even Alleyn had stated any man would sink into. A fenman told them that such an inexplicable flickering was known as a will o' the wisp.

By the time Alleyn arrived the skin of the wigeon had burned slightly and was giving off a tempting smell.

He announced, "We've been burying a man."

Macpherson looked up as he continued to baste the bird.

"Someone in another gang was shot today. They say he was trying to escape. The guards ordered the other prisoners to bury

43

him, but they refused. They couldn't shoot them all – that would have meant ten men less – and so they ordered some of our gang to do it."

He took a swig of water from the jug. "We agreed only because every man deserves a burial. We put him in the bank of the dyke. That way, he will not rot in water."

"Why did his own gang refuse to bury him?"

"They say he saw things others could not see, and so they were frightened of him even when he was dead. They made life hard for him, so perhaps he is better off now."

Alleyn sat on one of the thick pads Macpherson had woven from reeds to save them from having to sit on the ground. "And there is another reason why I buried him. In the first days of our march south, my younger brother was with me. But he was killed in a fight with another prisoner, and I left his body unburied and should not have done so."

As they swatted at the mosquitoes Alleyn said, "If it could be counted, I believe more of our soldiers have died since the battle than during it."

Macpherson thought back to the forest of pikestaffs, officers in red and black, tents, trumpets, helmets, horses, muskets, hills, disarray, yelling.

Alleyn recalled the military blunder, Cromwell's rallying call "Lord of Hosts!", the march, the hunger, the preparedness of those who were alive to leave the dead and injured, the guards' brutality, the exiling of men to the New World, the gradual disintegration of an army of thousands to a few hundred sitting on mats in hovels in front of fires hardly capable of producing a spit of flame.

He licked his fingers slowly.

Macpherson asked, "Did you mark the place where you buried that man?"

Alleyn shook his head. "He's one of many, and they'll all be forgotten. But if that dykewall stands when the floods come, it'll be thanks to men like him holding it together as well as to us bankers.

"And today I heard they're bringing more prisoners-of-war, but these ones are Dutch."

"Dutch?"

"They lost a sea battle against the English and they're being sent here."

Macpherson asked, "Is it better for an army to capture its enemies or kill them?"

"It depends on what it wants and why it's fighting."

"Why were we fighting Cromwell?"

"We were supporting King Charles."

"But he was executed."

"We were supporting Charles II, the son of the King Charles who was executed."

Macpherson said, "I swore to honour someone … was it him? Were we fighting for him?"

Alleyn put another turf on the fire. "We were fighting for each other. We were fighting to stay alive."

🐇 15th April 1652, near Thorney

Jenne was stroking Hibou-Bou's barred feathers. He was looking at her with his amazing yellow eyes. She loved the way he was restless at times with his eyes blinking, his good wing flapping, and how later he would settle to stillness and just sit and look his look of constant surprise.

When he was first found in a snare set for ducks she had prayed for his bad wing to mend so he could fly off back to the marshes, and Papa had said that when spring came he might try to get out. But his wing hadn't healed and he hadn't tried to get out.

The day had started early as her father had to ride to Denver to see the progress on the sluice he had been working on for so long. His mood was cheerful. This was because the end of all the work – on the New Bedford River, the Sixteen Foot Drain, the Twenty Foot River, the Forty Foot Drain, the Hundred Foot River, Tong's Drain and the sluices at Denver and the Hermitage – was in sight. Maman pointed out that his spirits rose as each project was finished, and she thanked le bon Dieu for that.

But Jenne's spirits were high for a different reason. She was going to Morton's Leam with Mathieu. She put the owl carefully back in his corner and closed the door with the stick and string.

"I don't know why you're so determined to go," Mathieu said. "People will wonder what you're doing there."

"Don't worry. If Monsieur Scribau's there I'll tell him you and Papa have talked so much about your work I wanted to see it."

"But Morton's Leam isn't one of the new dykes."

They picked their way through the fens which were becoming drier by the day. Ruffs and pintails flew up from under their feet.

When they reached the leam it stretched out to the left and right. The only people around were on boats. Mathieu pointed to one which seemed to be stationary in mid-stream.

"That's them. The one standing up is Mr Moore, the surveyor."

As well as Mr Moore, there were two men holding oars and two holding a chain. So, these were the prisoners-of-war from Scotland. They were all wearing brown outfits and orange caps and they all had beards.

A few words of what the surveyor was saying travelled across the water, "the width … silted up … tomorrow …."

After a few minutes Mr Moore sat down and pointed towards the bank. When he caught sight of Mathieu he held up his hand in greeting.

As the boat approached the surveyor's features became more distinct. The prisoners, bent alternately down and then up as they pulled on the oars, no longer seemed to be wearing plain brown but a mixture of white and beige and brown. It looked as if the dyes had run on their clothes. Mr Moore told the men to bring the boat alongside the small jetty. Holding a sheaf of papers, he climbed out and greeted Mathieu and Jenne.

"Have you come to help us measure the leam?" he joked. "We can always use extra workers. Or perhaps you intend to become a banker?"

All four prisoners were looking at Jenne. She blushed imme-diately, and decided to pay close attention to the conversation which had started up between Mathieu and Mr Moore. At the same time she was embarrassed and tempted to walk away but made herself stay because this was what she had come for. Not to be looked at, of course, but to see the prisoners. Anyway, where could she go? After a little while she turned slightly to get another glimpse of them and saw they were all still looking at her. One of them leant towards another and said something quietly. Yes, this was what she had come for.

Just then a boat passed too close, rocking the rowing boat and making the men hold on and shout at the other oarsmen. In that couple of seconds she saw their suits had once been white, but were now covered in mud. Then they all turned to gaze at her again.

She pretended to be interested in a garganey flying along the leam. No Huguenot man or even boy would dare to stare like that. No one had ever stared at her like that before. But being gazed at was much more interesting than the usual things which happened to her.

Mr Moore was walking towards the jetty. "Tell Monsieur Scribau I'll need these four for another couple of hours. Basically, it's too narrow and shallow – as we knew – but we'll have to live with it. Re-doing it can't be a priority." He stepped down into the boat and told the men to row.

Each of the four oars made a small pool where it dipped into the water, and the movement of the boat created a flat surface which led like an extending path between the stern and the bank.

Jenne watched the four men until they were in the middle of the leam. They did not take their eyes off her and she was sure they were thinking about her.

When they were out of earshot Mathieu said, "I shouldn't have brought you. Mr Moore will mention it to someone. He's friends with Monsieur Le Pla."

"He'll be thinking about his surveying. He'll have forgotten me already."

Mathieu broke a thin branch off a willow tree. "Not when those four are going to be talking about you all day. I should have thought of that."

"You should have thought of what?"

He didn't answer but just walked ahead swiping at things.

It was only when they were in sight of home that Jenne risked asking, "Where do the prisoners lodge?"

Mathieu answered angrily, "How should I know? All I know is that the Government sent them to work for the English and for us." He pointed his switch at Jenne. "Don't go near them. If you do, it'll cause trouble. Don't have anything to do with them."

Things carried on.

Jenne's knowledge of English was being reinforced by her increasing contact with English people. In the kitchen, she was learning how to pluck and gut smaller birds like teal and dotterel without tearing their skin. She completed the leaves on her embroidery and moved on to the first words of Psalm 120, *Au Seigneur Dieu, pour recouvrer lyesse.* She had just reached the second *e* of *Seigneur*.

Her father accompanied the Commissioners of Adjudication on their long-anticipated voyage to inspect the completed drainage works, escorting them all the way back to Ely. They were impressed and congratulated Vermuyden and the Huguenots for their industry and perseverance. All the planned changes were at last visible: rivers shortened, channels dug, banks strengthened, silt scoured, weed cut, and Denver Sluice all but finished. The Scots prisoners were kept out of the way because it could have soured the day if a guard had had to shoot one.

One evening in May Père put his knife down on the table and wiped his hands. "We need the rest of this year to complete Smith's Leam and Moore's Drain and to extend Conquest Lode to Whittlesey Meer. Then we'll have the winter to test everything, and from then on, grâce a Dieu, it'll largely be a question of maintenance."

He looked round at the family. "Drainage can teach us a lesson about life. There are times in life when you need to look at what's happening and address anything that's going wrong. It takes time and effort, but it's worth doing. And after you've finished you still have to maintain everything. Weeds – small troubles – will always appear. Floods – serious incidents – will swamp you from time to time. Silt will slow you down like sloth."

He picked up the knife again and sawed off a piece of bread. "And a family is like a piece of low-lying land. Unless it is protected, it can be ruined."

What did Papa mean? Did he mean something was wrong with their family? It was true there was trouble in some English families. There were men who drank too much, and recently a girl who wasn't married had had a baby (which probably meant she would never get married) and Mathieu had often said, "It's better to be Huguenot than English. We behave properly and do the right things. We're not like them." But Jean Fouchar had knocked his wife down twice, so it wasn't only the English.

Mathieu was sounding more and more like Père than Père himself. In fact, on the day when Père had been to Ely with the Commissioners and did not arrive home in time for the meal Maman had asked Mathieu to say grace. And recently, when Jacob had cleaned his – Mathieu's – boots, he had shouted at him because there was still mud on them.

"You're speaking to him as if he were a servant," Jenne had said crossly, "Or a prisoner. You're treating him like a prisoner, someone you can order about."

"Of course I'm not," he replied. "He's just got to learn to do things properly."

Jenne got up abruptly. "Oh come with me, Jacob. Let's give Bou-Bou another flying lesson. Teaching an injured bird to fly is much harder than cleaning boots, but you do it well."

"That's not the point," Mathieu called after them, "For God's sake, I'm talking about things that matter in life – not about *owls*."

They went outside to the small barn. Bou-Bou lived here in a corner behind a sort of fence Papa had helped them make out of thin sticks. Once inside the barn, they shut the door and let him free in the bigger space. He never went far, but usually managed to get up to the window ledge and sit there for a while before flopping down. Jacob liked to carry him up the ladder to the loft and let him fly down.

"He's looking out of the window again. Maman hates him being shut up in here. Can't we let him go?"

"It's too soon," said Jenne, as she extended the owl's good wing. She left his bad one alone because he snapped at her if she touched it. Even though he seemed well in himself that wing had not healed.

Jacob held out some bits of meat, and Bou-Bou pushed his head forward to reach them.

"Why don't we make him hungry?" said Jacob, "I mean not feed him in the evening and not the next morning, and then let him go. Then he'd *have* to come back."

"Let's leave it until the end of June, like Papa said. His wing might have improved more by then."

Bou-Bou suddenly looked straight into Jenne's grey eyes with his yellow ones.

"Jacob, I think he understood what I said. He knows we're going to set him free."

"No, he doesn't. Birds don't understand people. At least, not *words*. He knows when you open the door you'll bring food but he can't understand what we said about making him hungry, or his wing mending."

"He might do. He understands more than we think." She shushed the owl back through the cage doorway. "Good night, Bou-Bou."

"In you go," said Jacob, slipping the stick through the string to secure the door. "I'm going to tell Maman about when we're going to free him."

❧ Morning, 3rd June 1652, near Thorney

Jenne and Jacob were on their way along French Drove to the Le Pla's farm. They were carrying a bag of flour, four smoked eels and two reeves. When the reeves were lying on the kitchen table Jenne had drawn her fingers down their long beaks, through the exotic red-brown plumes round their heads and necks, and along their pink legs. Doing this renewed her determination to find a reeve's nest one day.

Butterflies were rising up in front of them, the sky was full of larks and the colza was becoming greener by the week.

When they were going down the slight slope they turned off the drove to play a favourite game which consisted of trying to see the most number of people in the landscape. At first glance anyone could have counted five or six, but the trick was to search and to wait.

Jenne did what she usually did – starting from the extreme left of the territory they had agreed on as the area to be looked at, she slowly and carefully shifted her line of vision towards the right, examining the whole view in a methodical way by dividing it up into imaginary sections. Keeping track of where you had reached was always difficult.

She could see two men in the distance with eel glaives over their shoulders. Her eye moved steadily to the next section which extended as far as a hut. Nothing. Then she altered a fraction further, towards the deer park. Yes, there were two women by the wobbly crossing plank. They were coming in this direction and carrying something but she couldn't make out what. And there were three boats. But how many people? Probably five. For a few seconds she forgot the game and thought back to the prisoners in the boat on the leam. To the even pull of their oars; to the steady gaze of their eyes.

"How many so far?" asked Jacob.

Jenne was tugged back to the game. "Nine. Ten, I'm not sure."

"I'm up to fifteen already!"

She shaded her eyes as she turned towards the sun. Unexpectedly close to the foreground she saw a man on his own, sitting under a bush. She glanced at Jacob but he was looking much further afield so might miss him. She could see men by a bridge. Perhaps they were mending it. Two of them, at least. She gave it one more go, counting them off on her fingers. And there was another group walking along a bank. First came two adults, then two children, then another adult. It could be the Petillon family.

Jacob won. He found nineteen people and Jenne made him point all of them out to her. Playing this game always pleased her – whoever won – because the landscape started off almost empty and then people revealed themselves if you were patient. It was as if, as you examined it, it came alive.

Picking up their baskets again they carried on to the Le Pla's. It was hot, the air nearly still, and they walked slowly.

As they were getting close to the farm they heard talking behind them. The two women Jenne had seen by the crossing plank had caught them up. She did not know who they were. They were certainly not Huguenots, but neither did they look

51

like the English they knew. The shoes they wore were not made for rough droves, their gowns were somehow different and as they were not wearing bonnets their hair swung about their shoulders. Each of them carried a bundle wrapped in a shawl.

Jenne stood aside to greet the women and let them pass, but they stopped, dropped their bundles to the ground and drew breath.

One of them began to wipe her face with her sleeve. "That's a relief – we've been walking for over an hour in this heat." She looked at Jenne, "Young lady, can you tell us where the soldier-boys are?"

Jenne was confused because she was not sure what the woman had said – something about boys. It was hard to understand English suddenly when they'd been speaking and thinking French all morning.

"The boys that's doing the digging," said the other woman. "The ones that's come from Scotland."

"You mean the prisoners?"

"Prisoners, soldiers, diggers, call them what you like," said the first, "Are they near here?"

"We've never seen them," said Jacob, "But my father will know."

One of the women pointed to the farm, "Is he here? Is this where you live?"

"This is the Le Pla's farm. We're just visiting." Jacob indicated the baskets he and Jenne were holding.

"Well, we'll keep going on this track. We're sure to come across them – unless they can't wait and come looking for us!"

At this, both the women started to laugh and then one said to Jacob, "You speak strange English. Where do you come from?"

Jacob pointed back along the drove.

The other woman laughed again. "No, she means where *did* you come from? What country were you born in?"

"Sandtoft."

"Never heard of it. That's not one of those new places across the sea where there's land for the taking?" She looked doubtfully at him. "He speaks foreign, doesn't he, Eliza?"

Just as they were about to pick up their bundles Madame Le Pla appeared from the farm, and they waited as she approached.

"Mistress, please may we have a drink of water?"

Madame paused a moment, taking stock of them, and then beckoned. She ushered Jacob and Jenne in front and the women followed her back to the farm. While she was fetching the water Monsieur Le Pla arrived from the field behind.

"Good morning. Where are you going to?" he asked.

"We're looking for the soldiers."

"There's none here."

"We heard they were in this direction, near Thorney."

"There's none here."

"But Papa told me …"

"Tais-toi, s'il te plaît, Jacob," interrupted Monsieur Le Pla. "I heard they've been sent somewhere towards Ely."

Madame handed the women cups of water, and told Jenne and Jacob to follow her inside. At the door Jenne looked back and saw Monsieur watching the women as they drank.

"Come on inside," insisted Madame, "I've got a jug of milk for you two."

"I'm sure Papa and Mathieu know where the prisoners are," said Jacob, "And they haven't said anything about Ely, have they, Jenne?"

Madame spoke before Jenne had a chance to answer. "We don't want women like that near here."

Monsieur came into the house. "They've gone," he said. "But keep an eye open, Judith, because there might be more of them."

More of them? Of whom? Jenne drank her milk slowly, wondering whether it was true the prisoners-of-war had been sent away. Jacob was right – no one had mentioned Ely. But the thought of Monsieur Le Pla lying was as impossible as the thought of her father lying.

Madame took them to see the kids. Born a few days earlier they were soft little trembling things and Jacob and Emily were given the job of taking them from the nanny and keeping them out of sight. Madame was surprised Jenne had not yet learned how to milk so she was shown how to tether the goat up by the wall, wedge herself on a stool against the warm flank, position the bucket, take a fat, pink teat in each hand and push and squeeze it upwards firmly, first one and then the other, until the milk began to flow. It felt awkward. Wouldn't it be better to squeeze downwards?

"Watch how I do it," said Madame.

It seemed so easy for her. Murmuring quietly she leaned into the nanny's solid side, her hands making a repetitive, even movement. Within less than a minute the animal was completely calm and two strong jets of milk were going straight into the bucket in turn.

"But what about the kids?"

"They won't go hungry. There'll be plenty more milk in an hour or two."

When the streams lessened and ceased she got up and passed the bucket to Jenne. Then she un-tethered the goat and re-tied her to a stake by the grass. The nanny went on complaining noisily until Jacob returned the bleating kids. Then she settled to eat despite being jolted and pushed from underneath.

The two set off home along the drove carrying a jug of cream and a bowlful of eggs.

"Emily asked me lots of questions about Mathieu," said Jacob.

"What sort of questions?"

"Where he's working. When he'll be visiting the Le Plas. If it's true he likes Amelia Sigee."

"What did you say?"

"I told her I didn't know."

They walked on. There was no need to hurry, but when Jacob suggested paddling by the wobbly plank they began to move a little faster.

Jenne was hoping Jacob would not mention the prisoners-of-war. She was still confused. She was sure they had not been sent to Ely. She was sure Monsieur Le Pla knew where they were. But who were those women? And why weren't they wanted?

To ward him off she said, "Let's let Hibou-Bou out again tomorrow. He loved it last time."

"Even though he still can't take off or fly properly?"

"He'll learn. He's getting better every day."

54

Jacob ran ahead and reached the crossing plank a couple of minutes before Jenne.

"Look – over here! And there! There's dozens of tiny fish. I bet I can catch some. Give me the bowl, will you?"

Jenne set the jug in a firm place in the grass out of the sun and carefully placed each of the seven eggs next to it. She lay on her stomach and pushed the long grass away from her face. As she watched Jacob studying the water she stuck her fingers through to the grass roots and the peat. Despite the sun it was cool and damp under there.

The light was making the lode's surface gleam. She half shut her eyes and half listened to Jacob's changing tone as he tried to catch a fish.

"Oh no! Nearly… Come here, you … now where … that's it, that's it, no! Jenne, I'm going further down where it's deeper."

She turned over and looked at the sky. Pale blue. From this position, that was all there was. Blue, blue, blue. She closed her eyes again. The breeze brought the scent of water-mint and ripe blackberries. As Jacob's voice faded she began to notice larks singing. She could imagine their uneven rising flight, their fast fall.

Somewhere close by there was a small trickling of water and an anxious duck. She heard a shout of delight from Jacob, but it sounded miles away.

Still on her back, she opened her eyes. The sky was dark with larks. They were flying in circles, hundreds of them. They weren't meant to be doing this but she couldn't stop them.

ᘒ Afternoon, 3rd June 1652, near Thorney

She was cold when she woke up, and her nose and lip were hurting. What was that noise? Where was she? Why was she on the grass?

"Steady now. Take it steady."

She rolled over on her side and tried to open her eyes, but her eyelids were gummed up. Instinctively she rubbed them, picked something off them with her nails. Then she brushed some leaves from her dress. She saw a man sitting next to her. He was humming, almost singing. Who was he? She felt exhausted.

The humming got louder and she heard more words.

55

"Just take your time. Steady now." The man was speaking in the voice mothers use to comfort children, almost a sort of lullaby. She yawned. The humming stopped.

"Good. You're back."

The sun was directly behind the man and she could not see his features – only the outline of his upper body and his head.

"Your parents will be here soon. Don't worry. Just stay where you are."

Her dress was wet and something was spilt on the bodice and down her front. It reminded her of the juice in mistletoe berries, but what was this yellow stuff? She touched her throbbing nose and found it had been bleeding. Her lip was swollen. Something was pricking into one shoulder too, like small pins, or insects. Lumps of her hair were stuck together. Then she realised the man had no shirt on. Everything was wrong.

"I'm thirsty."

The man encouraged her to sit up and drink from a leather cup. Her sore lip made it difficult.

"Where's my mother? I want Maman."

"I sent the bairn to fetch her. She won't be long."

Jenne turned on to her stomach again and began to cry quietly into the grass.

"She'll be here soon." The man leaned towards her. "Will you tell me your name?"

"Jenne."

"Jenne. That's like Jeanie. My sister's called Jeanie."

"I'm cold."

"You've got my shirt already."

She turned her face to the ground again and went back to sleep.

The next time she opened her eyes her view was of legs – Jacob's, her father's, Mathieu's and those of other men. Maman was kneeling on the ground beside her sobbing and the man with no shirt was standing on his own by the dyke. Everyone was saying things, but it wasn't a real conversation.

Her father's voice was quiet but angry. She had never heard it like that before.

"How could he have done this? *Souverain Dieu, aide-nous.*"

56

Someone else said, "She's only a child."

Maman kept repeating, "Ma petite chère, we'll soon have you safe and sound."

"They should never have sent us these Scotchmen."

"Poor, dear Jenne."

"He's hit her nose and lip."

"Put your shirt on," snapped Mathieu, "And your cap – you're supposed to keep your cap on all the time."

"Look, there's blood on him."

"But why didn't you come straight home?"

"Mathieu, va chercher les gardes. Vite."

"You grab hold of his other arm."

Carefully, Jenne was helped to her feet. Carefully, her dress was straightened. Someone wrapped a cloth round her waist, covering up some dark patches. She was supported by her parents. Although she told them it was her nose which hurt the worst they seemed to think she would find it difficult to walk. Behind her two men held on to the arms of the man who was there when she woke up. Or was it another man? She had lost track.

Jacob came last behind the awkward procession as it made slow progress along the path and up to the drove. By the time they reached the Causeway people had gathered to see them. Several women were weeping and holding their children to their skirts. Men held their scythes still and stopped talking. It was almost as if someone had died.

᭍ 4th June 1652, near Thorney

The guards took Alleyn to a strong cell. They kicked him, spat at him and pissed on him.

Now he was lying on some rushes watching a sparrow which must have been trapped in the cell before he was shoved in. It pecked at the floor, fluttered along the wall, and huddled in a corner.

He tried to move himself slowly into a kneeling position and began to pray. He prayed for his parents in Dunbar, for his brother Donald and for his sister Jeanie. He prayed for the men he had fought with. He gave thanks for the fact that he was still alive.

He had been so badly beaten he could not kneel for long so moved to sit with his back against the wall, facing the door. He prayed for the girl he had helped when she was ill but whom he had been accused of assaulting. For her family and his accusers. For himself. It occurred to him the only difference between his fate and the sparrow's was that the sparrow would die but he would be killed.

He thought of the day he had first seen Jenne, when he was on the boat and she was on the bank with that ill-tempered youth who had turned out to be her brother. Her unexpected appearance made it possible that life could be better, life *would* be better, that there were other lives to the one he was living. There had been coarse comments about her, but Alleyn knew it was not just the fact of her sex which caused him to feel elated.

That evening he had gone back to Macpherson and said, "I saw a lass today who made me realise that sometimes good things come when you are not looking for them."

Macpherson had asked, "What happened?"

"Not much. She just stood on the bank, but she was being seen as she had not been seen before. She had not expected that and she was pleased, and I had not expected to see her and I was pleased."

The sparrow was trying to fly upwards, but all it did was to raise the dust off the wall. Alleyn began to pray again using the words he had recited in church as a boy. He asked for deliverance from evil, for his trespasses to be forgiven. He lay down and went over all the events of the last day yet again.

Half way through the previous afternoon he and Macpherson had been trusted to find their own way to another dyke. It was particularly lovely walking through the fenland and they were feeling good. The day was going well and they had food for the evening – a sound state of affairs for prisoners-of-war. They cut across the land near where the religious group from Flanders had begun to farm. He was impressed by these Huguenots for they were almost the only people in this marshy place who attempted real farming. Their well-tended crops and their goats and cows reminded him of home.

The prisoners considered almost all the French who supervised the digging to be fair masters because they were neither harsh nor lenient but consistent in the way they allocated work and in their dealings with those in their charge. If a man was shot, they would always pause and say a prayer. One had told Alleyn that when this happened he prayed for the guard who had fired the shot as well as for the dead prisoner, and Alleyn believed him.

When they were about half-way Alleyn and Macpherson heard someone shout. They turned and saw a boy running towards them.

"My sister!" he had called out, "Please come and help my sister!"

They hurried after him and found a girl raving on the bank of the dyke. She was shouting and jerking her arms and in one hand she had hold of a small jug. Alleyn had seen fits before and immediately sent the boy to fetch help and Macpherson to tell the guards where he was. He tried to take the jug from the lass's grasp but she was seizing it tightly and in the struggle it struck her nose and his cheek. Then she loosened her grip and rolled on to her side. He grabbed the jug and threw it out of reach for safety and it fell into the lode. Now he could see that parts of her dress were dark with wetness and that some sticky substance adhered to her face and neck. As he moved round to place himself between her and the water, he felt his foot crunch something. It was an egg, and at once he realised she must have rolled into a nest and despite being in the middle of an emergency he remembered thinking it was late for nests.

And then her moaning began to cease, and she became calmer. Then she was quite still, but breathing loudly with blood bubbling from her nose which he wiped with his cap. There was not much more he could do except take off his shirt and cover her with it, for she would quickly become cold. As he did this he saw little pieces of broken egg shell sticking to her bodice, and egg yolk on her neck. Then he realised with surprise that the eggs were from chickens, not from wild birds. He found yarrow nearby, so picked some of the feathery leaves and held them by the girl's nose until the bleeding stopped and then washed his own bruised face and pressed more leaves against it. Then he waited, and while he waited he hummed quietly.

Ten minutes later the girl stirred and yawned. She was confused and unhappy but there was little he could do except reassure her, and she quickly fell asleep again.

While he went on waiting a swallow-tail butterfly alighted nearby on some milk-parsley. He studied the fake eye-spots, the long tails, the blue powder on the wing bands. It was an amazing creature. From time to time he surfaced from his observation and checked the lass was still breathing. It was not until the third time of attending to her that he realised she was the girl he had seen from the boat. How strange that he should find her in this way. How very different things were now from when he had first seen her.

He was impatient for help to come for it would be best if her family were there before she returned to consciousness. And at last he heard voices and saw a line of people hurrying along the pathway, following the boy. Relieved, he stood to greet them.

And now he was locked up, accused of those actions which people deemed to be the action of animals. They said he had lain in wait for her, had sent Jacob away so he could perform "acts of violation" on the vulnerable, innocent girl, and then attacked her when she tried to defend herself. When he asked exactly what these acts were, he was told they were "unspeakable and bestial". He thought back to the couplings he had seen between pigs, sheep and cattle in his village outside Dunbar. Did these people think he had raped the girl from behind? Or did animals do things he did not know about? Or were they just lying?

At first he was hopeful that these fair and honest people would listen to his story, but though they questioned him in English they spoke amongst themselves in French, and few attempted to understand his Scots accent. He looked to the boy to verify his explanation and the boy had spoken up for him. And when Jacob said "It was the same as when she fell in the Abbey Church" it gave Alleyn hope because it confirmed the lass had had a fit and so they would know he was not to blame. But everyone recalled Jacob's panic when he ran home and his words were dismissed as those of someone too frightened and too young to understand, just as Jenne's inability to remember anything at all of that day was attributed to her shock.

He asked them to call Macpherson but they said he was irrelevant. Alleyn's claim that the girl had hit herself with a milk jug was considered an obvious lie, for the bank was searched and no jug had been found. There was disagreement only as to why he had remained at the scene of the crime; one view was that he intended to assault the girl again, the other that he was ashamed and stricken with guilt.

People wondered if the incident meant that all girls were at risk from the prisoners, or whether Jenne had been singled out. But as she lived in Thorney, how could any prisoner have seen her or known about her? Whatever the situation, it was agreed a petition should be written immediately to get rid of these dangerous men.

Each person in the small party who had gone out when Jacob called the alarm had seen the state Jenne was in – her dress dirty and wet, her face bruised and bloody – but the real proof, spoken about only when the women and children were well out of the way, was the substance which had coagulated into a fine film on Jenne's cheeks, was visible on her clothes and had stuck the strands of her hair together.

The sparrow had stopped moving, and Alleyn realised from the cracks by the door that it was nearly dark.

He lay down weary of thinking of all the things he should have said.

⌘ 5th June 1652, Thorney

Au Seigneur Dieu, pour recouvrer lyesse et delivrer mon coeur de sa tristesse

Her parents had been talking for hours. Jenne heard their muffled voices and knew they were praying a pleading prayer by the side of their bed.

It had been a bad day. She was still tired and confused about being the centre of so much concern. The doctor had already been twice. The first time, he examined her nose and lip and bathed them saying they would heal quickly. Strangely, it didn't seem to matter to him that this was the second time she had had a fit of the falling sickness – she accepted now there was nothing else to call it, that's what it was – even though last time he had considered the condition very serious. But when he came back in the afternoon she had to do the worst thing she had ever done. She had to lie on her back, pull her knees up and open her legs. She had never been so embarrassed. Maman and the doctor were embarrassed too and the doctor apologised – to her mother, but not to her – for looking inside her skirt and even touching between her legs.

When he asked if he was hurting her she said "No" quickly, willing him to stop.

After he went, Maman had said he had had to do it to find out what the criminal had done. "He hurt you badly, but, grâce à Dieu, you can't remember it."

"I keep telling you I don't remember anything because I had a fit, but surely I'd know if I'd been injured? It would hurt somewhere, but I've told you it's my nose and lip which are sore. Down there it doesn't hurt at all."

Her mother had then explained, with some difficulty, precisely what they feared the man had done. Jenne knew what men did because her friend Ester had told her, but it was still strange to think of people she knew doing it. Is that what Maman and Papa did? Or people like Monsieur and Madame Frouchart? It must be. But could the Scotchman have done that to her without her knowing? It seemed as if everybody except her thought so, but no one expected her to know because she remembered nothing. She could not recall going to the Le Plas, or trying to milk the goat, or anything Jacob told her had happened that day. As before, she had lost hours, more than a whole morning.

A sudden idea came to her, If everyone believed a prisoner would have the Devil in him, the doctor must think that he might now be inside her *down there* and the real reason for examining her had been to find him and get him out. She recalled her mother's words, "He had to find out what the criminal had done". Could the Devil have escaped being caught by the doctor and actually still be inside her, now, at this very minute? Her whole body went hot and cold at the idea of it and she leaned out of bed, reached for the pot, and retched.

For the rest of the day she managed her fear through doing embroidery. She was on the last letter of *Dieu*. The rhythm of stitching in and out and tugging gently at the silk calmed her, slowed her. It kept things under control.

Now it was night, and more than anything she wanted her world to return to normal. She wanted her face to heal and her parents to stop being sad and worried. She wanted to be with her friends. And then there was Hibou-Bou, whom she'd almost forgotten.

She tried not to think about the fit but was well aware it had taken place before the six month period was up, the period which the doctor had said would, if clear, mean she was unlikely to have another.

Maman and Papa joined together in their final psalm whose first line she was gradually working her way through with her needle and coloured threads. It was a request to God, an appeal to God asking for the recovery of joy. Joy – that was what she wanted. *Lyesse*. It seemed a long way off.

᧔ 7th June 1652, near Thorney

It was morning.

The sparrow had edged its way towards a small pool of light. Alleyn leaned forward but it did not move, so he picked it up. It had almost given up the ghost.

He looked ahead of him. An ant was crossing an uneven whorl in one of the planks in the wall opposite him. He went on looking at the plank and found more knots, an even row of nail heads, distinctive marks made by an adze, a whole line of ants, splintered edges, a few carved letters, spiders, woodlice.

How had things come to this? Finding an answer took him back to his mother milking the dun cow, his father scraping mud off his boots, that stretch of water where the Firth of Forth met the German Ocean, the day he joined the Covenanters, his pride at learning to manage an unwieldy pikestaff. He remembered too the night before battle when they had been camped on Doon Hill, poised for victory. But twenty four hours later he was a prisoner-of-war on the move towards England.

And within a few days another prisoner, a dragoon, had argued and fought with his brother Donald in that walled field where they stopped. Donald was killed for a cabbage, and he – Iain Alleyn – had left his body there unburied.

He looked at the sparrow. It was a small scuff of feathers. It was dead. Suddenly the past no longer seemed to matter: he was where he was.

He wanted water. As well as needing to drink he wanted to wash his injured face. His left cheek and eye were so swollen he could not see properly. He got to his feet carefully, his left leg and his ribs hurting. His body needed time to heal itself, but there was no time. All the time he had in this world would be used up before the end of this day or the next day. They would get him over and done with as soon as possible.

Then he heard voices outside and the door was yanked open. Light poured in and he was blinded.

"Come out here, come on!"

Alleyn edged his way painfully towards the light. His foot caught the doorstep and he stumbled.

"Get up! Get up!"

He got up slowly, and was gradually able to see.

There were two men in front of him, one holding a musket, one a bucket. They were looking him up and down.

"Clean yourself up," said the one with the bucket, placing it on the ground.

Alleyn bent and cupped his hands to drink. He drank slowly. Then he cupped his hands again to wash his face. It tasted and felt wonderful, this water which he usually hated. It gave relief to his eyes, to his spirit.

"They want to see you again."

Alleyn pulled himself upright. He looked past the two men to the early morning sky, to the light in the east. That was better. For a sudden second he recalled the blue powder on the swallow-tail's wings and felt a sudden desire to stay alive.

They put him in a cart because it would have taken him hours to walk the few miles, but he hardly had the strength to hold on to the side and stop himself from sliding.

When they reached a certain farm, they left him waiting with one silent guard. Alleyn kept his eyes closed and faced the sun. He smelled meadowsweet and mugwort and heard the rustlings of a reed bed.

He had been alive for about twenty-five years. His father, he guessed, must by now be old – about fifty – so at this age would have had half of his life ahead of him. So, it was possible that he himself could be only half way through his life. There could be another quarter century for him too, if he was lucky.

But he was not lucky. He was on a cart waiting to appear before men who despised him because they believed him guilty of an appalling crime which they would not name and he had not committed. He reached out his hand to feel the horse's flank, wanting its solidity, its comfort.

"They're ready for him."

They led him indoors and into a large room where eight or ten people were waiting for him. He recognised several – including, to his surprise, Macpherson.

"This is not a court and I am not a judge," announced a gentleman. "I am the dyke-reeve here in Thorney. My name is Mark Le Pla. We want to know why you hurt our poor child, Jenne Deschamps. We Huguenots believe God will be our judge, and we believe He will forgive us if we forgive others. Forgiveness is the path to healing, and we want our child to be healed."

There was silence.

"I ask you, why did you hurt her so foully?"

Alleyn remained silent.

"You must speak," said Monsieur Le Pla.

"I did not hurt her."

"Her face is injured. You must have struck her."

"Sir, I did not. She struck me … she could not help it, she could not control her limbs."

The dyke-reeve changed his approach. "We have made enquiries about why you were not under guard that afternoon, but why did you go near the girl?"

He told them again about how the young boy had shouted,

and how he and Macpherson had gone to help. When he saw the lass he knew she was having a falling fit, so he did what he could.

"And what was that?"

"I prevented her from rolling into the water, I took the jug from her hand so she would not hurt herself with it again, and when she had calmed down I wiped her blood off and covered her with my shirt."

Monsieur Le Pla called out, "Doctor, you examined Jenne. You told me she had passed water. Is it the case a person may lose control and pass water if he – if she – takes fright at something?"

The doctor nodded.

"Do you know of any other reason why a healthy young girl would pass water?"

The doctor hesitated. "It's possible. There are conditions which are not fully understood."

"Is it true the girl had had some sort of fit several months ago?"

"Yes, but its cause was uncertain."

A latecomer entered the room but everyone was concentrating on Alleyn.

"And could she have had another falling fit on this occasion?"

"I doubt it … because … but … given all the circumstances … this man …."

"Please answer directly. Do you believe he forced himself on our poor daughter?"

The doctor paused. "I do not know. I examined her but she did not appear to be damaged. Of course, it is difficult to … I was not able to …. "

"We understand. Thank you."

Monsieur Le Pla turned back to Alleyn, "I told you our purpose today is to find out why you assaulted the girl so we may try to understand and forgive you, so healing may begin. We have asked your guards about you and there are those who think of you as trustworthy and unlikely to do such a terrible thing. But a search was made of your lodgings, and a pile of new clothes was found there. As you are a prisoner this makes you a thief."

"Sir," called out Macpherson. "I stole the shirts."

A rustle of interest went round the room but the dyke-reeve

continued, "And a dangerous weapon was also discovered concealed in the ground."

Alleyn knew several guards who might have placed a weapon in their lodgings, and he was wondering which one it was when another Huguenot man silenced the room by brandishing a stone which fitted his fist.

"You see this?" he called out, "Just imagine what the fate of our daughter might have been if the wretch had used this!"

Macpherson called out again, "That was my stone, not Alleyn's."

People began to murmur in French and ask for the stone to be passed round and Macpherson to be questioned, but the dyke-reeve asked for quiet. "We are not a court, and we must stick to our purpose, but I tell you again, if you are a thief we must assume you are prepared to commit other crimes."

While Alleyn gazed at the floor a different voice, but one he knew, spoke up.

"Monsieur le Pla, do not believe this other prisoner, Macpherson," said Mathieu clearly and loudly. "Alleyn once saved his life so they are as close as brothers. Macpherson would say anything to protect him. They both work for me and I have seen how they collude."

The dyke-reeve looked back at Alleyn, and indicated that he could speak.

"Sir, Macpherson is indeed trying to protect me. In truth, it was me who stole the clothes and sold them, but *he* found the stone which is not a weapon. I believe it was once a tool."

"Let us move on. Alleyn, had you ever seen Jenne Deschamps before the day you were found with her?"

"Yes, once. About a week ago she came to Morton's Leam where I was working with the surveyor."

There was another hum of interest.

"Was she alone?"

"No, she was with Mathieu Deschamps, the man I work for and who just spoke."

Immediately Mathieu retorted, "He's lying. I know nothing about Jenne going near any prisoner. I was certainly not with her."

At this, there were more murmurings.

"Monsieur Le Pla," called the man who had come in late, "I'm sorry to have to contradict Mathieu Deschamps. When I was surveying the leam last week I myself saw and spoke with his sister and with him."

Monsieur Le Pla's voice changed as he asked, "Mathieu, is this true?"

Mathieu stammered, started again, stuttered again, and nodded.

"Why did you take Jenne to Morton's Leam?"

"It was her idea, not mine. She was …." He struggled to get the words out, "She was fascinated by the prisoners. She begged me to take her to see them."

People began to exchange looks and words.

"Please. Silence please." Monsieur Le Pla leaned back to talk briefly to Jenne's father. He then announced, "We cannot proceed further today. Let the prisoners be returned to the cells."

Alleyn was pushed forward by the guard sitting with him. "Go on, go straight out."

He limped to the door and across the yard.

"These foreigners, I can't understand them," said the guard as he approached the cart-driver. "It's obvious why a man commits a crime. He's an evil bastard and he wants to gain something. Isn't it as clear as daylight?"

↷ 16th June 1652, Thorney

Mon Dieu, Mon Dieu, pourquoi de ce besoin m'as Tu laissé?
De moi n'as Tu plus soin?

Père needed to pray. Although he now believed his daughter had not been ravaged or hurt in any way he had learned that his son had acted wrongly, had lied to his own family and people, had failed to protect Jenne, and even Jenne – his only daughter – had not behaved as he would have wished.

Mère held everything together. She made more mistletoe medicine and watched Jenne drink it, treated Mathieu as if nothing had happened, continued to prepare meals and made sure Jacob did his lessons. When her husband spoke of his disappointment, she said, "This will pass. Our children are no different from what they were before. If they make mistakes we must find ways to help them."

Père forgave his children. What sort of a man was he if he could not do that? But he rued that his standing in Thorney was damaged and he did not know best how to repair it.

Despite his father's disapproval Mathieu counted himself lucky because he and Monsieur Scribau were now separated from almost all the prisoners. The work had just about come to its end. And things were even more in his favour when news came from the government that the prisoners-of-war were to be released in a month. Against all expectation and without even trying, this embarrassing situation would dissolve. Now he would be able to make a new, good name for himself. If he could prove he was honourable then perhaps Catherine, the girl he liked so much, might let him kiss her.

While these things were going on Jacob smuggled Hibou-Bou into Jenne's room.

"His wing's still not right."

"But let's try flying him tomorrow when I'm allowed out." Jenne stroked him gently. "How would you like that? How would you like feeling the wind and smelling all those scents?"

"I'd love to see him catch a vole, or a mouse."

"But he might not come back. I'll be sad if he doesn't, but he's not supposed to live in a barn, is he? He was born to be outside."

Jacob closed the door and they let him fly round the room. He had more confidence than before but his swoops were still lop-sided.

"I'd better put him back."

"Come here, Bou-Bou. You're beautiful. And tomorrow you'll be in the sky!"

"Papa's going to say something important at dinner this evening. He and Maman were talking about it and I heard him say, 'The sooner the better.' I bet it's about Mathieu."

Jenne continued to stroke the owl. "Or me."

"Seigneur, auquel gist la plénitude de tous biens, we give thanks for this meal."

Jenne was looking forward to eating at the table instead of in bed. Two perch lay across a huge platter, head to tail, and there was a dish of carrots and beans. Père served the fish and Mère passed the platters round.

"Merci beaucoup, Ann"

"Merci beaucoup, Mère."

Within a few moments Père announced, "I've been thinking about what opinion people have of us – of our family."

He held out his plate for some vegetables. "Do you remember when I said the principles of drainage can teach us how to live? Good. Well, it seems to me it's time we put some of those principles into practice."

Jenne pulled a small fishbone from between her teeth. Why couldn't they just go on as usual? It was true she had had the falling sickness twice and might have it again, but as her face healed her fear reduced. It was in the past and if the Devil had ever been in her at all he had disappeared, so why couldn't they just get on with their lives?

"I want you three to think of one thing which you could improve, something to help the family and perhaps other people here in Thorney. Your mother and I have already decided on what we can do together and now I want each of you to come up with an idea for yourselves."

"Will we have to do it for ever?" asked Jacob.

"No, not for ever. Let's say until St Bartholomew's Day – about two months away."

What Jenne wanted to improve was her health. She wanted never to have another fit. That would certainly help her family, and it would help others too because no one would have to worry about her. But even if she took that disgusting green medicine every day for a year it might not prevent the falling sickness and it didn't really count as doing something *better*. She had sat down at the table happy but was now unhappy.

They were all waiting for Père to speak again.

"Mathieu, you're the eldest. Have you any ideas?"

"Not yet."

"Then perhaps we should continue this meal in silence. That will help you to concentrate."

It would have to be something she wouldn't otherwise have done, so sewing another sampler would not count either. What would please her parents most?

Then Jacob indicated he wished to speak and his father signalled that he could.

"Papa, I could groom your horse and clean your saddle and reins. You could leave it all to me, I'd do it properly."

Mère smiled. "That's a good idea. It would be a great help if he did that every day, wouldn't it, Samuel?"

"Good boy," grunted Père with affection.

They continued to eat without speaking.

"I could go to church more," volunteered Mathieu.

This suggestion puzzled Jenne. Mathieu sometimes tried to avoid church, but even if he was trying to soothe his father there were plenty of other things he was more likely to have thought of.

Père looked at Mathieu and raised his eyebrows. "You want to go to more services?"

"Yes. I could go to the Latin ones as well as the French ones. It would improve my Latin, wouldn't it?"

Père stroked his neat beard. "Very well then."

"I'll start tomorrow. I'll go to the early service and learn more of the lessons."

Jenne was struggling for ideas and decided to say so.

"Never mind. You'll think of something as soon as you're completely well again." Père pushed his chair back. "Now let me tell you what we are going to do as a family. We are going to help that young man Iain Alleyn whom we wrongly accused. We Huguenots pride ourselves on our fairness, but we were not fair to him. Mark Le Pla gave him a chance, and I admire him for doing so. It is thanks to him that Alleyn is alive. But he was reviled and injured because of what we believed he had done."

"I thought the prisoners were to be freed," said Mathieu, "He'll be gone in a week or so."

"I have invited him to live here. I want to make up for what he went through because of us."

No one moved.

Then Mathieu said, "It wasn't just us. It was others too."

"I know. However, that does not alter the fact that we – you and me in particular – did him wrong."

"But he's a prisoner."

"He's a prisoner-of-war."

"He can't live here."

"Why not?"

"Because … he's … what would people …?"

"What do you imagine they are saying now? Some of them may be saying that you lied and that Jenne should have known better. And perhaps some of them are saying I am a bad father. Well, I want to be a better father and I want us to be a better family. Are those not good things to strive for?

"I have already spoken with him. He wants to return to Scotland but needs to earn money first. By giving him a home we will improve his future and our future just as the drainage work has improved these fenlands for others and for ourselves."

Then Père rose so they all stood for grace.

᧕ 24th June 1652, Thorney

He arrived a week later. Mère and Père greeted him and Jacob was charged with taking him to where a bed had been prepared, and to the barrel where he could wash. Mère had put some of Mathieu's old clothes out for him.

Jacob raced off to Jenne. "He's taller than I thought he'd be and he has a big, black beard. And he speaks Scottish so I can't understand what he says. He looks fierce."

Jenne wondered about Iain Alleyn as she embroidered the two s's of *lyesse* – the last word of the first line of her sampler. A stranger living in the house. A prisoner-of-war. Someone who had fought in battles, who had been to places she knew nothing about. During the previous week she had heard it said that people thought her father unwise to invite him into their home but she had no sense of danger even when Jacob described Alleyn as fierce. Père would look after them and so would Mathieu because he was really a man now. Jacob had found out why he had chosen to go to church more. He was interested in Catherine Amory and she and her family lived close to the Abbey Church, so the more times he went to church the more he was likely to see her.

Jenne put her needle in a safe place and examined the sampler. She must remember how she had done that double *s*, for she would have to do it again when she reached *tristesse*. And she had nearly run out of green.

She went over to the window. Jacob was sweeping up some straw in the yard and talking to a man whose long hair she recognised as that of Charles, the brother of a friend of Mathieu's who was due to return a borrowed axe. After a minute or two Jacob pointed to the barn where Hibou-Bou lived, then leaned the broom against the house and walked towards the barn door beckoning Charles to follow him. They disappeared inside.

It was time to help her mother with the washing, so she went to the laundry to fetch the basket of newly-washed clothes.

"I'll be with you in a minute," called Maman from the kitchen.

Jenne lugged the basket outside and began to hang up the linen.

"Don't do those big things on your own, " said her mother, hurrying out. "There's quite a wind."

As they were hanging the last sheets out Jacob and Charles came into the yard.

"Oh, there you are," said Maman. "Jenne, this is Iain Alleyn."

It wasn't Charles at all. She did not recognise this man in front of her. She knew he had been on the boat and with her when she had her fit, but she had no recollection of him. Nor did he look like the person Jacob had described because in the last hour he must have shaved. He had long, dark hair and was wearing a suit rather too broad and short for him.

"I am pleased to see you well, Miss."

Jacob was right. He spoke differently.

"Thank you."

The four of them stood beside the washing which was billowing out horizontally.

"Come on inside," said Maman. "Jacob, you can do that straw tomorrow, it's too windy now. Go and put the broom away."

As they walked back to the doorway Iain turned to Jenne.

"I like your houlet."

She did not understand.

"I mean that I like your owl. In Scotland we call owls houlets."

"Do you? We French call them hiboux – that's why he's called Hibou. But usually we call him Bou-Bou."

"I've thought of a way to help his wing to mend."

✿ 1st July 1652, Thorney

Jacob was holding Bou-Bou firmly against his chest and Jenne was holding the hurt wing out at an angle. The owl's face was very close to hers.

"Lean back," advised Iain, "He's not going to like this."

Iain bit off a length of Jenne's blue embroidery thread with his teeth and began to feel along the wing for the best place to secure the small stick he had chosen for a splint. Then he tied it to the upper part before, in a quick movement, twisting the bottom part of the wing from the awkward position it had been in so it aligned properly. Hibou squawked and tugged to get away.

"Well done. Keep him steady."

Iain carefully wound the thread round the stick and the wing in two places and pulled it tight. Then he stretched the wing out gently until Hibou resisted.

"There. It may never heal completely, but in two weeks we'll take the splint off and see if he can fly."

"Well enough for us to let him go?" asked Jacob.

"I don't know, but it's the best we can do."

"You're clever," said Jenne. "Thank you."

"Look at the black rings around his eyes. Aren't they wonderful?"

Jenne smiled at Iain and nodded.

"Can I hold him?" asked Jacob.

"Yes. Take him now because I've got to go."

Iain transferred the owl to Jacob, walked out into the yard and over to the cart he had promised to mend. He put blocks under one end to raise one of the rear wheels off the ground. He turned the damaged wheel and saw he was going to have to replace at least three new spokes so would have to borrow a spokeshave.

He set off towards the Caillots, whom Monsieur had told him had the best range of tools, and as he walked he reflected on the difference two weeks had made. From being a prisoner-of-war to a criminal to a guest in the home of his accuser. Everything had changed, and it had all changed for the better. Not only had the Huguenots retracted their accusations against him but he and the other prisoners had been released. He could never have expected this double freedom to arrive at all, let alone so suddenly. Briefly, he thought of Macpherson who had been so hungry for home he had taken the first opportunity to leave. Macpherson, he knew, would be pleased about him being invited to live with the Deschamps, but just as astonished as he was himself.

Iain was not sure how to live in this new world, but he wanted to pay attention to each of the family. Jacob and Jenne were easy to please for though they teased him about his accent they loved hearing his stories. They had particularly liked it when, armed with a glaive, he had demonstrated how a pikeman manoeuvred his pikestaff, though afterwards he had lain the glaive on the ground and said it was far better to use it for catching eels than for killing men. Madame liked him too for he was polite and appreciative, and although he did not talk much to Monsieur he was well aware the hospitality he was receiving was due to his host's determination to right a wrong. But Mathieu was difficult. Iain recognised that losing face was hard for him and what Mathieu needed was for something good to happen in his life. Until that occurred, it seemed likely he would go on excluding Iain in petty ways such as rarely addressing him directly, only speaking in English when he had to and not explaining things fully.

✎ 12th August 1652, Thorney

Jenne was making slow progress with the second line of words on her sampler. She was on the *u* of *coeur*. She had done her lessons that morning, had now been sewing for an hour and was bored of being on her own. She was thinking about how different Iain was to everyone else she knew.

"That's how the Scots are," he would say if she commented on the way he did things. "At least, that's how this Scot is."

"But are you a Scot any more? You'll become one of us – if you stay."

When she had finished *coeur* she realised it had started to rain hard. Soon, everyone would be back inside. She went through to fetch clean water for them. Iain had been working in the next field and was home first. When he had washed he came to talk to her.

"Can I see what you're sewing?"

She held the canvas up in front of him.

"That's pretty."

"There's only a few of the words left to do now."

"What does it say?"

She spread it out on the table so it was flat. "There you are," she said.

"I can't read it."

Jenne looked at Iain in surprise. Then she laughed. "Sorry! It's in French! I'll translate it for you. It says, "Lord God, to regain joy and deliver my heart from its sadness I've cried aloud in my ... in my something, I'm not sure what *deuil* is ... and my *ennui* ... I'm not sure of that either – something like misery ... and my God heard me.

"Iain, wouldn't it be good if you learned more French? If you read this psalm I'll help you pronounce the words properly."

Iain looked at the text again, to where Jenne was pointing at the first word.

He said, "I know that letter."

"The word is *Au* – it sounds just like the letter O in English."

"Jenne, I can't read English words. I can't read at all. I've never learned."

She stared at him.

"And I can't write, except my name."

"But how ... how do you ...?"

"I don't need to write, but I wish I could. I look at all of you, and the books on your father's shelves. Even Jacob can read, can't he?"

"He could read when he was six or seven. We all could. Everyone can."

"Not everyone. Not me."

Jenne was silent for a moment.

"Then I'll teach you," she said with energy. "That would be a good thing for us to do together. I know, it can be my thing to improve – the thing which Père asked us to do. Come on, let's start now. I'm going to borrow Jacob's slate to teach you the letters."

September 1652, Thorney

St Bartholomew's Day came and went. Monsieur Deschamps and his friends looked forward to the Thanksgiving Service to be held in Ely Cathedral the following spring to mark the completion of the drainage projects.

Jacob had kept up his tasks with his father's horse and Père congratulated him for it had been a substantial undertaking. Jenne had taught Iain the alphabet and they were moving on to words. There was no doubt progress was being made but the two of them often collapsed in laughter about the shape of Iain's *g's* or *k's*, or the way he pronounced a French word. Mathieu continued his dogged attendance at church, claiming that he liked going and demonstrating what he had learned by reciting several prayers in Latin. All in all, Ann and Samuel Deschamps were quietly pleased with the way the family was re-establishing itself as upright and dependable.

Père was impatient for late October, because not until then would there be enough rain to test the new channels and straightened rivers. But rain was only part of the story as the tides could sweep upstream, collapse the dykes and drown the land. He was keen Iain should know precisely the extent of the work which had been accomplished and what it was intended to achieve. He found the best way of explaining was draw him diagrams showing the watercourses, using single lines for the old rivers, dotted lines for the first artificial channels and hatched ones for the new ones. Iain did his best to make sense of these spidery marks which Monsieur Deschamps made on paper or, if it were closer to hand, Jacob's slate. Iain went to sleep with a new vocabulary of cloughs and cloots, gads and chains, roddings and haffings.

9th September 1652, Thorney

One Tuesday evening, when Mère, Père and Iain were talking in the kitchen after the meal, they heard a howl, a howl which wailed up and down and did not stop. Iain raced out to find Jenne for that sound could only come from her. She would be juddering on the ground, arms flailing, eyes rolling.

But it was Jacob. He was kneeling on the straw in the yard sobbing and sobbing, gasping for breath for the next howl. Hibou-Bou lay in front of him, his head twisted sideways.

Iain knelt down beside him, touched the still warm feathers, the bloodied beak. Jacob was beside himself, unable to put words together. And then Jenne arrived, imagining Jacob was yelling because he had cut himself with that axe he was not supposed to touch. She was puzzled when she saw her owl on the grass, and angry because Jacob had taken him out without her permission. Then suddenly she realised that Jacob must have hurt Bou-Bou, and she too began to weep.

Mère tried to comfort Jenne while Iain stayed with Jacob. Père held back and watched as the tears and noise gradually subsided.

"What did you do? What have you done?" sobbed Jenne.

Jacob set up another howl. "I didn't do anything! It was Mathieu!"

Iain kept his arm round Jacob who had curled up on the ground in his distress.

"What do you mean? What did Mathieu do?" asked Mère urgently.

"He killed Bou-Bou."

"But why?"

"Catherine, that girl Mathieu likes, thinks Jenne is a witch," wailed Jacob with his eyes tightly shut, "Because she has the falling sickness and she talks to Bou-Bou."

Iain continued to stroke Jacob's back.

"She says only witches talk to creatures so Jenne must have the Devil in her." He sat up, his hands clasping his head, and sobbed, "So he killed Bou-Bou."

Iain looked up to Madame who was in shock, her hands over her mouth. Monsieur had moved closer to Jacob, and Jenne and Jacob were weeping. The owl lay in the centre of the little group as if it were about to be offered to the gods.

Gently, Iain asked, "Are you sure it was Mathieu who did it?"

"He told me last week what Catherine said, but I didn't tell

Jenne because it would have upset her. And just now I saw him coming out of the barn with a stick. He saw I'd seen him, and he said, 'I should have done that months ago'."

"Where is he now?"

Jacob sniffed, "I don't know, but I hate him and I hope I never see him again."

Slowly, Mère led Jenne away towards the house. Then Jacob stood up, took his father's hand, and followed behind. Iain picked up Bou-Bou carefully and got to his feet. He went into the barn, found his old prisoner's shirt and wrapped it round the owl.

ᕮ 13th September 1652, Thorney

Mathieu hid nothing from his parents. He resented Alleyn living in his home. It was humiliating to have a prisoner to whom he had recently been giving orders eating at the same table. He should not have lied about taking Jenne to see the prisoners, but nor should everyone continue to hold this against him. It was unfair that people gave Jenne special attention just because she had nearly been a victim. They ignored the fact that although – not without reason – he had blamed the man whom he believed had hurt Jenne, there were plenty of others who had done the same including Père himself. He had not intended to make a false accusation but it seemed as if he was the only one being criticised for it.

It was sad about Jenne's falling sickness, but there it was. It would make life difficult for her and for others. He realised it probably meant she would never marry. But it was spoiling his chances too, because Catherine, whom he was serious about, had indicated that her interest in him would cease if Jenne went on having these fits. What Catherine really objected to was the rumour that Jenne was a witch. Everyone knew she talked to that owl as if it were a person so it seemed to Mathieu that if he got rid of it Catherine would think better of Jenne and all his family and thus he himself.

Jacob was a spoiled baby. By that age, he – Mathieu – had been expected to do many more jobs and to do real work as well as to study, whereas Jacob was allowed to play for hours with that stupid owl and hang around Jenne more like a sister than a brother. And did they know what he had found him doing recently? When he had gone into the barn for something he had found Jacob with the owl. Jacob had taken it out of the foul rag it was wrapped in, put it on an upturned box and was drawing it on a piece of paper which he must have taken – probably without permission – from amongst Père's maps. The bird was bloody and had lost its natural sheen, yet Jacob was so engrossed in drawing the horrible thing he had not even noticed Mathieu coming into the barn. That sort of thing was morbid, wasn't it? He should have been outside fishing or helping on the farm.

And it was true that learning Latin verses and going to church had not improved things for him or anyone else.

"So I'm a bad son. I accept that."

He stared across the table at the wall. Mère looked at his new, straggling beard, at how he was growing out of his doublet, at the way his hair grew like Samuel's.

Père sat for a minute with his eyes closed. Then he said, "Mathieu, you are not a bad son."

"I'm not good, am I?"

"You are our first-born son, and you are unhappy. We do not like to see you like this."

Mère asked, "What would make you happier?"

"I don't know."

"Try to tell us what you would like to happen."

Mathieu shifted on his chair. "I'd like Catherine to want to be with me as much as I want to be with her. I'd like people to stop judging me unfairly and believe me responsible, as they used to – as *you* used to – I'd like…."

"Yes, it's hard," said Père. "But you have to decide what to do and how to do it. You'll be nineteen next month, more than old enough to plan how to live your life. And unless you have some other plan you have to go on living here as our son, pull your weight on the farm again and make your peace with your brother and sister."

Mathieu looked at him sharply, "And what am I supposed to do about Alleyn?"

"You could at least be polite to Iain."

"I'm doing my best."

"Are you sure?"

Mathieu tipped his chair back.

"Don't forget he is our guest," said Père.

"No, he's not. He's not a real guest like Uncle Jacques, or the pastor. Real guests are real friends you choose to have in your house."

"We chose to have Iain Alleyn."

"Not because he was a friend. You only invited him because you had a bad conscience."

"Are you saying I'm wrong to act in accordance with my conscience?"

"I'm just trying to tell you why it's hard for me to accept him."

There was a pause.

"Anyway, when's he going back to Scotland?"

"I don't know."

"Well, he can't stay here for ever, can he? He doesn't belong in this house or to us, or to the English or to this place. We were here long before him – I was born here, I've been here all my life. For God's sake, he can't even read."

"Mathieu, it may be the case that you cannot do other than reject him, and if so, I regret it. But if you remain fixed in this attitude towards him then you will be stuck while he will continue to change and grow. I can't emphasise this enough: if you restrict and limit your attitude, it is you who will be the loser."

✒ 17th September 1652, Thorney

Jenne walked in front carrying Hibou-Bou. She had decided exactly where she wanted to bury him. Jacob and Iain came behind, wrapped in cloaks against the slanting rain.

After ten minutes she stopped. She pointed to the foot of a bank they knew well. "Here, because it's in sight of our house and when we look in this direction we'll remember him."

Iain suggested making the grave at the top. "When I first came here water lay at the bottom of every bank. Wouldn't it be better to bury him higher up?"

Jenne, uncertain, stood holding the owl in his brown shroud, her bonnet already wet through.

"Look at it this way," said Iain, "If it were you who was to be buried, where would you prefer to be?"

"Higher up," said Jacob immediately, "I'd want to have a good view, especially if I liked – had liked – flying."

Iain climbed further up. "Come and have a look up here."

Jenne followed him but as they reached the top the wind hit her so she turned back into the lee of the bank.

"Here, then," she said, "Half way up and half way down, out of the wind and out of the water." She looked at the wet bundle she was cradling.

Jacob said, "It's a shame his wing didn't heal properly."

"The splint would have worked if I'd been able to put it on earlier. It's best to mend things as soon as possible."

"I wanted him to fly off and be free, even if I didn't see him again." said Jacob. "But I *will* see him again."

"What do you mean?" asked Jenne. "Do you mean when you're dead too?"

"I can see him whenever I want."

Jenne looked at Iain who said, "You and Hibou-Bou must have a secret."

"We have."

"Then we won't ask any more about it. But he's free now, at least."

"Free?" asked Jenne.

"Yes. Death is a sort of freedom."

Jacob, who had insisted on lugging the spade all the way there, started to dig into the mud. Soon he was soaked through and struggling and passed the spade to Iain who started to work with strength and rhythm.

Jacob commented, "You're very good at digging."

"Of course he is! He was a banker, wasn't he?"

Jacob watched him scraping away the silty earth. "What are you going to be now you don't have to be a banker any more?"

Iain carried on digging as he said, "I'd like to heal people."

"I want to be a farmer."

"You'll be a good farmer." Iain stood up straight. "Now, Jenne, it's up to you."

She stepped forward. "I'm just going to put him straight in. I couldn't bear to look at him again."

So she laid Hibou-Bou, still wrapped in Iain's old shirt, into the bank and Jacob filled up the hole with the sandy silt.

Then she began to recite quietly her favourite chant from church: *O Souverain pasteur et maistre* and Jacob joined in.

As they walked back the rain eased off.

"Iain, you don't know the words of that prayer, do you?"

"No. We didn't chant like that in the church I used to go to."

"Your God is the same as our God, isn't He?"

"Of course. There's only one God."

"And there's only one Devil, isn't there?"

The fear had not gone away completely. Although her parents had been so upset when Mathieu killed Hibou-Bou and had never blamed her for doing anything wrong, they kept on saying those prayers about sins and transgressions and unworthiness.

"I don't know about the Devil," said Iain, "But I don't believe he's anything to do with the falling sickness. The falling sickness is exactly that – a sickness where you fall. I don't know why you had fits, nor why a boy in my village at home had fits. More than once I've seen him be like you were and recover just as you have recovered."

"But some people say I'm a witch."

She felt Iain's hand catch hers and slow her down. He turned her to face him and put his hands on her shoulders.

"You're not a witch, Jenne. You are a healthy young lass who is occasionally ill."

As they walked up the drove together, three abreast, Jenne felt different. It felt so much better that Iain had said she was not a witch, but how could he be sure?

She did not say what she was thinking but just before they passed the Abbey Church, Iain continued, "I can't prove it, Jenne, and I know I'm only a pikeman who can't read and write properly, but that doesn't mean I'm wrong. After you had the fit by the stream, people did not believe any of us. Not you, because you were ill. Not Jacob, because he's young. Not me, because I

83

was a prisoner. But we were all telling the truth, saying what we knew to be right."

They were nearly home, and as they approached they saw Mathieu. He seemed to be waiting for them, standing alone in the drizzle and looking miserable.

Jenne found herself running up to him, holding on to him, hugging him.

๑ December 1652, Thorney

October and November were already over and the rivers and channel banks were holding well. The men went out every day to inspect them and came back satisfied. Mathieu was beginning to show an interest in the technical side of farming and had ideas about how the ploughs pulled by oxen and horses could be made more efficient. Père and their neighbours were talking about preparing soil, breeding stock and buying seed.

While waiting for winter Jenne had begun to worry about whether Iain might decide to return to Scotland for recently one of her friends had asked, "Is that man going to live with you for ever?" and she had suddenly realised she was assuming he would.

Jacob had not forgotten Jenne had promised to take him on a long skating expedition now he was old enough. "You can come too," he told Iain, "And if you and Mathieu come Maman will allow Jenne to come."

"I'll have to learn to skate first."

"Mathieu will teach you. Everyone says he's the best skater in Thorney."

And at last the frost came, and ice formed on the Nene, The Twenty Foot, Morton's Leam and Bevill's Leam. Sometimes it melted for a few days, and slices of loose ice would slip downstream until the cold arrested them again and solidified them into a surface thick enough for horses and people.

Jenne watched Mathieu show Iain how best to strap the skates on to his boots and how to slide his feet and use his sticks. He told him too about how he wanted to copy skates from a new pair his friend Piere Roo had had sent from Flanders, but he needed metal and different tools. Iain suggested they went over to where the Dutch prisoners-of-war were working because they must be the experts.

"You'd better practise, Jenne," said Iain, laughing, "Once I get going I'll soon beat you."

Jenne looked round the table. Mathieu had stopped sulking and Père had stopped lecturing. Life felt good.

There were three things she was particularly pleased about: the falling sickness might return but she was not a witch; the land was no longer drowned but there were still plenty of places to skate; and even though it was possible Iain might leave, it had just occurred to her – during the dinner they were at that very moment in the middle of – that she might be able to influence whether he did or not.

They stood up.

Seigneur Dieu, nous Te rendons grâce de tous les bénéfices que nous reçevons.

Six months later, July 1653, Thorney

The Thanksgiving Service was a glorious occasion, but within weeks Vermuyden disappeared. The fens were full of rumours about him – that he was nearly bankrupt, he was ill, he had once again fallen from favour. Samuel Deschamps and Mark Le Pla discussed him for hours but to no avail for no more news was heard and, after all those years of work, he did not appear again.

As time went by Jenne found herself wanting a sign. A sign to prove Iain liked her *very much.* He was always polite and thoughtful – he was to everyone – but she wanted more than that. It was a pity their reading lessons had come to a halt, but Iain was needed on the farm for most daylight hours and somehow the two of them never managed to sit down alone together now that summer was here again.

This was partly because of Mathieu, who, Jenne believed, deliberately sought them out to interrupt them, for Jacob had whispered to her he had heard Mathieu telling their parents it was not suitable for Jenne to be on her own with Iain.

"She's already sixteen," he had complained, "Just at the stage where her head could be turned by someone like him – someone a bit different and with a foreign accent."

Père said, "She's perfectly all right with Iain."

"There are boys in Thorney who say Jenne thinks she's too good for them. She ought to be careful because she's not in a position to choose, is she? Not with her falling sickness."

"Don't be so unkind, Mathieu," said Mère. "Leave them alone, can't you?"

Jenne thought more about the idea of a sign. What would count as a sign? What would he have to say? 'I love you'? 'You're beautiful'? Or would it rather be something like the things which she wanted to say to him, words which would come out in an unstoppable rush: 'I think about you all the time and you make me feel happy and I always want to be with you and I want you to stay here and not ever go back to Scotland and I wish you would kiss me'. She no longer wondered *if* he would give her a sign; it was just a question of where and on what occasion.

She also gave some thought about what he might *do*. He had steadied her arm occasionally when pulling her across a ditch or helping her on or off a boat but he always let go immediately. Nothing had been as good as when he had put his hands on her shoulders that time they came back from burying Bou-Bou. She recalled their welcome weight and how the gesture seemed all the more important because his palms had left traces of earth on her cloak which she had never brushed off. If only he would do something like that again. She began to wonder whether she could create a situation in which he would have to touch her. She could stumble on the step, perhaps, missing her footing so he would reach out and catch her.

She imagined his flecked eyes, that small scar on his cheek and the way he tilted his head slightly when he laughed. She couldn't stop smiling when she thought about him, though she became more serious when she considered kissing.

But clearly nothing could be said or done unless they were alone.

"It's annoying," she told her friend Ester, "We're almost never alone."

"Just be patient. He'll find a way if he wants to. In fact, he can't fail to if he's living in your house."

Jenne trusted Ester's opinion for she was older and had more experience of boys. Piere Roo had been courting her for six months.

"At the beginning, how did you know Piere liked you? What did he do?"

"He told his sister to tell me."

"I'm sure Iain wouldn't give anyone a message. The only person he could give one to would be Jacob, and he certainly wouldn't do that. Jacob's far too young."

"Don't worry, Jenne. He'll find a way, believe me."

September 1653, Thorney

Although things were better than they had been for years there were still important decisions to be made. Should he forget the idea of returning to Scotland? Or should he abandon this warm Deschamps family and Thorney and go back to a life he found increasingly hard to recall? How important was it to him to learn to heal people? He could do that in Scotland, couldn't he? Would these Huguenots accept him fully if he did not adopt their faith? And would it matter if he changed faith?

At first, the central question running round his head was: Where do I belong?

He wondered whether the answer was to be found in a place – such as Dunbar, or Thorney – or with people such as with the Huguenots or with his family, but he had learned that sometimes it is best to leave a difficult question alone. Then, the solution might present itself.

And then there was Jenne. What about sweet Jenne? She was taking up more and more of him and it was becoming harder and harder to deny that first and foremost he belonged with her. He found himself thinking about her most of the time. She was a marvellous young woman. She was warm, good-natured, intelligent, mature for her age and very attractive. He loved the way she covered her face with her hands and smiled at him through her fingers and how she pushed her hair back over her left ear (but never her right) when she was concentrating. And her family mattered too. They were so steady that he knew she would remain centred and grounded if she were ever to face difficulties. When he imagined her with children he was sure she would be strong, patient and loving. And she worked well and cheerfully in the kitchen and on the farm too. Yes, she was everything. From time to time he thought about her falling sickness for that might always be with her, but it did nothing to weaken the strength of his feeling.

And he imagined holding her. He had only lain with a few girls in his life and the last time had been a few weeks before the Battle of Dunbar when a group of women had come to the edge of the camp and he, like many others, had paid some of their newly-acquired and still-shining coins to lie under a wagon with a half-dressed woman he could hardly see because they had been ordered to extinguish all lamps. The whole business had been over in a matter of minutes after which she had shoved him off and called for the next man. Jenne was as different from that woman as mountains were from the fens. He wanted to kiss Jenne, look into her grey eyes, tell her he loved her. He would cup each of her breasts gently. He would enjoy her and she would enjoy him.

So how, *how*, could he possibly be thinking of leaving her and returning to Scotland? Of course he would stay.

He was sure she felt the same way. Last week she had sought him way out by Old Wryde where he was having trouble with a broken cartwheel. Quite unnecessarily she had brought him some bread and cheese in case he was not home in time for the evening meal. He had looked up from struggling with the shaft and seen her approaching with her wide smile and those wisps of brown hair escaping from her bonnet. She was slightly out of breath from hurrying and he had found it very hard not to hold out his arms and embrace her there and then on the public road. When he had finished mending the wheel they sat and talked until dusk, and only later did he realise he had hardly touched the food she had brought.

But when should he say something? His place in the Deschamps' home, though secure, was unorthodox. Sometimes he felt like a son, sometimes a friend. He was unsure about the correct course of action. Should he ask Samuel Deschamps for his daughter's hand? Was he absolutely sure he could make his future in Thorney? He wanted to talk to someone about it, and resolved that the best person would be Mark Le Pla. Yes. That was it. He would look out for the right opportunity to approach him.

❦ 1st November 1653, Thorney

One cold, bright Sunday afternoon a week later, as Monsieur and Madame Deschamps and Jenne were setting out to see the new calves in the far byre and Jacob had run on ahead because he wanted to see them first, Iain asked if he could join them.

"Of course," said Mère, "You don't have to ask."

Jenne flashed a smile and slowed down so Iain could walk next to her. The path narrowed and Mère and Père went ahead, while Jenne and Iain fell behind. Jenne was swishing the grass with a thin stick, unable to hide her delight at this unexpected treat.

"I've been thinking," said Iain. "I've been thinking about my life and where I live it. I'm wondering whether I should go back to Scotland or whether I should stay here."

Jenne stopped walking and looked at him with an expression of dismay. "But …" she said, "But you can't … I thought you …."

Iain carried on along the path with his head down.

Just then Jacob appeared and squeezed in between them.

Jenne snapped at him, "Oh go away! Jacob, just go away. Can't you leave us alone for once?"

"There are three calves," he announced loudly, ignoring her, "One's almost white, one's brown and white, and one's sort of speckled like an egg."

"Why don't you go back and think up good names for each of them?" suggested Iain.

"You two just want me out of the way, don't you?"

Iain and Jenne said nothing.

"Everyone knows you're in love," he said, "It's obvious."

Then he sighed and said, "It's not surprising, I suppose. But it's very boring for me."

Jenne put her hands to her face in embarrassment and Iain burst out laughing. Then he caught Jenne's hand and said, "It's true, isn't it? You are the most important thing, the most important person in my life."

Jenne nodded, unable to speak a word.

"You feel the same way, don't you? Tell me you feel the same way."

She nodded again, and found herself sniffing and still speechless.

"I want to marry you, Jenne." Iain pulled her hands to his mouth and kissed them, "Will you marry me?"

Jenne went on nodding and crying and smiling at the same time.

"Then let's tell your parents, for they should be the first to know."

"It's too late," called Jacob, "They know already. I told everyone weeks ago."

↶ Six months later, 4th May 1654, Thorney

Mathieu managed to hide his disapproval at the wedding but it was as if from a distance that he joined in with the chants and watched the couple, the pastor and his family and friends.

How could his parents be so proud and pleased? Iain Alleyn had been a peasant before he became a pikeman. Then he had been a prisoner-of-war living on the very margins of a marginal world. Now he was more than that but he owed everything – *everything* – to the Deschamps and to Thorney. Granted, he had some skill as a farmer and a herbalist, but this marriage was a step too far. How had Père allowed it? If men like Alleyn were going to marry Huguenot women, who would be left for the Huguenot men? At this rate there would be no true Huguenots left. Their history and tradition would become watered down and lost. Iain probably only knew a couple of verses of the most common chants.

Now the pastor was performing the marriage itself, and then, within only a few minutes, it was over. Mathieu followed everyone out of the Abbey Church feeling wretched.

And how was it that Iain had found a wife so easily when he himself had such bad luck? One girl had said no to him as a suitor, it turned out another's family were quite unsuitable and when he traipsed all the way over to Crowland on that wet day to see a third one, she turned out to have a club foot so she was no good either. So for the time being he had given up the idea of courting and told himself it was easier to remain single. He thanked God that his work was becoming increasingly significant, for it was work which gave most meaning to his life.

But the new arrangements at home rankled him. He, the eldest son, had to move out from the room where he had slept before into the corner Iain had occupied in order to make room for Iain and Jenne. He grudgingly acknowledged that this was the only solution but on the wedding night he heard their love-making. They were in his bed, in his room, and he was relegated to being squeezed into a small room with his younger brother. He couldn't sleep. He was kept awake by the murmur of conversation and stifled laughter as well as by more urgent cries and groans he had no desire to hear yet found himself listening for. How was it that a defeated Scotchman could be doing those private things with his sister, the daughter of a respected drainage engineer and land-owner? What, he asked himself, would Cromwell have said about that?

He was soaked in sweat. He tried lying on his front, his side, his back. He threw off the covers only to pull them back a few minutes later. He got up to fetch water, to relieve himself, to go out into the cool air of the yard. He was taken over by resentment so strong it completely destroyed his peace of mind. He blamed his parents as well as Jenne and Iain but knew in his heart that what he was feeling was not their fault or anyone's fault. This rage was to do with he himself, but he could not understand it and had no idea how to be rid of it.

He sat out in the dark yard for an hour until the night air stilled him and he was able to return to bed, settle down and sleep.

But the next morning he woke wanting a woman. Not a wife, but a woman – any woman. When he went outside to the barrel to wash he met Iain.

"You first," he said curtly, conscious he was being ungracious. What reason did he have to be gracious to this man? He leant against the wall and watched Iain splash the water over his face and arms with energy, pull a clean shirt over his head and smooth his hair down.

There was no denying it: the lucky, lucky bastard was glowing with vitality and joy, and he was not.

ᷤ One year later, 17th May 1655, Thorney

"Look at her tiny nails."

Jenne leant over the baby. "I keep checking to see if she's breathing."

"I can't believe she was inside you until three days ago."

"It's a miracle – babies are the best of God's miracles."

"She's waking up."

They watched the baby turn her head, lift an arm and make small sucking movements.

"It's extraordinary to think of all the things those little hands will be able to do."

"And she'll be walking and running on those tiny feet."

"And skating!"

They stood marvelling at their first-born until Iain said, "I've got to go. We've a lot on today. I'll be back as soon as I can." He kissed Jenne and the baby and went out.

Jenne picked Magdalen up out of her cot, held her against her shoulder and walked around the room. She pushed her nose into the baby's neck to smell her sweet smell and relished the feeling of holding her close.

Was it possible to be happier than this? She had everything she could ever want: a loving husband, a healthy baby, a home and family and more than enough in respect of material things.

Yet again, she found herself praying:

"Notre bon Père tout puissant, We thank Thee for blessing us with our daughter Magdalen. We beg forgiveness for those sins we have committed which have led Thee to be displeased with us. We recognise our unworthiness but beseech Thee to grant us Thy clemency and grace. Amen."

There was a knock on the door.

"It's me."

"Come in, Jacob. I'm just going to feed her."

"Then I'll come back later because I want to draw her. That'll be all right, won't it?"

"Of course it will. It's a lovely idea."

Jacob held his finger up to Magdalen, and stroked her hand.

"She's holding on to my finger."

"Yes, she likes doing that."

"She's trying to suck it!"

"That's because she's hungry. Come on, Magdalen, let's settle down comfortably so I can nurse you."

Jenne sat down on the low chair and asked Jacob to put a cushion behind her.

"I'm off now. Goodbye, little niece."

Jenne loosened her clothes and put Magdalen to her left breast. She watched her nuzzle urgently round the big, brown nipple before finding it, latching on to it and starting to suck steadily. She was only three days old and she knew exactly what to do. Her mouth and cheeks moved in a rhythmic, strong movement. Jenne had never imagined how feeding a baby might make her body and spirit feel, had never thought it would feel so good and right. She was reminded of the far stronger feeling she had had when she and Iain were married and first made love for then too she had been completely unprepared. Why had no one told her how extraordinary and amazing it would be? She was sure she was changed by it but why did no one ever say that? She thanked God again.

After four or five minutes she moved Magdalen to the other breast, but even as she did so she felt the fullness of the baby's little belly. Did she have room for any more? A trickle of the almost blue milk was running from the baby's mouth and she wiped it with her finger and licked it. Its sweetness surprised her.

"Come on, ma petite. Don't go to sleep yet."

But Magdalen had had enough and was already asleep. She did not wake even when Jenne undressed her, laid her on her back and cleaned her. It was quite wonderful to see her naked. Jenne stroked the little thighs and knees. She patted the rounded stomach. She touched the small strange knot, evidence of how she and Magdalen had been joined, and she gazed at the soft and swollen crease which announced this baby to be a girl. How could the creation of new life be at the same time so commonplace and so extraordinary?

"Père éternel qui nous ordonne, grant us Thy grace for this day and this night. We beseech Thee to help us avoid displeasing Thee and to support those who have suffered for Thy sake but who, like us, have transgressed."

Mère came in just as Jenne finished putting Magdalen back in her cot.

"I didn't know how much I'd love her. I didn't know it would be like this."

"But you're happy?"

Jenne burst into tears. "Yes, yes, I'm so happy. I've never been happier."

"Come here, ma petite."

She held Jenne to her and stroked her back until she stopped crying.

"Isn't it strange," said Mère, "How sadness and happiness can sometimes be so close?"

1658

⤷ **Three years later, September 1658**

Mathieu came running into the room and threw his jerkin on to the bench.

"Have you heard? Cromwell's dead! He died last week, and he's named his son as his successor."

Iain looked up, then slowly dipped his fingers in the mixture he was working to a paste. "Like a son succeeds a king?"

Mathieu looked at him in surprise. "Yes. I suppose so."

Iain went on making the poultice he was preparing for Monsieur Frouchart.

Mathieu hurried out calling, "I'm going to tell Père."

Why was he so excited? What difference would it make to their lives? It certainly might do, but Mathieu always seemed to respond to things in an extreme way – he would violently oppose or support things without giving them enough thought.

Samuel would know what it might mean. Samuel always sought news from travellers, and said, "We live on our little island of Thorney. We have few visitors and we rarely go far ourselves.

But we should not forget that things which happen in other places might affect us. History shows no one should ever believe their prosperity and safety are secure. Bad events – and good ones – can appear out of thin air."

Was it right for a man of power and authority to name his son as his successor? Surely no one can know how their child will turn out? Even a general or a wise man might have a son who was no good as a soldier or leader. And surely a man who sought such an office should be chosen on his own merits, not on his father's? It was different for kings, of course, for they ruled by Divine Right.

It was only after he had poured the poultice into a jar and was walking along the causeway to deliver it that he realised Cromwell must have died on the very anniversary of the Battle of Dunbar, the battle he and his fellow soldiers had fought in, been taken prisoner at and been marched south from. Perhaps it was Cromwell, not he himself, who was the cause of him living a completely different life than he would otherwise have had. He would never know whether his life would have been better if he had stayed in Scotland.

He regretted the loss of his family. He rarely thought of his mother and father, his sister and brother, but when Magdalen was born he had wanted more than anything for them to see her. Sometimes he had the feeling that he had betrayed his family by not going back to them, but what good would going back do now? If his parents were still alive he hoped that his sister had a child to live after them, but there was no telling as to what had happened.

And now Cromwell, whose soldiers had indirectly brought about the death of his brother and had killed so many men he had known, was himself dead. What might this lead to? Could Charles II could be restored to the throne? Could the king he had fought for become king again? If so, would a war be necessary?

One war was enough. The thought of another here in this place where they were peaceful and comfortable was difficult to imagine. He remembered how General Leslie had destroyed all the crops and stock round Dunbar so Cromwell's troops would be short of food. What if that were to be done in Thorney? All their industry would have come to nothing. And if he had been unable to protect his brother, would he be able to protect Jenne and Magdalen?

1661

They have made the fen-ground into land, meadows and pastures in those places which lately presented to the eyes of the beholder but great waters, and a few reeds scattered thinly here and there.

Bedford Level Charter of Incorporation

If we weigh the great inconveniences which these over-flowings have produced, certainly the advantage by the general draining ought the more to be prized; for in winter-time, when the ice is strong enough to hinder the passage of boats (as hath been by some well observed) and yet not able to bear a man; the inhabitants upon the hards and the banks within the fens can have no help of food, nor comfort for body or soul; no woman aid in her travail; no means to baptize a child, or partake of the Communion, nor supply of any necessity saving what those poor desolate places do afford. And what expectation of health can there be on the bodies of men, where there is no element of good? The air being for the most part cloudy , gross and full of rotten harrs; the water putrid , yea full of loathesome vermin; the earth spungy and boggy, and the firre noisome, by the stink of smoky hassoks.

From Dugdale's History of Imbanking and Drayning

↶ Three years later, 5th May 1661, Thorney

The child was making her unsteady way through the long grass in pursuit of a tabby cat, but when the cat jumped on to the window ledge she could no longer see it. She stood still and looked in every direction except upwards.

"He's up here. Look," Jenne pointed to the cat and helped the child up on to a step. "Stroke him gently, like this."

The cat submitted to being stroked but jumped down and ambled off towards the barn when his fur was pulled.

"Gently, Magdalen, or he could scratch you." Jenne set the girl down again, stood up straight, put her hands to the small of her back and eased her shoulders forwards and backwards. She

96

was still slim but she was cautious about picking Magdalen up in case she miscarried.

Mère came out of the house. "How are you feeling? Shall I look after her for an hour or so?"

"That would be good. It's so hot today."

"Go on then. Go and rest." Mère smiled at her daughter and called to Magdalen. "Viens, ma petite. I'll take you to see the cows."

Jenne turned to scoop a jug of cool water out of the barrel. She carried it inside, poured a cupful and drank it slowly. She took off her shoes and pulled back the top cover from her bed, ready for sleep.

How many times had she lain in this room, awake or asleep? It was in here that she had recovered from a falling fit and it was in here too that she recovered after giving birth to Magdalen. And then, not much more than twelve months ago, it was in this very bed that she gave birth to a baby too small to survive. That event had nearly knocked the heart out of her. She recalled Iain carrying the tiny coffin to the churchyard on a day made for rejoicing. It was early autumn and the leaves were beginning to change colour. It was a day to give thanks to God for His goodness and grace. Their quiet procession had stood grieving in the warm sunshine before the pastor consigned Isaac to his small grave.

She wondered about the meaning of *recovery*. The re-finding, re-gaining of something important which had been lost such as well-being, good health, information. Each of her significant experiences in this room had been different, and each had led to her coming to know something she would not otherwise have learned so vividly: the randomness of illness; the joy of giving birth; the pain of losing a child.

Now she had her precious Magdalen whom she loved, she hardly dared admit, almost more than Iain. But surely a baby – indeed *any* baby – could not have too much love? It was only after having one which died that Mère told her she too had lost a child. That had helped Jenne for it showed her how life went on and how things could improve.

And when she and her brothers were babies, had Mère loved them more than she loved Père? Probably. Probably all mothers loved their babies – even those who had yet to be born or had died – more than their husbands. But if Magdalen had all her love now, would she be able to love the next baby as much? Might it be possible to run out of love? Surely mothers – or anyone – couldn't just keep on extending their love to more and more children? Wouldn't their love become weaker, watered down?

Since missing her courses and knowing she was pregnant she had added to her usual prayers an extra one for her unborn child as well as for the dead one. She gave thanks too that she had only twice had the falling sickness since her marriage, but she was fearful for Magdalen. The thought of her or of a baby having a fit was quite terrible. Someone had told her that if a child was seized by a fit it should be plunged into cold water up to its neck. She had imagined getting hold of Magdalen and lifting her up and then setting her down into that dark water in the barrel which stood in the yard, the one she had just taken water from. She imagined the child's little dress she had so carefully smocked puffing out with air before it became soaked, and then Magdalen's screams, her shocked face and body. Jenne had resolved never to subject her to this.

The older she became the more there was to pray for. Her parents prayed for Mathieu, for her, Iain and Magdalen, for Jacob, for their deceased relatives, for other living relatives, for those they knew with responsibilities or difficulties, and they never forgot the victims of the Massacre even though it had taken place a hundred years ago. And when Mathieu and Jacob married – Mère and Père were probably already praying for Mathieu to settle down with someone suitable – there would be more prayers for their wives, and then their children. The list would go on and on growing as more things happened but never leaving out important things from the past. So, if her parents could go on extending their love and prayers, she also should be able to.

Iain never criticised her parents for their lengthy French prayers, but his were always short, almost the same and to the point: *"Holy God our Father, thank you for our lives and for the lives of those we love, and for this world you have given us. May we have peace in our hearts. Help us to live well and do what is right. Amen."*

He didn't even mention sin and when Jenne pointed this out to him he said he was not interested in evil and that in order to do what God wanted his time was better spent checking dykes, feeding sheep, mending tools and preparing herbal medicines than praying.

He was out in search of herbs that afternoon. Jenne imagined him walking along a bank by a dyke of almost still water. He would be stopping every few yards and squatting to identify a leaf or to see if a certain plant was yet flowering. Ever since their betrothal they often walked together, usually slowly and with little talking. However, having Magdalen with them made it a different experience and once she was able to walk they held on to her for fear she would fall in the water. Their progress these days was far from silent but just as enjoyable.

*

There was something wrong with the mare's mouth. A tooth had festered and come out with the slightest of pulling, but the gum remained bloody and sore, and the creature had hardly eaten for days. It would be a great misfortune if she were to die.

It was always difficult to heal mouth sores, especially in a big animal, but Iain was hopeful that plantain would work on the horse. He needed a large quantity and had already collected a bag full of stalks and leaves as well as some whole plants complete with roots. It was a good day for finding them for they were robust and, topped with the thick parts that reminded him of tiny bulrushes, they were easily visible amongst the bending grasses.

Just as Jenne was falling asleep and he was about to return home he noticed some shepherd's purse. He stooped to pull it, for only last week when Magdalen had fallen and bruised her knee a poultice made from this herb had soothed it at once. Learning about herbs was fascinating and recently he had decided to make a map of where each one grew on good paper Matthieu provided from his engineering studies. Iain was taking great pleasure in writing the name of the place and the herb's name and uses beside it although this was proving increasingly complicated as he gained more knowledge about the various powers of the different parts. Each part of the plant – the roots, leaves, petals, seeds and fruit – might affect the body in different ways as might the various methods of preparation.

Now in his thirty-fourth year, it seemed as if his life was making progress at the same pace as that in the drained fenlands. While he had a home, a family, a wife, a child and new skills and knowledge, the farm was producing onions, peas, hemp and woad, and cattle and sheep were grazing on the other side of the dyke. All those years of digging and draining had been a success, and his own life felt stable and established.

There was still plenty of undrained land where the fenmen could snare birds and catch fish and eels as they had always done, but this did not stop them complaining. Only last month there had been rumours about how the rivers' outfalls into The Washes were being clogged up by incoming tides and outgoing silt. But there was probably little substance to what was said. Some fenmen were always complaining and criticising; that was just how they were – they exaggerated problems and looked on the worst side of anything they did not approve of. The single thing that had forced them to make actual changes was the sluices. They were too small for the Humber Keels to pass through so cargoes had to be unloaded from one and re-loaded on to another, which resulted in delays and increased cost. Eventually the Keels would be replaced with the smaller Fen Lighters, but that would take years and more money than most fenmen could afford.

Samuel was right. no one could have done more than they had. The plans envisaged by Vermuyden and carried out by the French and others – he never forgot to acknowledge the Scottish and Dutch prisoners-of-war – would last for generations. As long as the banks were maintained winter floods would be a thing of the past except for those which were supposed to run into the Ouse washes between the Old Bedford River and the Hundred Foot River where they were rendered harmless.

As he walked home Iain surveyed the all-but-level landscape. It was only when he had stopped working on the embankments that he perceived the land as a body whose flesh had been opened up and dug into deliberately. Every path and drove, every river and dyke sliced through it like knives. So much was still new and raw. This image of wounding disturbed him, for he thought of himself as a maker, not a destroyer.

Out of the corner of his eye he caught sight of a marsh harrier, dark against the pale sky. What a view it must have of those lines which stretched to the horizon, those fields whose straight-banked edges showed they had been drawn along a ruler.

He leaned against the balustrade of the bridge and watched the clouds. There was no point in troubling himself about the land. What mattered this evening was to see how the mare was and to hold Magdalen to him and see her smile before Jenne laid her in her cot for the night. He would continue to live as he had always lived: doing what had to be done at a steady pace and being thankful for what he had.

✒ 7th June 1661, near Thorney

The geese were panicking and trying to escape from a fenced-in area. The air was full of desperate squawks, feathers and swear words. The hair and clothes of the two boys who had the task of catching them were covered in white down. Thomas laughed at the sight of them stumbling through the frightened flock, losing track of the goose they were after and finally grabbing any one they could reach by its wing or a leg and clutching it to them firmly until they could hand it to one of the waiting men. He had done the same job when he was a boy and knew that plucking geese was always like this – comical, hard work and profitable. They had been at it for an hour and already there were two half-filled bags, one of down and one of quills. It looked as if they were going to get a good weight this time.

Thomas knelt down and signalled to one of the boys to bring him the next goose. He jammed the bird's head and one wing sideways under his arm and started on the other wing. Geese were noisy creatures at the best of times but when they were being plucked they struggled and cried with pain and fear each time the down was pulled or a quill tugged out. He cursed at the fuss this one was making and worked his way round the body until it was bare, then threw it over the fence where it scuttled off to join the other freed birds. Without their feathers they looked starved and shrunken.

He always considered these pluckings, which left the men and boys covered in shit and feathers and the geese naked and sometimes bloody, very satisfying. Even better, they earned him a goose to take home. But the job needed to be done five times a year: on Lady-day, at Midsummer, Lammas, Michaelmas and Martinmas. In fact he could sometimes recognise the very same geese coming back time after time until the day their feathers no longer grew properly and they died from cold or ended up over someone's fire.

While he was choosing a bird as payment, his pinched-looking wife and scrap of a son arrived.

"Take that one," said Janet, pointing. "It's a good size, looks healthy."

Thomas caught it with a boy's help, yanked its neck over a stick and killed it there and then.

Janet watched for the two or three minutes it took until it stopped moving, and said with satisfaction, "It'll keep us going for days."

One of the boys had put Daniel, Thomas and Janet's son, in the enclosed place with a goose which had escaped plucking because most of its feathers had already been pecked out by other geese. It was much bigger than Daniel but was cowering in a corner.

"Go on, chase it," called the older boy. Then, impatient for action, he said, "I'll make it move."

He ran off to fetch something to poke the goose with but Thomas lifted the child back over the fence. He laughed. "Not yet, my lad, but you'll be in there one day, won't you? In a year or two perhaps."

They set off home. On the path they saw a few raw-looking geese which looked as if they were not going to survive. Daniel, curious, ran up to one and squatted down in front of it.

"Don't touch it. Geese can hurt you." said Janet.

"Leave him alone. He's got to learn that for himself, hasn't he?"

When they reached their hut Thomas put the goose on the ground before stooping to go inside. The roof was made of wood he had taken last autumn from the cargo of a Humber Keel when it was being towed up Bevill's Leam. For some reason nearly half a load of timber had been unloaded on to the bank. Next morning the men had set off to haul the boat upstream and he had expected the abandoned planks to be claimed. He had kept his eye on them for two days but they were not collected, so, one by one, he and his brother carried them home. Now he was lucky enough to have a roof nearly high enough for a man to stand in without knocking his head. The walls were made with turves and reeds, and each summer he put another layer of cow dung on the windward side. He was pleased that this year no rain had come in at all.

Thomas took a board from inside the hut, settled himself with the goose and took out his knife.

"Go and watch your Da," said Janet, pushing Daniel outside. "I'm going to get the fire ready."

The child went up close to his father and watched him chop off the head, cut off the wings and take out the guts.

"Get a bowl from inside," he said, and Daniel fetched one.

Thomas put the innards, heart and liver into it and then wiped his slimy hands on the grass. He looked at the carcass again. "It's still too big for the pot, so I'll have to cut the feet off too." He held the heavy knife high and brought it down sharply. One of the goose's feet flew up into the air and he reached out and caught it. He laughed and made to chop the second one off. "Are you ready?" he asked Daniel, before bringing the knife down again. The boy watched the severed foot fly over his head but stumbled as he tried to catch it. He picked it up and gave it to his father who told him to throw it away for there was no meat on it and anyway they had a whole good goose to get through, so he threw it behind the hut with the old bones.

Later that night Janet and Thomas slept side by side by the fire. Daniel, lying on his back with his arms above his head, was asleep on the new, dry hay they had brought in the previous day. Looking at him like that, Thomas felt a rare surge of warmth towards him. He remembered his own father, his sodden body lying on the sodden ground at Murrow after he had been swept off the bank by a flood. Had his father ever thought of him with warmth? He had no idea. It seemed to him he had hardly had a father, yet here he was, twenty five years old, living with a woman he had married too quickly and already a father himself.

Before he slept he thought about his eel nets, a different place he'd just found for fishing, and about the strange news his brother had just told him. He had said some of the riverbeds were rising. This was not possible, but as Peter was not often mistaken about things he'd promised to go with him to see what he was talking about.

9th June 1661, Thorney

In the yard, Jacob was holding the mare's mouth open while Iain painted the gum with the infusion he had made from the plantain leaves. Much of it was spilling out. The mare was trying to shake her head free.

"Could you put the mixture in the feed?"

"She won't eat. But this is useless." Iain stood back from the horse and nodded to Jacob to take her into the stable. " I'm going to make an ointment with lard and stick it into the hole in her gum. It might remain there long enough to have some effect."

He took the bowl back into the kitchen and began to work another batch of cooked plantain leaves into a handful of fat. There was plenty of the mixture, enough to make some spare pellets for another time.

Iain had learned that finding the right cure for an ailment was often a question of trial and error. Sometimes it was best to make an infusion from dried leaves, and sometimes to grind up the seeds or roots and administer them in a potion. Only practice would give confidence about quantities and strengths, and even then the ripeness of a herb and the season of its picking could affect its ability to cure. It was also the case that different preparations of the same herb could work on the body in several ways. Because it was so much more a skill than an art he was determined to record everything accurately.

He dipped his fingers into a small pile of oatmeal, took from the bowl a quantity the size of his thumb and rolled it into a ball.

Jacob came back into the kitchen with some papers. "I've been making some drawings of herbs. I thought we could make a book with my drawings and your descriptions and recipes." He held up a page in each hand.

Iain rested his floury hands on the edge of the bowl. "They're beautiful, Jacob. Yes. A book would mean more people could be healed from pain and disease. Especially with illustrations. People could even heal themselves. I still have much to learn but I'm beginning to believe that herbs can cure anything – anything at all – that ails a man."

⟡ 20th June 1661, near Thorney

Kyme Pitts was beginning to smell stagnant and was alive with mosquitoes. While Peter walked round to the other side Thomas waded into the shallows, parting the reeds and sedge to get a glimpse of the surface. There were plenty of plants providing shade and food for the fish and eels. This particular mere was one which usually remained full every summer, and the fact that it had not done so this year was yet more evidence of how the drainage had altered things. No one could rely on the fen in the way they used to. This year Thomas had found fewer nests and therefore fewer eggs to eat and birds to trap, and there seemed to be far fewer numbers of some types of duck.

He squelched back on to dry land as Peter returned.

"What do you think?" asked Thomas.

"It's big enough, and there's plenty of pochard over there. Let's come here next week, at midsummer."

The decision made, they set off towards the north bank of Morton's Leam in order to see where and how much the river bed had risen, if, indeed, it had. The level of the water was quite low.

Peter called out to a passing fen punt, "Is it true the bed is rising?"

The boatman slowed the boat down, stood up, held his quant upright and pushed it downwards. The top part stood well out of the water. "There," he said, "That's bottom. It's never been as shallow as this before."

"But that's because it's summer."

The boatman pulled his quant back into the boat and sat down. "Not necessarily. Last winter there were times at Earith when boats became grounded. That never used to happen."

"So what happens if a boat is grounded?"

"Someone pulls it off, or heavy rain floats it, or they unload some of their cargo and make two journeys instead of one." He spat over the side. "Those Adventurers are only interested in planting and harvesting their crops. They don't care what else goes on."

As the boatman moved slowly away from them Peter called out, "If they'd known we'd still get floods they wouldn't have believed it, would they?"

The boatman shouted back, "You can't change what's meant to be. They shouldn't have tried to do better than God."

The brothers sat on the bank watching the progress of the punt along its dead straight course – a broad band narrowing to a glinting line – until it was out of sight. It was evening now and the river was quiet but they could hear teal calling.

Thomas said, "They've always been our fens, our washes. The French should stop farming and become fenmen like us, or leave."

They got to their feet and began to walk back to the new wind machine where Peter had recently started work.

"Those timbers we took from the bank to make your roof must have been left there to lighten a boat."

Thomas nodded. There was nothing he could do about it now, even if he had wanted to. Anyway, finders were keepers, weren't they?

They approached the wooden sails and the great scoops which ladled water out of the field and emptied it into the river. In winter these saved land from being drowned. More and more of them were appearing everywhere, creaking, clacking and flapping like giant birds perched on solid bodies in lines along the straight watercourses.

"What matters is that the fens become ours again," said Thomas.

"It's too late now. They never will be."

"But they could be. Then you wouldn't have to be a millman. You could go back to fishing and fowling."

"I need a proper wage and so will you when you have more children. Being a millman will be steady work."

Peter had four children already, and Thomas thought of Janet after she had lost her second and third babies. He supposed all women would be as she had been, but she'd just have to get over it.

"So is hassocking."

"Hassocking," repeated Peter derisively. "I'd never go hassocking."

"And I'd never work lifting water out of a rich man's field to make him richer."

They reached the doorway of the mill with its still sails. Janet was there with Peter's wife and Daniel was playing with his cousins by the water's edge. They were floating small boats they had made of reeds and Daniel ran up to show his to his father.

Thomas looked at it briefly, then beckoned Janet and set off home after nodding goodbye. Damn Peter. It always felt as if he was right. There was nothing wrong with hassocking and it had to be done. It was just work, like any other work. He walked ahead of Janet. She could not have kept up if she had tried and she was keeping back to be with Daniel who was somewhere behind her.

As he strode on he had to acknowledge it was not his land that he pared the turf off, nor his seed that he sowed, nor his crop that he harvested. In the end, he was no different to Peter: the work he did made rich men richer. In particular, it made the Deschamps family richer. Not that they were a bad family to work for, although it was a good thing the eldest son was now involved with other work. Few people liked working for him. But that Scotchman who had married the daughter kept a close eye on what was going on and, he had to admit, treated the workers fairly.

Thomas was feeling renewed resentment in respect of both those he worked for and the foreigners' interference. What would happen if boats were prevented from moving easily up and down the rivers? They all relied on boats, but even without the mud and silt the rivers were still not clear for navigation. The horses or the men towing the boats kept having to make way for people cutting weed or repairing banks. Would the draining never be finished?

Perhaps the men in Whittlesey were right. That morning he had decided not to mention them to Peter but he presumed he knew about them. Under cover of night, they were breaking down banks. They had asked him to join them but so far he had not given them an answer. Would Peter do anything like that? He wasn't sure, even though Peter sometimes echoed his complaints about the way things were going.

Yes. He ought to think about it again. Taking action would be doing something towards getting rid of the outsiders, and then they could reclaim their fens and set their nets when and where they wanted. Why had he been hesitating? For a moment he imagined going out at night with a group of men – people like John Alderson, and Richard Everitt and his brother – and digging through a bank. As the water started to pour through they would make their separate and unnoticed ways home along the dykes and droves. Even the idea of it was exciting.

Why in God's name had he been hesitating?

He realised he was nearly home. He turned round to look for Janet, and called to her to hurry for he was hungry. The thought of more of that fat goose pleased him, as did the prospect of a few hours sport on the little mere he and Peter had visited that morning. He swatted at the mosquitoes as he walked on.

✐ 26th June 1661, Thorney

Mathieu was doing well. He was not interested in crops and stock, but had developed a sound knowledge of specific aspects of the drainage system: the construction of piers and floodgates, the strengthening of banks and sasses. He had notebooks full of sketches and calculations. Recently his attention had been devoted entirely to wind-engines, but now that the design of these was well established he was wanting to do something different.

"Just wait until we don't need wind," he said provocatively at the evening meal.

"We'll always need wind," said his mother. "How could mills turn without wind? Unless you mean using oxen and horses again."

"There's more than wind in this world."

"What do you mean?" asked Père.

"I meant there are other sorts of power."

"Yes: the God who created us. God is the source of all power."

"Of course He is. But I mean we can find other ways of making energy." Mathieu broke off a piece of bread and spoke as he chewed it, "You've seen what happens when there's a very hot day down on the fen, haven't you?"

"The fen dries up. The moisture rises," said Jenne.

"What dries it up?"

"The heat of the sun."

"Exactly! The sun has the power to melt and to dry and to evaporate water."

"But you can't have sun machines like we have wind machines."

"Perhaps not, but there may be ways of using the sun's energy." He finished his mouthful, "And one day we'll discover them."

"In my lifetime?" asked Père.

"Who knows? Years ago no one would have considered it possible that the fens could be drained. But they have been – and in your lifetime too. In fact, it's been done in *my* lifetime."

"By the grace and power of God and the labour of men."

"And the skill of Vermuyden and other engineers, including you. You worked out a way to do it, didn't you? And in future people will work out other ways to do other things. Père, I promise you'll see many more advances before you die."

Mathieu looked round the table. They were all looking at him. Did they understand?

"Think of any tool." he said urgently, "Think of a spade. Once men dug with their hands, but when they discovered how to use and make tools they could do far more. They were able to build, to farm properly, to do things they'd never imagined. That's what I mean – as time goes on we learn better ways of doing things."

"That's obvious," said Jacob. "But if you didn't use wind what could scoop the water off the fields?"

"I don't know yet. All I'm saying is that there must be a way. There *must* be other sources of power we can use to improve our lives."

"Power can make things worse as well as better," said Père. "Powerful men ruin civilisations. Powerful elements ruin lands."

"We *need* power," said Mathieu.

"Yes, but it must be used wisely."

They stood to say grace and Mathieu caught the glance exchanged between his parents. He was sure they were thinking: 'How Mathieu has changed!' and 'How full he is of passion and ideas!' and probably 'May God help him find a good wife.' Well, they were right, for he had changed, he was full of ideas and one day he would get married. He would show them that he, the son who had once caused them so much anxiety, would make good in some way that as yet they – and indeed he – could not imagine. He would work well and marry well, and they would be proud of him. The whole family, the whole of Thorney, would be proud of him.

But now he excused himself and hurried off to his drawing board. He was trying to design a system on a specific site near Guyhirn to create a greater lift and remove more water. Could there be two mills next to each other? How close should they be together? Should they be the same size?

As he searched for the calculations he had been doing before the meal he recalled what his father had said. It was true power could be used in different ways, some good and some bad, but surely it was better to explore and understand sources of power rather than to fear them? Père could be so old-fashioned.

Or what about building just one wind-engine but giving it more sails?

❧ 28th June 1661, Thorney

Jacob was already courting. A few months earlier, at Easter, he had met a girl at the Le Pla's house. Her name was Alice Le Roue. He had told Jenne almost every detail of his progress with her.

"She's very pretty."

"I'm sure she is."

He had gone back to the Le Pla's farm with Bastion after a day spent sowing peas. Unlike some of the English who still just broadcast them on to the soil, they had made shallow drills and laboriously sown them properly and covered them up. Bastion Le Pla had started to complain about his aching back so Jacob did most of the bending and by evening they were ready for a flagon of beer. They poured out a draught even before they washed.

While relaxing and stroking one of the dogs, Jacob heard girls' voices. He recognised Emily's voice but not the other which was slower and deeper so he was curious when the girls entered the room. He stood up to greet them, and was introduced to Madame's cousin Alice. She was staying with the Le Plas for two days.

He liked her at once. When Monsieur Le Pla went off to wash she and Emily stayed with him as he sat down again to finish his beer.

"Have you been here before?" he asked Alice.

"Yes. In summer I come when they can spare me from home to work in the dairy here."

This was good news for it meant it would be easy to meet her again and he began to do so. Soon he was making an increasing number of visits to her home at Parson's Drove where there was another small French community. It was only a little over five miles unless he had to go the long way round in order to deliver something to Murrow, and it seemed as if he was spending the whole summer walking, usually on his own, backwards and forwards along the increasingly familiar route. He enjoyed the time this gave him to think about drawing as well as about Alice.

"I don't believe you," Jenne had interrupted when he told her this, "I don't believe you'd think about a plant rather than Alice."

"It's true!" he protested, laughing.

He would stop to examine the leaves of a sow-thistle, or the pattern on the bark of a tree, or the way a purple loosestrife flower grew from its stalk. He liked too to make little sketches for Alice but had not yet told her he would like to draw her portrait.

Now they already knew each other quite well. It felt a little strange that he, younger than his brother by eight years, should have a sweetheart when Mathieu had not shown any real interest in anyone except that girl a long time ago.

"Don't let that stop you," said Jenne with conviction. "Younger brothers don't have to wait to start courting until their elder brothers are betrothed. If that were the case you might be waiting for ever!"

Alice was *interesting*. She was pretty but not sweet, nor giggly like some girls and never intense as Emily could be. Alice listened to what he'd done on the farm and told him what had been going on at Parson's Drove. She liked walking out with him too, and, on one of the occasions when she was staying with the Le Plas, Jacob had asked Monsieur for his permission to walk with her on Sunday afternoon along the Causeway and back.

"As long as you bring her home by milking time." He looked at Jacob rather fiercely. "I can't have you stealing her, can I? I need her to help in the dairy, not be dreaming about you."

But Madame said, "You should hear her when she's milking. She sings to each cow, has a different song for each one, and as soon as they hear it they let down their milk."

The idea of Alice singing as she milked made Jacob smile. And he smiled more to think he would see her twice on Sunday, first in church and then for a walk along the Causeway. What could be better?

⟡ 29th June 1661, Thorney

So the next Sunday he set off to the Abbey Church with all the family. Mère was walking with Magdalen, picking her up every now and again. Although Jenne was pregnant she walked with energy. However, she would be going to the wall today because she was finding it tiring to stand throughout the service. Once inside, the family went to its usual place, but Jacob shifted slightly closer to the front to see if Alice was there yet. She usually went to the church in Parson's Drove and it was a treat for him if she came to the Abbey Church.

Most people had already arrived. Iain and Père were nodding to the Massingarbe family. Magdalen was leaning against her grandmother's legs and seemed placid enough for the time being, but she might have to be taken out later if she became noisy.

And here were the Le Plas. Alice entered behind Emily and

Jacob could see her searching for him. She returned his cheerful smile immediately. Monsieur Le Pla moved his family forward into the centre of the church, closer to the Deschamps and so nearer to Jacob.

With a little more shuffling Jacob and Alice ended up much nearer to each other than either had expected, and Iain gave Jacob a particular amused look which signified he had noticed this.

The two greeted each other in whispers, and then Alice turned to speak to Emily, and then leant towards Jacob again.

"Where's Mathieu?" asked Alice.

"Working. He's busy with some new project so he'll be going to the evening service today. Why do you ask?"

"Emily wants to know!"

"She doesn't give up, does she?" said Jacob to Alice who then passed the information on to Emily.

When the chanting began Jacob listened for Alice's voice. Wanting to hear it clearly, he lowered his own voice and did little more than mouth the words. It was true, she had a beautiful voice, clear and steady. There were only a few hours to go before they would be walking together. He'd ask her to sing for him. She couldn't refuse. After all, she sang for the cows.

Later that evening Jacob sat drawing plants – he was illustrating an entry on henbane for Iain, who was writing. Magdalen was asleep. Jenne was sitting in her chair where the evening light slanted through the window and fell on the cushion she was embroidering. Mère was finishing off a job in the kitchen and Mathieu, having returned from the late church service, was reading his notebook. Occasionally someone spoke, or moved their chair slightly, or adjusted their position. The tabby cat ambled up and rubbed itself against Iain's legs.

When Père returned half an hour later after the stroll he liked to take on summer Sundays he entered the room and stood quietly in the doorway. Jacob paused in his work and looked up at him. His father was standing there with his eyes shut, and Jacob knew he was thanking God for blessing him with such a home and such a family.

*

As for the decay of fish and fowl, which hath been no small objection against the public work, there is not much likelihood thereof; for notwithstanding the general draining, there are so many great meers, and lakes still continuing, which be indeed the principal harbours for them, that there be no want of either; for in the vast spreading waters they seldom abide, the rivers, channels and meers being their principal receptacles; which being now increased, will rather augment than diminish their store. And that both fish and fowl are with much more ease taken by this restraint of the waters within such bounds we daily see; forasmuch as all nets for fishing are better made use of in the rivers and meers, than when the waters are out of those narrower limits; and that decoys are now planted upon many drained levels, whereby greater numbers of fowl are caught than by any other engines formerly used; which could not at all be made there did the waters, as formerly, over-spread the whole country.

From Dugdale's *History of Imbanking and Drayning*

🐿 30th June 1661, near Thorney

On the evening before they were to get the birds, the brothers and a boy lugged their punt out of the river and across the few hundred yards of fen until they got it to Kyme Pitts. Their arrival caused a commotion but they pushed the boat into the reeds and left at once, knowing the fowl would settle down overnight and be completely peaceful again by morning.

At dawn they approached the mere slowly, each carrying a basket and, over the shoulder, a pole the length of a tall man. The boy had only a couple of sticks and he quietly made his way round to the far side giving the mere a wide berth. Meanwhile Thomas got into the punt and Peter passed him the poles and baskets before getting in himself. Then they edged the boat out from the rushes opposite where the boy was, put down their oars and picked up the poles. For a few minutes they sat motionless as the sun began to light up the slightly wrinkled surface. The sky was still pinkish, the air sweet and damp. The only sounds were from the fowl on the opposite side of the mere.

Then Peter nodded to Thomas before giving a long, low whistle. Immediately the boy shouted and banged his sticks causing the birds to call out and fly into the air in an almost single movement which billowed like a wave. They flew away from the noise and directly towards the men who were now standing in the punt with poles held high and at the ready. As the body of birds flew over they swiped at them fast and hard. Each time a pole struck a wing or a beak or a head a bird fell or swooped down fluttering. The boy continued to holler, the birds to cry desperately and Thomas and Peter to thwack until, within only a few minutes, every one of the flock had either been brought down or had managed to escape.

They surveyed the result. Some of the damaged fowl were flailing for dear life with disjointed wings, some were nearly drowned but kicking with their remaining good leg so they rotated lopsidedly and some were still scurrying for the reeds. Feathers lay on the rippling surface.

The men smiled at each other for it was a surprisingly good haul for such a small mere.

Thomas poled the boat into the centre to reach each bird. They put the quiet ones straight into the baskets and hit the awkward ones over the head to still them.

By the time they had finished collecting up their harvest the boy had made quite a pile of the birds he had picked up from the shallow water and the ground. His method for shutting the noisy ones up was to stamp on their heads.

Thomas and Peter stepped out of the punt and pulled it out of the water. Then the three of them half-carried and half-tugged it back across the fen to the river. Though the two men were wet to their thighs they felt exhilarated, and the annoyance Thomas had felt in respect of his brother over the previous weeks had disappeared. Peter was good company and they must do more things together for it was good to have a brother and they should always be firm friends.

Peter opened the basket and invited the boy to choose a couple of fowl. Delighted with his reward, he asked them to drop him off by the bridge. His mother, he said, would be very grateful.

Then they made their way upstream slowly with oars, the four ends of their poles extending from the ends of the punt like legs from a giant water boatman. They were extremely satisfied with the already warm sun, their successful morning's sport and themselves.

Now was the time to tell him, now when they'd just enjoyed doing something which, if the fens continued to be interfered with, they might not be able to do in future.

So, sitting in the punt in the early sunshine, Thomas told Peter about the men who were determined to undermine and destroy the drainage work. He told them how they hacked through banks, forced flood gates open, stopped up channels and even bored through dykes. He told him the names of some of those who were involved and stressed that these men were not bad but just wanted to keep the fens as they should be and retain the old way of life, the way of life which had supported everyone until the foreigners had ruined things. Taking action like this was all they could do, for they had no influence where it mattered. The only friend they had ever had was Cromwell, and he had deserted them as soon as Charles 1 was dead. And anyway, now Cromwell himself was dead.

Peter listened without interrupting, then asked, "Are you going to join them?"

Thomas looked up and down the leam, squinting against the sun. He watched a snake make its zigzag way across the water, its head just above the surface.

"Yes," he answered, "And will you?"

Peter did not reply.

"It'd be better if we did it together. Safer."

"I can't go out at night and do that."

"Why not?"

"I've got a wind engine to attend to. I need my job." They drifted past a small group of willows. "It won't work," he continued. "No one can undo what's been done here. All these improvements are here to stay."

"But they're not all improvements, you've said so yourself. What about the navigation? What happens if the channels are clogged up?"

"I'm saying no. If you want to get involved with these Fen Tigers, it's up to you. But you'll be taking a risk."

"A risk? It's a risk to leave things as they are. They're getting worse, can't you see? By the time our children are grown up the fens won't be anything like what they were, or even like they are now. The fowl will be gone, the fish will be gone, the boats won't be able to sail and the place'll be covered with someone else's oats and wheat." He threw his arm towards the bank in a wide gesture. "Don't you want to save this? Keep it as it was, as it should be?"

"I'm saying no."

Peter picked up the oars, ready to row.

"And I'm also saying that if you get into trouble, don't expect me to come and help you. Yes, you're my younger brother, but it's you who has to deal with the consequences of actions like this. Keep me out of it."

↪ Three months later, evening, 10th September 1661, Thorney

Iain had spent the day with the ploughing team at Guyhirn. There had been trouble with a share and they had had to stop for a blacksmith to mend it, but now the day was over and he was on his way back to Thorney. He had a handful of long white goose quills which he had found near the place where they did the plucking, where the ground was covered with soft down and green and white goose mess. He would cut the ends of most of them to make pens – they were ideal for the work he was doing with Jacob – and he would give two to Magdalen. She'd love them.

It was much later than usual and he was hurrying because that morning Jenne had complained of an ache in her belly.

"Do you think the baby is coming?" he had asked.

"No. This feeling is different. It's not how I felt when I started to have Magdalen or the other baby." She winced. "But I'm going to stay lying down."

It would be good to get home to her and to wash and eat after the long day.

From the direction of Thorney a figure on horseback came

into sight riding towards him along the foot of the bank. The dust was rising so whoever it was was moving fast. Iain stood aside for him to pass.

It was a man from the village he knew slightly. He slowed down but did not stop as he called out, "I'm going to fetch the doctor. They need the doctor."

The doctor? Who needed the doctor so urgently?

Iain watched the retreating figure. Why hadn't the man said more? And why had he just let him ride off without asking anything? He hurried on home, full of anxiety. Surely the baby could not be born so early? Something must be wrong if it was coming now.

May Jenne be safe. May she not die. May she not die. May this baby not die.

Only that morning there had been talk about the problems women faced when giving birth. The wife of a ploughman over towards March had recently died in childbirth and the man's cousin had said, "She was fit and healthy, but something went wrong and the poor woman bled to death." Then, when they stopped to rest at midday, other men told similar stories until Iain had had to walk away. He had stood stroking the horses and then bent to rinse his face in the shallows by the bridge.

Now he stumbled along the path with his bag bumping against his thigh, telling himself it was someone else who needed the doctor and not Jenne at all.

May she be safe. May she not die. Please may she not die.

Soon the house was in view and he ran the last quarter mile, hoping, against all his feelings of natural fairness, that it was not Jenne who was ill. But Jacob was waiting outside and came towards him without his usual smile.

He called out, "Have you seen Mathieu?"

Why was he asking about Mathieu?

"Is Jenne all right? What's happened?"

"It's Père."

"Samuel?"

Iain dropped his bag and the quills to the ground.

"Tell me."

Jacob could hardly get the words out, "He drowned."

"Where? How?"

"They were replacing timbers at the Dog and Doublet and he was knocked into the river and as he fell he hit his head on the stone pier."

"But they've brought him home? He's alive?"

Jacob broke down and covered his face with his hands and said, "Mathieu, where's Mathieu? He should be here."

Iain went inside. He found the others in the room with the big bed. Samuel, wrapped in a blanket, was lying on his side. Ann was sitting beside him, leaning towards him and holding her hand to his cheek. Jenne was standing at the foot of the bed. They all looked up as Iain and Jacob came in.

Ann turned back towards Samuel, and moved her hand away gently.

"He doesn't need a doctor now," she said.

She leaned back, closed her eyes and lifted her chin so her face was turned to the ceiling. Strands of her greying hair had come loose from her coif. Iain noticed the slender stretch of her neck, her slight shoulders, her drawn jaw.

"I knew something like this would happen. He gave so much of his life to water, and water has brought him death."

They stayed in silence. Each person was praying but they were praying alone. There would be time to say prayers together, but now they were separate even while they stood close to one another.

Iain felt himself close down into a stillness. He was suspended in a place and time he did not know but which protected him.

"Maman! Maman!" Magdalen was calling from outside the room.

Jenne moved towards the doorway and whispered, "Come here, little one."

Magdalen said loudly, "Look at my feathers. I found some feathers by Papa's bag." She held up a white quill in each hand.

"Sshh, sshh," said Jenne, picking her up.

"Why's Papi lying down?"

"Sshh, Magdalen."

"Let her come to me, Jenne," said Ann. "Viens, ma petite."

Jenne set the child down and she went to her grandmother, holding the quills upright like white tapers.

Iain watched Ann take Magdalen on her lap, hold her and rock her as she must have once rocked Mathieu, then Jenne and then Jacob. When her grandmother began to weep Magdalen held up the feathers again.

"Look, Mamie. Look at my feathers."

Ann nodded. "They're beautiful. Shall we put them beside Papi?"

"For when he wakes up," said Magdalen.

While all this was happening Mathieu was making his way home. He had followed Whittlesey Dyke and Morton's Leam and was now heading north. As the sun went down to his left, his shadow stretched out to his right. He would be home within the hour and he was almost singing because he had just been given the job as assistant sasse-keeper at Stanground near Peterborough. He looked on it as a step to enable him to learn first-hand about the operation of sasses. He was finding that while people were interested in his designs and ideas they considered his knowledge insufficient and his youth a disadvantage.

"It's all very well having plans on paper," he was told, "But plans made by much more experienced men than you have failed."

He had grown up seeing what could go wrong but was also well aware that some plans had succeeded. However, he had to accept that in order to place himself in an advantageous position for the future he would have to do more than produce drawings. His work would not be taken seriously unless he proved he knew every practical detail about the control of water by sluices. Moreover, nobody would pay him for his plans unless they were going to use them.

But now his work and efforts had been endorsed by securing this post. He might even be able to buy his own boat. The work would mean living away from home for a few months, but that could be interesting. He would be near Peterborough, a city where there would be different people to those in Thorney whom he had known for years. His family would be delighted at this appointment with responsibility for an essential part of the whole drainage enterprise. So would men like Mark le Pla and

Monsieur Roo. Although his study had been interrupted a few years earlier he had picked it up again willingly. All along he had known that his father had been right and it was up to him to find a way to get out of the position where he had cornered himself. If he did not, Iain would have continued to gain all the credit and might even have come to rival his status as eldest son. He smiled as he thought about how Iain might react to the news. He would certainly *say* he was pleased. Yes, he should be fair to him – he would be genuinely pleased. But he had to admit that even now, despite Iain having been married to Jenne for some years, he still regarded him with some misgiving.

He decided to take a short rest. Seeing that Bamb Weare was covered in mosquitoes he pressed on as far as the wooden bridge, shrugged his bag from his shoulder and drank a long draught from his leather bottle. But within only a few minutes he was eager to be up and off and heading for his bright future. There were only a few miles to go until he would be able to tell his father his good news.

September 1661, near Thorney

After declaring his willingness to help undermine the so-called progress Thomas had gained new friends amongst the Fen Tigers. They consisted of two groups: firstly, the thoughtful ones – mainly fishermen, wildfowlers and boatmen – who were determined to hold on to what they considered to have been theirs for generations; secondly, those who felt aggrieved by what had happened and wanted to gain revenge. Although Thomas earned most of his living directly from the fens he was regarded as one of the wilder ones because he often expressed resentment.

He began to spend more and more time with these men. At dawn he would check his nets, then return home to eat and then go to the fields to work. By the time he reached home again Janet had usually managed to get hold of some white poppies, steep them in boiling water and make tea. This did not stop her coughing, but it helped her settle and manage to make a meal. Then, when he had eaten he would go out again.

"Will your brother be with us?" asked one of the men.

"No."

When asked why not, Thomas hesitated.

"He's a millman, isn't he?" said one.

"Yes."

"Then winter might see him changing his mind and joining us," said another.

Thomas had already identified this particular man as someone who opened his mouth before thinking, but even so the threat hit home. It had not occurred to him that Peter could be harmed. The thought was worrying but he dismissed it for he had gone too far now to back off.

Winter. That was what they were waiting for. Winter meant rain, full rivers, darkness, fierce tides. Winter was by far the best season to carry out damage, because although the risk was higher more could be achieved. They could breach whole sections of dykes. They could break those bloody wind machines and allow the water to once again spread where it wanted.

As he became more involved Thomas learned more about the effects of the drainage. Although the engineers still denied it, or at least denied the significance of it, some of the rivers and new channels were definitely silting up. Worse still, the land around them seemed to be becoming lower. This meant that some dykes were ending up higher than the fields alongside them which obviously put the pastures at risk again from being drowned.

In September, as water-levels heightened, increasing numbers of wind-engines were beginning to pick up their scoopfuls of water from watercourses on one level and tip them into others at a higher level. Peter had said some millmen tipped the water on to the next farmer's land rather than into the rivers or drains. It was an easier way of getting rid of it, and as the men were paid as long as the scoops were working, did it matter what water went where?

"Of course it does!" exclaimed Thomas. " Doing that is no better than what I'm going to be doing. It's working against the drainage."

Peter argued that it was not deliberate damage.

"It is. It's making the wind-engines do useless work, work which does nothing to reduce flooding. Tell me, would a farmer be happy about water being lifted on to his land? Of course not."

Thomas and one of the men he liked most began to make regular walks along Morton's Leam and the Twenty Foot. Others did the same along Whittlesey Dyke, Bevill's Leam and the Old Nene. They wanted to be familiar with every yard so that when the time came they would made the best decisions about where to strike. They noted weak points. They noted shallow banks. They found out which farmers were active in carrying out repairs promptly and which were lazy.

ᕦ Late evening, 10th September 1661, near Thorney

When he got home late and after dark Janet complained he had been gone too long.

He merely said, "What I'm doing is important."

Janet's coughing increased when she lay down, but she did not talk about it to him, thank God. In fact, unlike some wives he heard about, she said little to him at all. It was true he had become even less interested in her since he had met the Fen Tigers at Whittlesey. They provided him with a cause, and that cause meant much more to him than she did. She couldn't have changed that if she tried. That was how it was. And that was what happened in many marriages, wasn't it?

And now, just when he wanted to sleep, Janet started to shiver.

"I'm so cold," she said. Ten minutes later she said, "I'm so hot."

There was no denying it, this was the ague and poppy tea was the only remedy for it.

He turned away so he would not be disturbed by her coughing and shaking. Daniel, on his back with his arms above his head as usual, was stretched out by the smouldering fire. He was only young but one day he would be old enough to help him. Boys were useful when it came to putting up duck, catching geese and baiting grigs.

Janet was not asleep yet but he had nothing to say to her. She would not understand about the Tigers' plans for the winter, and it was safer if she did not know them because she was a woman and therefore bound to tell someone about them.

Mathieu was weary by the time he approached Thorney, but the sight of the Abbey Church gave him new energy.

He had decided to speak to his father on his own first and was rehearsing what to say. 'Père, I've got a job. A real job.' Or 'Now you can be proud of me.' Or 'You wanted me to change and I've changed.' His father might be so pleased that he would take it on himself to make a special announcement to everyone and Mathieu was already imagining the great satisfaction he would feel if this were to happen.

No one was around as he hurried along the Causeway to the house. Strangely, the cows were in the byre and not in the field. Why was the milking so late today? Someone must have let something slip.

As he reached the house he saw Jacob squatting with his back against a tree. It looked as if he was waiting for him and he rose to his feet but did not call out his usual greeting. What was the matter?

"What's wrong, Jacob?"

Jacob began to cry.

"For God's sake, what's the matter?"

"Père's dead."

Mathieu stared at him and hurried past into the yard, across to the door, up the steps and to his parents' room. It wasn't true. It couldn't be true. His mother was kneeling by the bedside and he went round the bed and knelt beside her. Each of them reached out an arm out round the other. They did not speak.

Mathieu's head was howling, his heart thudding. This was not what was meant to happen. Père should have lived for years. It was not fair of him to die today – this day of all days. He was not supposed to be dead.

Why did these things always happen to him? Why did things always go wrong for him?

Mère said, "Try and be still, mon fils."

Mathieu had not realised he was shaking with emotion. He had thought the candles were shivering in the sconces, but it was him.

"Will you pray with me?"

He nodded.

His mother started to chant *O Souverain pasteur et maistre* and he joined in with a voice breaking both for his father and for himself. As the verses proceeded he felt Mère fading and needing to be pulled along so he made his voice stronger but feared he would not be able to keep it up.

"Go and get ready to eat," said Mère when they finished. "I'll come soon."

So he got to his feet and went out to wash before going into the kitchen where Jenne was preparing food. He embraced her and Jacob and accepted Iain's warm handshake and arm round his shoulder. He sat down and let Jacob explain what had happened.

Jenne fetched Mère when the meal was ready and they stood while Mathieu said grace, then ate slowly and in near silence. Mathieu felt his news burning into him like guilt. He had no desire to share it with the family because it was not for them. It was for his father who was lying in the other room, and he was still determined to tell him first.

They sent for the laying-out woman, and Mère and Jenne helped her to wash and dress Père. Then they arranged a vigil and in the morning a stream of visitors began to arrive. Mathieu, Iain, Jenne and Jacob took turns greeting them, accepting condolences and looking after Mère. Two sets of neighbours visited who themselves had recently been bereaved, and Mathieu began to realise how they must have felt when he went to their houses. But had they had such special, such crucial information for the deceased person? He was sure his grief out-griefed everyone else's except his mother's.

✎ 11th September 1661, Thorney

The next afternoon, when the usual tasks were being undertaken once more, Mathieu resolved to sit with his father again. He did not want to be interrupted, so he asked everyone to stay out of the room for an hour.

"He must do what he needs to do," said Mère to Jenne when she expressed surprise. "Samuel's death will have a different effect on each of us now and in the future. Let Mathieu have his hour. There are more than enough hours for us all."

So Mathieu entered his parents' bedroom alone.

His anger subsided as soon as he closed the door behind him, but at first he could not bring himself to look at Père. Instead, he looked at the candles, at the black Bible on the small table by the bed, at one of his mother's gowns hanging behind the door. He looked at the covers lying across his father, showing the shape of the body underneath.

As he walked toward the head of the bed with his head lowered his father's arm came within his sight. Mathieu studied the palm of the hand extending from the sleeve of the deep blue linen cloak. Numerous small scars were hatched against the grain of the deep lines which covered it. Someone who had not known Père would have guessed this was the hand of a workman who had spent his entire life digging and dyking and hewing. One forefinger was slightly crooked from when it had been broken years ago. Every nail was ridged and had white marks on it, hairs grew on the back of his hand and at the wrist the veins were visible under the skin.

He told himself to look further up the body to the shoulders and neck, but found himself glancing quickly at Père's face. He made himself look at it again and go on looking at it. Compared to the previous day, his skin was not like the skin of a live person although it was hard to say what was different. But he certainly was not asleep. He was dead. His face was dead. All of him was dead.

His bushy eyebrows seemed bushier than usual, and his nose, Mathieu realised for the first time, was not quite straight. And there were three small moles on his father's left cheek. How could he not have noticed these before?

His jaw was held closed by a cloth tied round his head. This was the mouth which had said so many wise things, had praised and reprimanded him, and had prayed day after day, decade after decade.

Under these eyelids were the eyes which had envisioned the drained fens and a solid family in Thorney.

This was the high forehead which had until only yesterday contained so much thought and hope.

Mathieu felt weak and sat down on the chair by the bedside. He should touch Père. He was sure that as the eldest son he ought to touch him.

He thought of the women preparing the body for the burial and of the intimacies that task would have required of them: washing every inch of him; easing his heavy legs and his long arms into his clothes; brushing his hair.

He reached out to his father's shoulder, felt its firm shape and withdrew his hand.

He would speak to Père first. Yes, that was the best thing to do. That was what he most wanted to do. He leaned towards him.

"Père, please listen to me. I want you to know I've been given a good job at Stanground, working on the sluice. I was sure you'd be pleased." He paused, and reached out his hand towards his father's. "I came racing home to tell you, but you'd died. You died before I became what you wanted me to be. And I'm so sorry. I'm so very, very sorry."

As he started to cry quietly he moved his hand to within half an inch of his father's, and when he finally touched the cold, hard fingers he found himself repeating, "I love you. I loved you. I love you."

He stayed by the body until he heard the cows being called in.

⚘ October 1661, Thorney

Things were different without Samuel.

Mère wept for a month during which she coped with the funeral, the family and the neighbours. She had lost her beloved, good husband of nearly thirty years. But soon she picked herself up and continued her work: feeding the poultry, doing the cooking, making clothes, washing and gardening. Although she was determined life should change as little as possible she chose to spend hours on her own, something she had never done before. There was no alternative to coming to terms with the fact that Samuel had gone and would never come back.

Jacob had twice found her late in the evening standing by the wall and looking down over the fen for so long that her skin was covered in goose pimples.

"Come inside, Mère. Please come inside now."

Mathieu's anger remained a vital part of his grief, but the rawness he felt from having been cheated made him doubly determined to capitalise on his new job. Père's death sealed his will to do well and nothing else was going to prevent him from creating the career he craved. Although he wanted to be regarded as the responsible eldest son, he simultaneously longed for all this domestic tragedy and upset to be over. He found himself longing for life at Stanground and the new start it would give him.

Jacob was lost in his grief. Père had died far too soon. There had been no time to share the success of what they had done together. Within three years, or two, or perhaps even within the next twelve months, their system of crop-rotation would have become established and the orchard would have been bearing fruit. He and Alice might have been betrothed and Père – who liked Alice so much – would have rejoiced, would have laughed that full-bodied laugh of his. But now he had to look after his mother for Mathieu was not doing so. In fact, anyone could see Mathieu was impatient to get away. So, it was up to him to be the head of the family.

As soon as Jacob saw his dead father he was determined to draw him, so just before the funeral he had sat at the end of the bed and sketched him. Drawing was always good, for finding the right lines and shadings kept his emotions at bay. As he drew he realised with sad satisfaction that drawing might help him if – when – he was faced with other deaths.

Jenne retired to bed, exhausted. She did not know whether her fatigue was due to Père's death or to being in the last stages of her pregnancy, and she did not care. What she desired most of all was to sleep and to dream her father back, but sleep would not come and she lay in bed trying to fend off Magdalen who wanted her attention much more than usual. For the first time she found herself snapping at her. She complained to Iain that Magdalen was too big for her to pick up now, and was showing signs of becoming a whiny child.

Iain tried to stay steady. He had survived battles, injury, hard labour in desperate conditions and near starvation, but this situation was different. The world he and the family which had adopted him lived in had been shaken hard. When Samuel was alive it had almost always functioned in harmony. Although over the years there had been various difficulties about politics, the farm, Mathieu, the lost baby and more, each had been dealt with or at least lived through. And so, he supposed, would this death. Ann was finding her way, and she had the support of the priest and many friends. Jacob cared greatly about her, but at present he was in such distress himself that his help consisted of staying near his mother and putting his arm round her. Mathieu was hopeless. There was no other word for it. He paid little attention to his mother's grief other than to encourage her to go to church as often as possible. Then he'd take out his notebook again or sit down at his drawing board.

But Jenne, dearest Jenne. She had taken it so badly. She had retreated into a place where he could hardly reach her. She cried several times every day, found Magdalen difficult and refused the bugloss and sorrel he suggested would calm her down. And she found praying no longer brought her hope or comfort. She had said bluntly, "There's no point. I can't pray properly and God isn't listening."

What should he do? Try to reassure Jenne, who seemed to want little from him? Be a better brother to Jacob than Mathieu? Face Mathieu and tell him what he should be doing? Reach out to Ann, his gentle, grieving mother-in-law?

How insecure things were. How the death of one person could so disturb what had seemed solid and grounded. No wonder the deaths of thousands of soldiers caused immense changes to countries and empires. But was it the deaths which caused those, or the responses to those deaths? And if it was the responses, then was it possible for people to choose how they responded? Surely it *was*. But it seemed as if his family had no choice now: one person was sad, one lost, one angry, one overcome. Had he escaped the worst of it himself? Or was he experiencing the worst in that he had to observe the others? Despite Ann's steady presence and industry, Iain felt responsible for the whole family but did not know how to heal it.

And through all this he was himself aching for Samuel. The

man who had taken him, a prisoner-of-war and a stranger, into his family to right a wrong. The man who was wise, full of faith, hard-working, honest and generous. The man Iain had come to love as well as respect.

He tried to remind himself that life had been good and would be again. A man had died, but the family still had their house, their farm and their faith as well as each other. They would get over this. The situation was sad and difficult but every family had to deal with the loss of parents, and it was nothing compared to war.

🦎 1st November 1661, Thorney

Iain needed air so walked out into the yard and saw Magdalen sitting on a pile of straw watching the chickens scratch and peck at the ground.

"Hallo my wee girl! What are you doing there in the cold?" he asked. "And you've made your smock all dirty."

Without looking at him Magdalen asked slowly, "Where did Papi go?"

"A long way away."

"Can I go too?"

"No."

"Why not?"

"You're too young, and this is where you live."

Magdalen scuffed the straw into a pile with her feet.

"Come on," said Iain, "Let's go and find Maman."

"No!" shouted Magdalen, and she scrambled to her feet and ran to the far side of the yard.

Iain went to her and attempted to hold her but she struggled to get away.

"I know," he said, "Shall we look for Mamie?"

Magdalen stopped kicking out and pushing against him and let Iain take her indoors to her grandmother.

🦎 18th December 1661, Thorney

About two months after the funeral Jenne's travail started. She was hanging washing out in the yard and felt wetness running down her legs.

"Hurry and fetch Mamie as fast as you can," she told Magdalen.

She said to her mother, "My waters are coming out of me."

The incident seemed to cause Mère to regain her former spirit immediately. She reassured Jenne that the breaking of the waters probably meant birth was imminent. She made her sit down and pressed her to take the decoction Iain had prepared for precisely this occasion. She sent a neighbour's boy to give a message to the birthing woman, the same woman with whom she and Jenne had recently laid out Samuel's body. After Magdalen had helped her collect the eggs and feed the chickens she found some coloured beads on a string for the child to play with.

When Jenne called to her and said the pains were beginning Mère sat with her. After two hours the pains were stronger and Mère sent another message to the birthing woman, asking her to come at once.

When Jacob returned home through the rain he was worried immediately for as he approached he saw the washing was still out and soaking wet. He hurried inside and found Magdalen squatting in the middle of the floor poking her finger into a broken egg.

"It fell down," she said. "All by itself."

As Jacob pulled off his cloak and went to look for his mother he heard a loud moan coming from the bedroom and realised at once what was happening.

Half an hour later Iain arrived at the same time as the woman who was to assist at the birth. Jacob told him Ann was happier than she had been since Samuel's death.

"It's because there's going to be a new life in the family," he said, "The birth is a turning point for her."

But the birth was not a brief point in time. The travail went on past dusk, past the hour when they usually ate their meal and past when they usually went to bed. Still the baby was not born. Jenne's cries grew to an uneven crescendo, then dipped, then rose again. Iain found this too difficult to listen to so took himself off to the furthest part of the house where he could not hear it. On the way he decided to look in at Magdalen whom he had not even seen that evening, and discovered she was not in her cot. He searched for her and found her asleep on a couch. The sewing box was open beside her and she had wound skeins of pink and yellow silk round her fingers and put a thimble on her thumb. Iain freed her fingers, put the scissors and thimble back in the box with Jenne's embroidery – a box Jenne had not touched since Samuel's death. Magdalen must have been looking for something to do when all the adults were occupied.

She woke when he picked her up and he carried her out into the black yard and showed her the pinpoints of stars which he and Jenne had often looked at together. As they stood there an owl appeared and floated past like a huge moth. Silently it crossed in front of them, then flew round in a low, wide arc, then back past them so close they could see the markings on its pale face turned towards them. It went off towards the fen. Iain told himself it was wrong to envy it, but he did.

Dear Lord, Please help this family. Please help my wife and her baby. Please grant us your grace. Amen.

Iain took Magdalen inside and tucked her into her cot, then went back to be with Jacob who, like him, was willing the long travail to be over, and at last the calling out ceased and a thin cry came from the bedroom.

"Mère!" said Jacob as his mother appeared. "Is Jenne all right?"

She nodded.

"And the baby?" asked Iain urgently.

"Yes. Another girl." Ann smiled at her son and son-in-law. "I was very worried, but both are alive, grâce à Dieu."

Iain's heart surged with joy. Now everything would be better. Now they could move forward again. He kissed Ann and shook hands with Jacob. Jenne was safe, and so was the baby. Soon things would return to normal.

Thank you, dear God. Thank you.

❧ Late December 1661, in the fens

Winter had been well-established for many weeks and Daniel's mother was coughing more and more, causing his father to want to be out as much as possible. The season for hassocking was over, so, having made sure there were enough turves to keep the fire alight all day, he would either go out with his nets or off to Whittlesey to meet the Tigers. Daniel used to stand at the doorway of the hut and will him to turn and wave. But it never happened. His father would just go along the path and disappear into the mist, his bag hanging from his shoulder, his stave in his hand.

On bad days Daniel stayed in the hut with his mother who alternately told him to cover her with a blanket or fetch her water. Even without looking he could tell how she was feeling. When she was cold she breathed more slowly and uttered sighs and moans. When she was hot he could hear the quick in-and-outs of her breath and the reeds rustling beneath her shivering body. Cough, cough, cough, cough. It went on and on. When she said she might cough her heart out he shut his eyes tight for the thought terrified him.

But twice a day she would crush up some poppy seeds, put them in a pot of hot water and stir them over the smouldering fire. She would add a little honey before pouring out a small cupful of the liquid for herself and giving a spoonful to him.

"This is what we need, isn't it? Thank God for this good medicine."

Daniel liked the tea. Not for the taste, although it was sweet, but for the warm, comfortable feeling it gave him. He saw it was the same for his mother. As she sat there with her hands round the bowl of the cup, sipping slowly, she relaxed. When these times came he could not be more content. His mother's bouts of coughing became less violent and less frequent, she saw the world differently and she talked to him.

She would says things like, " I heard a cuckoo today," or "Let's hope your Da brings home a good fish" or, occasionally, "Shall I tell you a story?"

Her stories were about what she and her brothers and sisters did when they were children. She would start off well enough with a beginning which took his attention: "Once we found a snake's nest. There was a heap of small white eggs in the grass and Will was sure they were pebbles ..." But gradually the story would become vague, and she would pause and then start up again in a disjointed way which made no sense. And then she would fall asleep for perhaps an hour or more, and this sleep would hardly be disturbed by coughing.

At some point his father would come squelching home through the wet and the dark. He'd shake off his outer cloak, glance briefly at his wife and then attend to the turves. If she was coughing a lot he would eat quickly and leave, and if she was not he would say a few words to her, pull the only chair closer to the fire and stand Daniel between his knees. With his father's heavy hands on his shoulders and his big knees holding him tight and the warm fire in front of him, Daniel felt enclosed and protected. But if his mother started to cough again his father would tense up and say it was impossible to get any peace and that her having the ague was enough to drive any man away.

He'd finish up by saying something like, "Me and the boy'll have to go. There's work out there we can do. We can't listen to you all night."

And he would stand up quickly, releasing Daniel, and make as if he was going to take up his cloak again.

When Janet asked what work he could be doing during the night he would wave her questions away and sit down again and refuse to speak.

⸎ 8th January 1662, in the fens

One night he did not come home. Daniel sensed his mother's anxiety although she did not say anything. She gave him something to eat, and told him to go to sleep. He lay there listening to that rough cough, to her getting up for the poppy tea she usually saved for the middle of the night, to the change in her breathing as she drank it and the short silence which followed this. And then, as usual, he heard her begin to cry.

So he got up and went to her. She pulled his blanket close and he settled down at her feet. Soon, lulled by the familiar sounds of her coughing and crying and coughing again, he fell asleep.

He was woken by his father's voice.

"What a night of it! We made a hole in the bank so great a herd of cows could have walked through it." He was waving his jug of ale as he spoke.

"Don't tell the boy," urged Janet, "You don't want him telling others what you've done."

"I want him to be proud of me, proud of his father," he replied, tipping his head back for another draught.

Daniel had no idea what his father was talking about.

"We broke down a dyke. We started where it was weak and we dug along the top of a section to make it lower. Soon it was only just above the water level so we cut a V to let the water trickle through. Within minutes there was a stream as thick as my thigh and soon it was as big as this ...." He stretched his arms out to show what he meant. "And then, in a matter of minutes, the bank was just washed away for yards because there was no strength, no weight in it."

He threw back his head and laughed. "What a night! What a good night!"

Though weary he stood up with energy and fetched in another stack of turves, then put his cloak on again.

Why was he so pleased to have broken a dyke? It didn't make sense.

"I'll go out now and check the grigs. Keep the fire hot and I'll be back soon with something for you to cook."

He made as if to go and then stopped and looked at Daniel. "If anyone asks where I was last night, tell them I was here." He leaned over and asked, "Do you know what will happen if you say the wrong thing?"

Daniel smelled his father's beery breath and shook his head.

"The Bailiff will get you. The Bailiff of the Marshes."

Then he picked up his stave and went out into the dark dawn.

☙ 23rd January 1662, Thorney

Jenne looked down at the baby at her breast. They had called her Helen, after Iain's mother. She had a tuft of pale hair and was prettier than Magdalen had been when she was newly born.

Surely she had had enough milk by now? Jenne pulled herself away but the baby kept her mouth open and turned her head from side to side trying to find the nipple again. Jenne gave in and let her suck, then, a few minutes later, moved her to the other breast. The sucking lessened as the baby became satisfied, and then she fell asleep, then woke for a moment and sucked again, and then slept again and did not wake when she was lifted against her mother's shoulder and patted on the back.

Jenne settled the baby back in her cot and lay down on the bed. Within minutes she was weeping yet again.

She did not know why. It wasn't just because Père had died. There was another reason, but she did not know what it was. She felt no delight in this baby whose birth had exhausted her spirit and torn her body, and she seemed to have lost interest in Magdalen and indeed everyone and everything. She appreciated Iain and realised she was causing him concern, but felt tired and miserable all the time. She was supposed to be happy with her family and the new baby, but she wasn't. She resented Helen crying in the night and had to make herself get out of bed and pick her up. And Magdalen was being so difficult, always trying to climb on her when the baby was feeding, then picking things up and putting them down in the wrong place. She would hardly leave Helen alone, and Jenne kept telling her to stop stroking and touching her.

"For goodness' sake let her sleep, Magdalen. I don't want her waking up again. Go and find something else to do."

It was all too much. She had no idea where what Père used to call 'the light of her soul' had gone, and she no longer cared.

A few days earlier Mère had persuaded her to take up her embroidery again. She had fetched the sewing box and as soon as Jenne saw it she immediately felt a small, positive shift in her mood. She had quite forgotten she was in the middle of creating a delicate chain of yellow celandines around the edge of a piece in whose centre she had stitched

Magdalen
14th May 1655

As she settled herself comfortably Mère took Magdalen away so she would not interrupt her mother. For almost the first time since the baby was born things felt better.

As soon as she opened the box she saw her silks and scissors had been moved, but when she took out the piece she was working on she found a corner had been cut off. Deeper down in the box, pushed under the balls of wool she used for mending the men's clothes, she found the missing piece with the severed celandines.

Her wail of anger brought her mother hurrying back into the room, and she held up a piece of cut cloth in each hand.

"Look what Magdalen's done! Iain told me she'd opened my box, and look what she's done! She's ruined it."

"Jenne," urged her mother, "Calm yourself."

"But she's spoiling things!"

Magdalen had followed her grandmother into the room and was holding on to her skirts.

"Dearest," said Ann, "She's only a little child. Don't say that of her."

Jenne had got up from where she was sitting by the table and tried to grasp Magdalen, shouting, "You're a *bad* child. You're a *wicked* girl."

As she reached out to smack her Magdalen had run screaming out of the room.

Jenne had sat down, put her hands to her face and started to sob again.

Even now, days after the incident, she could recall her anger. But the child seemed to have forgotten it although she stopped asking her why she was crying and showed less interest in the baby, and Jenne thanked God for that.

*

The Point in Question, is the perfect Draining of the Great Level of the Fennes, called Bedford Level; some are for cutting the whole Level into Dykes and Banks; others, to let the Sea to flow into the Level, to lodge its Silt, for the repairing of the Banks; beside several other wayes, which, upon experience, and after infinite Charge, have been found fruitless at last. That which I propose is, briefly to effect the thing; and to make appear in this Discourse, to any unbyassed person, the facility, and the certainty of doing of it; and finally, of doing it upon such easie Tearms, that the whole Charge shall not amount unto much more, than hath formerly been spent in a Year or two Reparations: and for satisfaction herein, I shall referre the Reader to the Account and Calculation which follows.

A Breviat of the whole Charge of the Works mentioned in Colonel Dodson's Designe, for the perfect Draining of the Great Level of the Fens, called Bedford Level

	£	s.	d.
Imprimis,			
The great sluce and soss at Germans near Magdalen, as they are designed to be builded with brick, stone, flood-gates, fall-gates, soss-gates, iron-work and workmanship, and allowed by workmen, will cost	9833	15	6
The making the river through Marshland, from the river called the Horseshooe to Germans-bridge, with banks and in-drains, at 5*l*. a pole, will cost	12800	0	0
The purchase of the land in Marshland, where the river, banks, and in-drains, are cut out of, at 15*l*. an acre for the purchase, will cost	1575	0	0
The purchase of the land, with the making of banks and in-drains of the new cut, from the river of Owse to the great sluce, will cost	384	7	6
The making of Sandy's River, from Ely to Littleport Chair, at 1*l*.15s. a pole , will cost	1680	0	0
The sluce and sos at Guyheirne, allowing the timbers of the sluce and sos at Saltor's Load, there to be delivered, will cost 500*l*. otherwise the charge of that sluce and sos will be double	500	0	0
The sluce and sos at Ditton by Cambridge, allowing the timbers of Knowl Sluce, with the timbers at the brick-kills, there to be delivered, will cost 200*l*. otherwise the charge of that sluce and sos will be double	200	0	0
The taking up of shelves and flats in the rivers of Owse and Grant, will cost	600	0	0
The making of the two dams, one over the river of Owse by Magdalen, and the other over the river called the Horseshooe below Wisbidge, will cost	600	0	0
The making of the pit for the great sluce at Germans,			

or near Magdalen, may cost	200	0	0
The tarras to be made use of in and about the great sluice and sos, may cost	200	0	0

The Total of the whole Charge of the Works : £27563 3 shillings 0 pence

Collonel William Dodson, The Design for the Perfect Draining of the Great Level of the Fens

March 1662, Stanground

Mathieu's life was dominated by the sluice: the huge wooden gates which he helped raise and lower slowly, the resistant pressure of their movement through the water, the Humber Keels and Fen Lighters with their crews and cargoes, the horses, the shouted conversations between boats, the silences and pourings of the river. While he had been growing up his attention had been focused on drainage but in the last few years, he had been more of a farmer than a riverman. But now he was back where he wanted to be: working with water.

It wasn't easy. Learning the tasks was straightforward enough for he was well-informed and had a good man to teach him. But within his first couple of days he came to appreciate the difficulties.

While it was the case that there was now a better network of routes for boats to take inland or to the coast, these were not as successful as they should have been. Although only completed seven or eight years ago, their hard-won banks were proving less than robust. The packed-down peaty soil they were made of had begun to dry out as it had lain exposed to the weather. Last spring the blows had carried it off in thick brown clouds which made men turn to protect their faces. The fine soil dropped from the air on to the fields or, worse still, back into the water it was supposed to contain. Mathieu's heart sank when he saw how much of Vermuyden's work was so easily undone.

But that was not all, for the ground itself was sinking. No one believed this at first, thinking the land looked lower because the water level was rising. But Mathieu was shown posts stuck in the ground which proved the earth was shrinking. Notches had been cut each year to show the reducing levels. The peat itself also seemed to be disintegrating: where a man had once been able to hold a handful of moist, fibrous soil in his palm it was now little more than flaky dust which slipped through the fingers. How in God's name could things change so much? No one knew, but no one could deny what was happening.

In addition to these things it had become clear that the gradient of the newly-straightened rivers and channels was so slight there was insufficient force to clear sediment downstream. It sank on to the river bed and collected on the inside of bridges and sluices where it reduced the depth of water, making it too shallow for larger boats. By the time it reached the sea the sluggish flow clogged up the outfalls with mud. Simultaneously, the incoming tides carried their sand along and deposited it inland.

All this meant that navigation in the Fens was becoming harder instead of easier. This had an impact on travel and trade and particularly affected getting the crops of wheat and barley to market.

An engineer visiting the sluice told Mathieu, "You can't change a whole landscape without altering other things."

"But what can be done?"

"You must keep those wind machines turning at all costs, and you must repair the dykes and you must clear the sluices and bridge footings of mud and sand and weed."

So there was no end to the work and Mathieu was relieved when he had a chance to return home for a day.

Despite the ongoing pain of his father's absence it felt good to say grace and then sit down to a meal with the family. Iain, Jacob and Mère were interested in and concerned about what he was telling them but he decided not to dwell on the problems because more bad news wouldn't help them or Jenne who was looking so unhappy. Mère had warned him that she was taking a long time to recover from the birth and it was true – she was not her usual self at all.

ᔆ Morning, 14th March 1662, Thorney

When he was next at home Magdalen came to find him. "Hallo, Uncle Mathieu."

"Hallo. How are you?"

"Look, I can hop on one leg."

"That's good. How's your little sister?"

Magdalen changed legs. "And I can hop on this leg too."

"Yes, but I want to know about your baby sister."

"I don't like her."

"But she's your sister!"

At that moment Mère came into the room and Magdalen ran to her saying, "Uncle Mathieu's here."

"Yes. Isn't that good? Are you going to take him to see baby Helen?"

Magdalen turned and ran away out of the room.

"What's the matter? Why doesn't she like the baby?"

Mère sighed. "It happens like that sometimes, just as it happens that some women are sad when they've given birth. These things will pass, God willing."

Jenne was standing by the window holding the baby. Despite having had an undisturbed night she felt exhausted. The very thought of undressing Helen and bathing her and dressing her again tired her still more. She wanted to lie down, not be responsible for anyone, and sleep.

Outside some men were delivering a load of hay to the yard and she watched the chickens scatter and the loose stalks fly off as they unloaded it. Alice brought out a jug of water and talked to the men as they drank it. Someone must have said something funny because they all laughed at once and when one of them jerked his thumb out towards the fen they all laughed again.

She was annoyed they were not getting on with their work and turned sharply away from the window. Helen was beginning to whimper although she had only just been fed. What on earth was wrong with her now? Jenne spread a cloth on the bed and began to undress her. She was dirty and needed a wash, but Mère had taken the basin away and not yet brought it back so now she would have to wrap Helen up again and go and look for it. Why were things always so difficult? She almost cried with frustration as she tried to cover Helen and hold her at arm's length without getting herself dirty. She found the basin, filled it with warm water and washed the baby. The whole operation seemed to take hours but at last she put Helen back in her cot and threw herself face-down on her bed.

How could she be so tired? How could it be so hard to look after this baby whom she ought to be adoring?

After an hour she rose and went to seek her mother who was preparing food and talking to Mathieu.

"My dear, come and have some bread and cheese. You're not eating properly."

"I'm not hungry."

"You need to eat to make milk for the baby."

"I know that, but I'm not hungry," snapped Jenne. She caught Mathieu's expression and saw he was shocked by her sharp response, but who cared?

"Jenne, you've had less milk recently. You must think of Helen."

"Why? Why must I always think of her? Can't I ever think of me?" She put her hands to her face and covered her eyes. "I wish I'd never had her. I shouldn't have had her. I don't want her and I don't want Magdalen."

Mère led her back to the bedroom slowly, settled her down in a chair and picked up Helen who was crying bitterly.

She held her against her shoulder and rocked her. "There there, ma petite. There there."

ᑐ Afternoon, 14th March 1662, Thorney

Mathieu helped Jacob on the farm and saw one or two neighbours before it was time to return to Stanground. As he rode back he reflected on his brief break at home. Mère had been more settled, Jacob was taking more responsibility than he had expected and Iain was clearly doing his best with poor Jenne who was in a far worse state than he had realised. Thank God he himself was going back to his work with new energy. Tomorrow he would dydle the west side of the sluice gates thoroughly.

When passing Matlade Flottons he came across a man fishing on the bank, and stopped to talk.

"Have you heard?" the man asked, "A dyke has been broken near Whittlesey. They came in the night and breached it, causing a whole field to be drowned. Five sheep died."

So the rumours were true. Things were so bad that fenmen were now taking action right here in this part of the fens.

"Do they know who did it?"

"They've a good idea. They're out searching for them today."

As Mathieu went on his way he became increasingly adamant that he and those responsible for the drainage would have to do something. They couldn't just allow the saboteurs to destroy the dykes. He began to think of setting traps to catch men, of arming himself and hiding on a bank, of forcing those ignorant slodgers into the water and making them swim for it or even drown, for that was what they deserved.

He remembered how Père and his fellow Huguenots had suffered hatred and assaults on their dykes and homes in Sandtoft for years before giving in and moving away from the trouble, and even then it had happened again here near Thorney and Guyhirn. Surely it couldn't happen now? Please God, let it never be like that again.

But if it was, he would not just give in and move, as Père's generation had done. Why should he? He would fight bitterly for all the land they had won from the water.

ᕦ Six months later, 17th September 1662, Thorney

One day, after a night when he had not been home, Thomas arrived with a good-sized eel and skinned it outside in the rain. Janet curled it round in a pan, covered it with water and cooked it. Soon the three of them were eating it and licking their fingers, and then Thomas announced he needed to sleep as he had not slept for hours and probably would not do so for many more. But instead of lying down where he usually did he said he was going to where he went in summer. Although it would be wet, it would be safe.

"Come with me, Daniel. I need you to know where I am."

Daniel did not want to leave his mother whose shivering was worse than usual.

"Get up and stop sniffing," said his father as he picked up an armful of dry reeds.

Daniel followed him out of the doorway reluctantly, and the

sounds of his mother's coughs gradually lessened until all he could hear were his and his father's feet slurping in the mud.

Thomas's shelter rose above the level like a big molehill and was hardly distinguishable from the ground. He ducked and entered the dark space slowly, careful of the puddle which formed inside every time it rained. The place stank of mud, smoke, dankness.

He stepped across the puddle and spread the reeds on the ground on the far side.

"I'm going to stay here for a few days, and you'll have to bring me food. It's too risky to be at home. Can you find your way back?"

Daniel nodded.

"Then go now, and come back with bread and beer later on. And don't speak to anyone on the way."

But what if he met the Bailiff of the Marshes and the Bailiff spoke to him?

"What are you waiting for? Go on. Go home now."

Daniel went out into the rain and started to run but it was slippery and he had to slow down.

Then he saw someone coming towards him and feared the person had seen him, so there was no getting away. Who was it? As they neared each other he saw it was a man he knew, and the man called out a greeting and asked, "And how's your poor mother? Is the Bailiff still with her?"

He replied, "No. She's on her own. No one's with her," and then doubted whether he had said the right thing. Perhaps he should have said that his father was with her.

Daniel continued on his way more slowly. Could it be that the Bailiff really was at home? If so, would his mother be all right?

When he reached the hut he stood still and listened for voices, but all he could hear was coughing so he entered cautiously. Everything was the same as usual: his mother half-sitting half-lying, half-awake and half-asleep. No one else was there.

She opened her eyes and smiled at him. "Fetch me some water, will you?"

He willingly fetched it and looked around more confidently. There was definitely no one else there.

Then he found a warm spot by the fire. By the time he had been asleep for half an hour thin steam was rising from his clothes.

Loud talking woke him. His mother was answering questions from someone whose voice he did not recognise. It must be the Bailiff. He kept his eyes shut and did not move.

"Was Thomas Ridman here last night?"

"Yes."

"Are you sure?"

"Of course I am. Where else would he be?"

"Do you know where he sets his nets?"

Cough, cough, cough. "No."

"Where does he keep his boat?"

"I don't know."

"Where is he now?"

"I don't know." Cough, cough.

Another muffled voice came from the doorway.

"When will he be back?"

"In an hour or two, I expect."

"Then that's when we'll return."

The other voice called, "Let's leave this place or we'll end up with the ague too."

When Daniel heard horses being mounted and the shluck of hooves in the mud he sat up. His mother could hardly speak for coughing but gestured to him to fetch her cup of poppy tea. She sipped it slowly and gradually the fit of fever subsided.

"Go and tell your father they were here looking for him and that they'll be coming again soon."

The Bailiff had been there, in his own hut, but he had not hurt them. Daniel was glad he had not looked at him but did not want to meet him outside.

"Be off, then. Give your Da this bread, but make sure they don't see you." Then she started to shiver and moan, and Daniel was torn between leaving her and taking a message to his father. Half-coughing and half-speaking, Janet wrapped some bread in a cloth, pushed it into his hand and shooed him out of the doorway.

He looked first to see if the Bailiff and the other man were still nearby, but they were not, and he found hoof prints leading away from the direction he needed to take. It was not yet dark and he felt better once he set out. He found his father exactly where he had left him that morning – hidden at the back of his shelter in a pile of reeds.

"Ma said to say the Bailiff's been and he's coming back."

Thomas sat up quickly. "What bailiff?"

"The Bailiff of the Marshes."

Then his father laughed and asked, "Is that food you've brought me?"

Daniel passed him the bread, confused as to why his father had laughed.

"He wanted Ma to tell him where you were."

"That wasn't a bailiff. That was one of the dykemen." He bit into the bread and seemed to gain immediate energy from each bite. "I'm not going home. I've been thinking. I'm going back to Whittlesey next week and you're coming too. We need someone small, and you'll be just right."

18th September 1662, Thorney

Iain was making a syrup out of sloes. There were two full bowls of the blue-bloomed berries on the table and he was rolling up his sleeves ready to work. His hands and arms were covered in scratches from the blackthorn bush he had stripped of fruit that morning.

Magdalen was standing on a stool watching him. As he scooped some berries into a large mortar and began to press it with a pestle she picked up a sloe which had rolled towards her, bit it, and screamed.

Iain went to her at once. "Oh, Magdalen! Spit! Spit it out! Don't eat it! They're horrible!" He comforted her and wiped her face. "Never mind. Here's an apple to take the taste away."

She calmed down and Iain went on with his pulping, and soon she asked if she could do it.

"No. It's difficult, and it's messy. The juice will stain your clothes. Look what it's done to me." He held up his hands which were blue to the wrists.

"Will your hands always be like that?"

"No. It'll wear off after a few days."

He poured the squashed fruit into a cloth strainer and started on the second bowl.

"What's it for?"

"It's for people who are ill with a fever."

"Is Maman ill with a fever?"

Iain went on pounding and pressing.

Magdalen asked again, "Is she ill?"

"No, she's not."

"Then why does she take medicines?"

Iain paused before saying, "So she's got plenty of milk for the baby."

Suddenly, Magdalen heard a horse coming into the yard. She got off the stool and ran to the window.

"Uncle Jacob's here!"

Jacob came in saying, "The dykemen have been asking about Thomas Ridman. They want to know if he's worked for us recently."

Iain looked up, holding his dark blue hands still above the bowl. "He usually hassocks for us in the summer, but he's not been with us much this year. Why do they want him?"

"They're fairly sure he's involved with trouble over towards Peterborough. A dyke was breached last night."

"They should talk to his brother. He's a millman somewhere out beyond Whaplode."

"I'll tell them."

Magdalen asked, "Uncle Jacob, will you draw me a picture?"

"Not now, I've got to go off again. I'll do you one when I get home tonight."

She went outside to see him ride off and came back in to find her father covering the bowl of thick blue-black liquid with a cloth and putting things away.

"Go and see what Mamie's doing," he said. "I've got to go out to Singlesole Farm."

Magdalen wandered around for a while, and went to look at Helen who was awake and lying on her back.

It was then an idea came to her. She went back to the kitchen, searched for a sloe and found one which had fallen under the table. She pushed it hard against the sharp edge of a knife to puncture its skin and took it back to Helen. Then she put it in the baby's mouth, ran away and hid behind Papi's desk.

She curled up in the rug he used to put over his knees when he was reading in winter, made a nest for the tabby cat which had followed her, and went to sleep.

Jenne had a bad fit of the falling sickness while Magdalen was sleeping but the child was not woken by the shouting and grunting, the crash of a falling water jug and the callings out of her grandmother and uncle attending to her mother. It was not until two hours later that Ann realised she was missing and started to search for her.

"My poor dear Magdalen," said Ann, hugging her tightly. "Thank goodness. We couldn't find you, but there you were, hidden away in the corner! What on earth were you doing there?" She led her through to the kitchen. "Look Jacob, I've found her, and it looks as if she's had a sloe in her mouth too. How strange."

"But thank God she's all right."

"Poor, poor Jenne. She'll come through this fit as she did the others, but I pity Iain. Mon Dieu, why did this have to happen when she is already unwell? I'm so glad you were with her." Ann set Magdalen down off her lap. "Even though it's frightening to see her have a fit I always worry that one day it will happen when she's alone."

Jacob nodded towards Magdalen, "At least this little one didn't witness it."

"Now we must make sure she rests and that her face and arm heal up." Ann stood up and straightened her dress. "But I just don't understand why Jenne gave the girls sloes."

Magdalen began to cry and Jacob sat her on his knee. "It's all right. Maman will get better now."

"Papa said she wasn't ill."

Ann reached out to stroke her hand and said, "Well, she was suddenly ill today, but she's getting better already, grâce à Dieu."

"Here's Iain. Mère, I think it best that you tell him." Jacob stood up with Magdalen in his arms. "Come on. We'll go and see if your Maman is all right."

When they went into the bedroom Magdalen saw that pieces of the best blue jug were lying jumbled on a chest. Jacob carried her to the bedside and she looked down at her mother. She was asleep and her arm, wrapped in a white bandage, lay above the covers. There was a big blue bruise over one eye and her nose was swollen.

Magdalen began to howl.

☙ 21st September 1662, by a river

Daniel was crouching on the far side of a river several miles away from where he lived, with two lit lanterns at his feet. His father had told him exactly what he had to do: wait in the sedge until he could no longer hear the sound of the punt being poled back across the water, then take up the two lanterns and, holding one in each hand, walk upstream along the dykebank as far as the stone bridge. If he heard anyone nearby he was to put the lanterns out and hide. If no one came he was to leave them alight until he reached the bridge where he was to hide until he was collected.

"If you do that," said his father, "The dykemen will think we Tigers are on that side of the river and they'll cross over when really we'll be on this side. It'll give us time to reach the sluice."

"But what if they find me?" asked Daniel.

"They won't find you because you're small. You can go deeper into the rushes than they can. They'd sink in, wouldn't they? But don't try to swim or you'll drown."

So he had been ferried across the river in the darkness watching the wet quant gleam each time it was lifted from the water. As he heard the calls of small birds he worried alternately about not returning to his mother and the task he was about to carry out for his father, but when the boat reached the bank and hissed into the reeds he scrambled out at once and was passed the lanterns.

Then his father got out, struck a spark, lit the lanterns, got back into the punt and pushed off. Daniel listened to the sound of the boat receding until he could no longer hear it.

He picked up the lanterns and began to walk. Within a minute or two he found he could not hold them out with straight arms. He had been told to do that so the dykemen would think he was more than one person, but the lanterns were far too heavy, and if he held them by his sides they lit up the track and helped him see where he was going. He kept looking across the river in the hope of seeing a light to prove he was not the only person on this dark, unknown riverbank. He forced himself onwards trying not to think about will o' the wisps.

He heard a noise of slithering and stopped dead. What could that have been? Something quite big. Bigger than any duck or rat. He suddenly felt his stomach contract. He put the lanterns on the ground and hurried to loosen his clothes. He crouched there in the dark and relieved himself, looking at the two over-lapping domes of lamp-light each surrounded by darkness. He shut his eyes to concentrate on listening, but there were only the noises of night birds. It occurred to him that perhaps what he had heard was an otter. He picked up the lanterns and continued.

There was nothing to measure his journey by. Most dykeside paths were the same, especially at night, for they were all straight and bare of any growing thing except reeds and bulrushes. He could only recognise the ones close to his home because of the elder bush which leaned sideways, the tying-up post, the shallow place where the cattle waded. On this bank it was as if he was in the middle of nowhere and walking to nowhere. He slowed down a little, wondering if his mother would be able to get her poppy tea or if because he was not there to get it for her she was coughing and retching.

Suddenly he heard voices and turned to check where they were coming from. He looked back down the river, and saw lights moving across it. They seemed to be floating by them-selves but they must be on a boat. That meant men were coming after him. How far away was the bridge he was supposed to reach? Could he risk going further on while he counted up to fifty? When he reached fifty he would hide. In his haste he lost his shoe in the mud but wasn't going back.

It was quiet again so he hurried on and started counting from one again, but still there was no bridge, so he looked for a marshy den to hide in. Finding one he sloshed in too fast, dropped the lanterns into the river, stumbled and found himself in water up to his chest.

He strained to listen above the hammer of his heart, and wanted to cough but had learned early in life how to stifle his coughing. So, gasping with cold and with his eyes less than a foot above water-level, he waited in the slight light that leaned on the surface.

The next sound he heard was not the voice of a man but the bark of a dog. Dogs? Why hadn't Da said anything about dogs? Dogs could go anywhere, could smell anything – he had often seen them bounding along to retrieve fowl. He would be forced to swim for it if a dog came near him, and if he swam he'd drown.

As he waited he heard more voices, more barking and then saw the flicker of lights coming nearer.

A man called out, "Find him, Nab! Find him," and Daniel heard a dog crashing through the reeds and panting. He imagined its pink tongue rolling, its wet nose sniffing first his shit and then his shoe.

"Is he in there? Good dog, good boy."

There was nothing to do but swim for it so Daniel struck out from the bank away from his hiding-place in the reeds.

"There he is!" yelled another voice. "Get him, Nab. Get him!"

A sharp pain tore through his heel and within minutes he was yanked back to the bank where men he did not know surrounded him.

"What are you doing out at night?"

"So the Tigers are getting children to do their work now."

"Who is he?"

"What's his name?"

"What's your name?"

"He's too frightened to speak."

"Look at his ankle."

"Nab did a good job, then."

He was hauled across someone's shoulder and despite his left foot hurting as nothing had ever hurt him before he thought of his mother in their hut and his father poling the punt away from him.

It seemed to be hours before the man stopped and laid him down in a warm, dry place.

When he woke up an old lady was looking at him, and at once he called out for his mother.

She spoke softly to him. "Shhh shhh. Your mother isn't here. We're looking after you because a dog bit your foot."

He asked for his father and was told no one knew who he was or where he was.

The old lady said, "Can you tell me his name? What's your father called?"

"Da."

"And what's your name?"

"Daniel."

"Daniel who? Daniel what?"

"Daniel Ridman."

"Where do you live?"

"By Jackwater."

A man came into the room. Daniel was terrified when he saw that he had blue hands.

"Good, you're awake. We're going to give you a wash."

A wash?

The woman pulled back the cover and told him to stand up, but he lurched forward and fell against her when he tried.

"Careful," she said, supporting him.

Then another man brought in a big pot and began to fill it with jugs of warm water. They took off his clothes which were covered with wet mud, then told him to try to put his right foot into the water.

"Even half of you is better than nothing," said the old lady, smiling.

But he could not put any weight on the hurt foot so she sluiced him down gently where he stood.

Then the man with blue hands said, "Ann, will you hold him steady, please? I want to undo the cloth round his foot and have a look at where he was bitten."

Daniel had never had all his clothes off at once before except when playing in water with his cousins. He stood petrified while he waited for the blue hands to touch him. Would they be slimy? Or would they sting? Everyone was staring at him.

The old lady said, "Look at his little chest. You can count his ribs."

The man with blue hands felt carefully round his ankle and under his foot and pressed the skin near the wound. Then he said, "Good. Apart from the swelling, it's no worse than it was last night. I'll crush some more horehound leaves and make another poultice."

The other man asked, "What are those marks on him?"

The man with blue hands turned Daniel's back to the light.

"Ringworm," he said.

A small girl looked in through the doorway and saw the boy, but almost immediately someone appeared behind her, picked her up and took her away.

🐾 28th September 1662, Thorney

Mathieu was arguing with Iain.

"My father would not have brought that boy into the house as you have done."

He was insisting that this child Daniel was in a completely different situation from the one Iain had been in years earlier. Iain had, Mathieu granted, been wronged then, and could therefore be said to be owed something by Père. But this boy had been trying to wrong the French drainers in general and Stanground Sluice in particular. He was obviously connected to the Fen Tigers who wanted to destroy everything the Deschamps family and the Huguenots had worked for, everything they stood for.

"For God's sake, why didn't you ask me first? Is it true he's been here a week already?"

"Be reasonable," said Iain, "You weren't here to ask and I talked it over with Ann and Jacob. The bairn can't be more than eight years old, and two days ago his mother was found dead from the ague in her hovel over by Jackwater. Are you suggesting we should send him back there on his own?"

"Send him to another relation then. He must have more than a dead mother and a criminal father."

Iain had already visited Peter Ridman but he told him he had been estranged from his brother Thomas for years. Iain had hoped he might have accepted the boy into his family but saw at once he would not.

Matthieu continued to complain. "The point is that he's Ridman's son, isn't he? And Ridman was trying to damage my sluice. I can't believe you're treating his foot and feeding him, especially when all this is going on with Jenne. There's only one good result that can possibly come out of all this."

Iain looked at him enquiringly.

"Soon enough his father will come and collect him and then you'll have your man. You can apprehend him and hand him over."

Iain had thought of this too but it gave him little consolation for the child was under-nourished, unhappy and likely to be lame for life and it was hard to see how having his father sent to prison would improve things. When told of his mother's death Daniel had retreated into almost complete silence. But since then he had accepted Magdalen following him around wherever he went and even seemed to want her to be with him.

That was a further reason for Mathieu's disapproval. "If you let Magdalen go around with him there's no knowing what habits he'll teach her and what she might catch. I bet he has lice or something worse. I wouldn't let him anywhere near a child of mine. For God's sake, Iain, can't you see he's a nasty little bastard?"

7th October 1662, Thorney

And then, about ten days later, Iain found Magdalen in tears because Daniel had disappeared. They searched for him in the house, the yard and the fields.

"Where's he gone?"

"I don't know. Perhaps a long way away."

"I want to go with him."

"You can't."

"Why not?"

"You're too young, and this is where you belong."

Iain sat down by the fireplace and stared into the smoky fire. He reached out for the ancient stone Stuart Macpherson had found years ago, for he liked to feel it cool in his hand and admire its ridges and bevels. But it was not on the shelf. He checked underneath but it had not fallen there.

The loss of the stone disturbed him for he had come to think of it as a talisman. Perhaps Magdalen would know where it was. He would ask her the next morning.

Well, he had done all that he could. Perhaps Daniel's leaving was for the best.

As he sat there his mind went back to the readings he had heard the previous Sunday in church. They were taken from the Book of Job and described a man who was virtuous, wise and wealthy. His family were so rich and his land so large *"he was the greatest of all the men of the east"*. But despite his status he was always aware that one of his family might have done wrong unintentionally so he took the precaution of making burnt offerings to God every day.

However, Satan asked God about Job and God allowed him to test Job through a series of terrible events – his stock was destroyed, his children killed and he himself made to suffer a plague of boils. Despite all this he was never tempted to lose his faith.

Iain's attention had waned when the story became more complicated and three friends urged Job to confess the sins they believed God must be punishing him for, but he listened when it came to Satan. The pastor had read out

And the Lord said unto Satan, "Whence comest thou?" Then Satan answered the Lord, and said, "From going to and fro in the earth, and from walking up and down in it."

Did Satan really walk up and down in the earth? Was he the cause of things going wrong? Of Jenne's loss of vitality and withdrawal from him? Of her falling sickness? Of Samuel's accident? Of his difficulties with Mathieu? Of the on-going problems with the drainage? Of the recent sabotage? Of the way Magdalen was changing from a happy child into an unhappy one?

He thought too of Jacob and Alice. They were enjoying each other so much. How could it be that some people seemed to live easily, while others had so many troubles?

Iain did not consider his life to be anything like Job's, but he was almost overwhelmed. He had never felt so sorry for himself. He had never felt so low and lost in his life.

Everyone else in the house was asleep so he banked up the fire and looked once more for the stone but it wasn't there.

When he went out into the wintry yard to rinse his face a particular phrase from the reading came back to him. In complaining to God about his desolation and despair, Job had said,

> *"I am the brother of dragons and a companion to owls."*

Job had expressed it perfectly. That was exactly how he himself was feeling.

8th October 1662, Thorney

The next afternoon Iain put his head round the door to tell Jenne that Ann had asked him to visit Samuel's grave with her.

Jenne nodded.

Why did she say so little? Why?

He stood hesitating by the doorway and said. "It's stopped raining now."

"I know."

She was dressing Helen but why didn't she even smile or look at him when she spoke to him?

"Magdalen is playing in the kitchen, and Jacob is drawing in there. We won't be much more than half an hour. Perhaps an hour at most."

How can I reach her? How?

Iain and Ann set off for the Abbey Church. It was a bright autumnal day with big, clear skies and the oaks beginning to shed their leaves. Things felt a little better immediately. Surely Satan was not going to and fro in the earth on a day like this?

Ann took his arm and they walked slowly. After a while she asked, "Do you know what I particularly miss about not having Samuel?"

There were so many things they all missed about him and he could not guess which one she meant, so he just said, "Tell me."

"I don't speak French so much."

He waited for her to say more.

"We used to speak French together most of the time, but now I – we all – speak English more and more and I miss it. And it's only when I'm on my own for a long time that I even think in French."

"I'm glad you sometimes speak and sing in French to the children."

Ann smiled. "I like doing it. It's important to me, and it was for Samuel too."

They walked on, talking a little about Jacob and Alice, about Mathieu and his work and greeting an elderly neighbour they met on the Causeway, but Iain couldn't get a recent incident out of his mind. He had been leaning over Jenne's shoulder to look at something she was holding when she had snapped, really snapped at him, "Oh leave me alone, can't you? Just leave me alone."

When they reached the Abbey Church they made their way to the grave and stood beside it. The air was quite still, the sun just strong enough to warm them. Ann had cut some sprays of still-red rosehips and placed them on the grass by the grave.

Iain said his usual prayer for Samuel but his mind was on Jenne. Did she care about him or the children any more? She just seemed to get through her tasks, and sit and sigh. And sometimes she was even hostile – that was the only word for it – towards him. Even though she had recovered some strength since the fit, she had not recovered her spirit at all. What had happened to her? How could he heal their marriage? He had tried to get her to take his medicines and had even put some in her food without her knowing, but nothing had changed. It was so difficult.

"Are you ready to visit Isaac's grave now?"

Iain nodded and they made their way to the small hillock with its small cross. Seeing it made him sigh a long sigh, and when Ann put her hand on his arm he could not stop himself from crying.

"I don't know what to do." He pressed his hands to his face. "I'm doing my best and I don't know what else to do."

Rooks were cawing above them. A horse and cart rumbled in the distance. A woman called her child.

"You must listen to God."

"I don't know how to."

"Try."

He thought of Jenne's listlessness, of her almost total refusal to be touched by him since Helen was born, of her disinterest in Magdalen. Could God change all that? Could He change things back to how they were before?

He said, "Miracles only happen in the Bible."

"God can't make things just as we want them," said Ann, "But He can help us to accept things as they are."

"I refuse to accept them as they are," said Iain with vehemence, "I can't live my whole life with Jenne as she is now, and feeling as I do now."

"God can change how you feel about your life and her life."

"But it *can't* be right to be like this."

"I know it seems wrong," Ann sighed, "And it makes me too very unhappy to see Jenne as she is."

Immediately Iain was ashamed of himself for being so insensitive. Ann had lost her husband and now her daughter seemed out of reach. How could he not have noticed that she was suffering too? He reached out his hand to her.

"I'm sorry," he said, "I didn't ... I haven't ...."

"It doesn't matter, Iain. When we are in pain it is difficult to see the pain of others."

They walked on round the outside of the Abbey Church to the main doorway, entered the high nave and sat on the bench by the wall. Looking up, he could see the tops of trees through the windows. He was familiar with the place but although he joined Jenne's family in their worship each week he did not believe as they believed.

"There's no need to pray," said Ann. "Just be patient. Just be open."

So, knowing nothing would come of it, he waited and tried to calm himself. He realised Jenne had been right when she said she could not pray and that God was not listening, for it was the same for him. But he stayed there because he did not know what else to do and to please Ann who was trying to help. She was the only person he could rely on and perhaps it was good that she had seen him weep.

Then, out of the silence came words he had not thought of since he was a boy. They were the words of the prayer his mother had learned when she was a child growing up in Stonehaven. She had often recited them by his bedside.

Oor Father in Heiven hallowt be Thy Name,
Thy will be dune on the Yird as in Heiven.
Gie us oor breid for this incomin day.
Forgie us the wrangs we hae wrocht,
as we hae forgien the wrangs we hae dree'd,
An say-us-na sairlie but sauf us frae the ill-ane.
An thine be the kingdom,
the Pooer an the Glory,
noo an forivver.
Amen

He recalled her soft accent from Aberdeenshire, and the words tugged him back to his home on the hillside, to the bed he shared with his brother and sister, to the way his mother paused after she said *but sauf us frae the ill-ane.*

Whose voice was it? His mother's? Or God's? It did not matter. What mattered was that he felt better.

He sat with his head bowed until Ann gently laid her hand on his arm and said, "It's time to go."

They walked home together in silence, and when they reached the house Jenne was standing at the door, holding the baby and beckoning.

Iain's heart jumped with dread as he hurried forward. What was it now?

But she greeted them saying, "Come and see Jacob and Alice. They have good news for us!"

PART II

1669

Alice lifted Benjamin from where he had wedged himself into a corner. By six months he was already robust and solid, able to roll himself over from his front to his back leaving him waving his arms and legs like a helpless beetle, and now he was constantly on the move and trying to climb on to everything. Christian, her first son, was playing with Magdalen. He was quite a different shape, leaner and longer, more like Jacob. She watched him hold the ball up into the air ready to drop it, wanting to be the one to win by grabbing it first.

Alice watched them, half-expecting Magdalen to abandon the game and disappoint her small cousin. It was so hard to know how best to deal with her.

Jacob and Ann were the ones who found it easiest to accept Magdalen's changes of temper. They felt she had had a bad beginning because of Père's death, the difficult birth, Jenne's weeks' long withdrawal into herself followed by a serious fit and the attention which had to be given to the new baby. Ann was philosophical about it, recognising that this was perhaps how things were always going to be

"Any child would find all that hard," she said. "So we have to do our best with her."

Ann and Jacob reasoned with Magdalen when she answered back and distracted her when she was determined to have her own way. Jacob took her out with him on the farm from time to time and Ann would sometimes successfully prevail on her to attend her lessons and complete tasks properly. Helen, a biddable child, did not complain that she was relied on far more than her older sister when it came to tidying up and looking after her little cousins. She had never known Magdalen to be other than she was now: alternately energetic and lazy, often rude or selfish, and usually preferring her own company to that of others.

"She'll grow out of it," said Jacob. "All we have to do is wait."

But she was already thirteen years old. Jenne, after her gradual recovery from the fit and her low mood, had done her best to reach out to her first born, but by then Magdalen had moved too far away. As for Iain, he was so hungry to re-connect with Jenne that he relied on Ann to cope with Magdalen.

Christian suddenly gave a loud yelp and Alice whirled round.

"She bit me!" he cried, "Magdalen bit me!"

Alice sat down on the bench and pulled Christian to her. He held out his finger and showed her a ring of small red teeth marks.

"Magdalen, why did you do that?"

"I didn't."

"You must have done."

"I didn't. He bit himself."

"I didn't," wailed Christian. "She did it."

Alice got up and took the hands of both her boys, "Come on," she said comfortingly, "Let's go outside."

Magdalen pushed past them into the yard, hurled the ball over the wall and ran off on to the fen.

⟡ 20th May 1669, in the fens

Daniel Ridman was in his hut.

He was repairing the roof with new branches while thinking about how to prevent the rain from running in through the entrance. Last year he had built a lintel, but this had stopped any wet inside from getting out.

In order to make the roof firm he used his knife to peel the bark off the pale, supple wands and then jammed them in tightly. He pushed against the new branches to test them. They gave slightly under his weight, but the roof felt better. Later he would cover them with reeds.

Perhaps he should raise the level of the floor? That might be possible. His father could help, but at present he didn't know where his father was. However, he would turn up soon enough as he always did when he wanted help or a safe place to hide for a couple of days.

The fire was going and the potful of water already hot, so he brewed himself some tea, sat down outside the hut and watched the sun go down beyond Bassenhally Moor. Over the last week or two he had noticed how it was staying light a little later, and this pleased him.

He thought again of his father who until now he had been content to have staying in the hut if he wanted to, but increasingly he wished to have the place to himself. He wanted to be alone when Magdalen came to see him again.

His father didn't even know Magdalen existed. All those years ago, almost as soon as Daniel had run away from the house in Thorney he had found his way back to where he had lived, taken one look at it and run off again. Without his mother, it was no longer home.

After a few days he was re-united with his father and they had found a way of existing by occasional paid work but mostly by fowling and fishing. At first they moved between the huts they found or made and the homes of the few people who took pity on them because Daniel was so young, but as time passed Thomas became more confident and stopped worrying about the law so they moved less often. But his temper remained as violent as ever, and one day when he came home drunk again Daniel decided he no longer cared about him, and set off to make his own hut which he vowed he would never let his father enter.

He knew Magdalen quite well by now. He had known her from all those years ago after he was caught in the dyke and taken to her house. She had wanted to be with him and she had given him that special stone.

He had not seen her for at least three years after that, but one day he was fishing in a place where he was not supposed to be and a man with a girl and boy came walking towards him along the bank. He recognised the man at once – he was one of the men in that house where he'd been looked after, but not the one with the blue hands. He had to get away before they reached him so quickly collected up his fishing things and hurried off. Behind him he heard the boy ask, "Papa, why isn't that boy walking properly?"

"He's lame," said the man.

"Will he be like that for ever?"

"I'm afraid so."

Daniel had looked back and seen the man and the children standing in a line watching him. Then the man picked up the little boy and continued along the bank, but the girl stayed where she was until the man called out, "Come on, Magdalen. Christian's tired so let's go home."

And then, a year after that when he was about eleven, he had seen Magdalen again, and she had given him an apple. Then, still later, they had met when he was taking a short cut across her family's farm, and he had given her a striped caterpillar he had just found.

And so they began to seek one another out to exchange or show each other things: a sheep's tooth, a good blackberry bush, a broken but useful blade, a cake intended for Helen, a fish with no eyes, a handful of hazelnuts.

But Daniel had only seen Magdalen once during these recent winter months. It was too wet or too dark for her to get away unnoticed, but every week she put bread for him under an unused punt. Once he had hidden close by and watched her arrive, push the small package into the agreed-on place, pull her red scarf close and hurry away. Watching her do this for him gave him great satisfaction.

And then one day in January when both land and water were solid he heard voices calling so went to the fen to watch the people out there on the ice. From where he stood at the far end he tried to pick Magdalen out, and after a minute or two he recognised her red scarf. He had not seen her skate before and was surprised to see how easily she sped backwards and forwards.

At last she caught sight of him standing alone and allowed herself to come to a halt. He saw her look round and hesitate, unsure about whether to skate over to him or not. Someone came towards her and she bent down as if re-tying her skates.

He willed her not to approach, and while she had her head

down he limped away into the fen, leaving his uneven footprints in the shallow snow.

That was nearly two months ago, and every day now he was impatient for her to come to his hut. She had been in it before. She called it his den.

ᙖ 22nd May 1669, Thorney

"What are these words?" asked Iain, pointing at the writing under the Coat of Arms of the Bedford Level Corporation.

Mathieu pulled the map nearer. "It says *Arridet aridum*."

"But what does it mean? You know I can't read Latin."

"A rough translation is 'The dry land smiles', because obviously that's what the Corporation exists for. To ensure that the fens dry out to create good, dry land." Mathieu stood back and appraised the Coat of Arms with pride. "Père would approve of it, wouldn't he?"

"Yes, " said Iain, "He would. And he would be very proud of you."

Matthieu was feeling extremely pleased with himself, and had every reason for being so. He had been given the very job he most wanted – sluice-keeper for the now well-established Bedford Level Corporation which had been founded to manage the entire system of drains, banks, sluices and bridges and to protect navigation interests. Things were working out in just the way he had been hoping they would. Iain, Jacob and his mother were all impressed, and here was Iain saying that Samuel would have been so too.

When Iain left the room he rolled up the map and stood looking out on to the road where his horse was tied up. Even though the window was closed he sensed warmer air and greener trees. It was just the right time of year to buy a better horse, perhaps think about a new saddle, or at least new reins.

But the question increasingly occupying his mind was, Is now the time to find a wife? Sometimes marriage presented itself as exactly the right thing for him to do next, but when he considered every young woman he could think of he discounted each one in turn.

He came away from the window and sat down at the table to

re-read the paper he had been given by the Bedford Level Corporation Committee.

Sluice-keepers

The sluice-keepers, when the passage of the water is required for the purposes of drainage, should use their utmost diligence both by day and night, that the doors be opened as soon as, and as long as, a run can be obtained; and when the ebb doors are required to be closed for keeping up the navigation, it is their duty to take care they are kept shut. The sluice-keepers, however, are not allowed , on any occasion, to admit waters into the rivers without a written order from the engineer or superintendent.

It is also the duty of the sluice-keeper to do all in his power, without committing a breach of the peace, to oppose any person who shall attempt to pass through any of the sluices at a time or in a manner which may occasion any injury thereto, or who shall force open the doors, or draw the lighters in by horses, or force the lighters in before the doors are properly open, or leave any barge &c., either in the sluice, or so near thereto, as to prevent the opening, shutting, or using thereof; or, when the same is open for the drainage of the fens, who shall place, or continue, a barge, lighter &c., so as to obstruct the passage of the waters draining through the same, or who shall attempt to do any other injury; and he is to communicate all that happens to the superintendent, that the offenders may be immediately prosecuted by the corporation.

Denver Sluice, Salter's Lode Sluice and the Old Bedford Sluice, being contiguous to the tidal river, require the constant care and presence of the sluice-keepers: it is consequently their duty not to be absent therefrom, for any purpose whatsoever, without the consent of the engineer or superintendent; and when that consent is given, the absence is to be as short as possible.

It is also a part of the sluice-keepers' business to keep their respective sluices in good order, and, particularly when necessary, to croome, dydle, or remove sands in the sluice, or at the backs and fronts thereof; and when there is ice, to break it, and to do anything consistent with their duty as sluice-keepers, as the engineer or superintendent may think requisite on the part of the corporation.

Each sluice-keeper is sworn, immediately after his election, to the

diligent discharge of the duties of his office. The oath is always adminis-
tered by the register, in the presence of the board.

Bedford Level Corporation

Yes, despite all the problems which kept on arising he could do all that was required and two days ago, in the presence of the board, he had sworn to do so.

At least now that it was understood how the drainage had caused the peat to dry up and shrink, they could actually get on with strengthening the banks. That was what it always came down to: strengthening the banks. But this was the job of others, for he had new responsibilities.

So. A wife. Is that what he needed?

It probably was, so now all he had to do was to meet the right person.

Perhaps he should look further than he had so far. He had not met as many new people in Stanground as he had hoped, but what about March? Or Wisbech?

But he couldn't just turn up somewhere looking for a wife, could he? No. He needed help. He didn't want to ask his own family, so who could he go to? Piere Roo would have been the obvious choice until a few years ago, but now he had his own wife and child, and it would somehow be embarrassing to ask him. What about Bastion Le Pla? He was courting that girl from Gedney. He – or perhaps even she – might know more girls.

Girls. When he came to think about it, he realised he didn't know much at all about girls and women.

He tried to imagine the sort of wife he wanted. She wouldn't be too young, for he had left it late, though there would be nothing wrong if she were ten years younger than him. She would have to be steady and sensible like his mother, competent on the farm and in the kitchen. She'd have to be pretty, too.

And what about children? He thought of his four nephews and nieces. Helen was a sweet little girl, and Benjamin was a placid baby. But Alice had been tearing her hair out for months about Christian because nothing she or Iain tried would get rid of his worms. He'd be fine for a couple of weeks and then he'd start scratching himself again. And as for Magdalen, what could be said?

Nevertheless, he imagined a meal-time with him at one end of the table, his wife at the other and children on either side. He imagined saying grace, and making sure the family was polite and obedient. They would all be proud of their father the sluice-keeper. But when he thought about it, he realised that within ten years he would probably have been promoted.

Yes, Bastion was the best person to confide in. He'd ride over and see him the very next day.

🐇 23rd May 1669, Thorney

Magdalen had collected up a handful of candle-ends. no one missed them and she hid them down the front of her dress.

If she went out through the side door the only person who might notice her leaving would be her grandmother. Now that Mamie's sight was poor she liked to lean out of the window on warm evenings and turn her face to the light.

Sometimes, when she caught sight of one of the girls running, she would call out, "Who's that? Is it Helen?"

"It's me, Magdalen."

"Where are you off to?"

"I've to take a message to Uncle Jacob."

Revelling in her escape Magdalen ran past the side of the house, on to the Causeway and across towards the fen.

When she became out of breath she slowed down and relaxed, for once she was on her way to Daniel things always began to feel better. It was much more exciting to be with him than at home. He would thank her for taking him bread each week as well as for the candles, but she was already wondering what he would have for her this time. She always tried to guess but she had never yet guessed correctly and that was because the things he found her were much more unusual than the ones she found. She remembered how he had dared her to hold that strange fish with no eyes. It had been silvery white except for the fins, which were orange. She had imagined it swimming with its mouth open, trying to catch things it could not see.

It was possible that Daniel would not be in his den now, but there would be no better opportunity for a day or two. She hurried on with her fingers crossed.

But there he was, sitting outside his hut. He got up to meet her and she saw at once that he had he grown a couple of inches over the winter and also had the beginnings of a thin beard and moustache.

"Here I am! Have you missed me?"

"Sometimes," he replied. He took a step nearer her. "What have you brought?"

Magdalen put her hand into her dress and brought out the five candle ends.

"Good. They'll be useful."

Magdalen smiled.

Daniel said, "And I've got something for you."

"I'll try to guess. Is it alive?"

"No."

"So it's dead?"

"No, it's not dead either."

"Then it must be a stone."

Daniel shook his head, went inside the hut and returned with some small brown objects in his hand.

"What are they?"

"Owl pellets."

Owl pellets? She was disappointed.

"Come here and look at them properly."

Daniel took the broken-bladed knife Magdalen had found on the edge of a field, put the pellets on a flat piece of ground and carefully half-cut and half-pulled them open. They were composed of soil rather like peat, but within them were little cream-coloured twigs of a hard material.

"Those are bones," said Daniel. "The owls hunt mice, voles and shrews and eat the whole creature. Later they cough the pellets out, like this." He mimicked an owl moving its throat in the way she had seen a cat cough up a ball of fur. Then he poked the pellet again. "Look at it. There's part of a feather and that's a jaw bone."

Magdalen leaned towards him. She pretended to be interested in the various scraps he was indicating but what she focused on was his smell. He smelled different from how he had smelled before winter. He smelled like a man and not a boy.

Daniel brushed away the peaty parts of the pellets but kept the longest bone in his hand. It was curved and nearly an inch long.

"A vole's bone," he said. "This is what we need."

"What for?"

"So we can become blood brothers."

"What are blood brothers?"

"They're people who mix their blood with the blood of someone else and then swear to be friends for life. We can do that now we've got a bone from an owl's pellet to mix the blood with."

Magdalen hesitated for she knew this was another dare, another test, but the thought of being friends for life with Daniel excited her.

"All right."

"We'll do it now."

He pushed his sleeve up, placed the knife point on his forearm below the elbow and put pressure on it. Its point pushed the skin into a little dip before it penetrated. When he squeezed his arm above the cut several drops of blood appeared.

"See? It's easy."

He passed Magdalen the knife and she held its point to her forearm but could not bring herself to make the cut.

"Go on. Do it."

"I will when I'm ready."

But she sat there without moving.

"I'll do it if you can't," said Daniel.

"Just give me time."

With a quick movement she screwed up her eyes, pushed the knife in and felt a small unexpected surge of excitement and relief.

She heard Daniel laugh and opened her eyes to see red running down her arm and on to the ground.

"Now we have to mix it up."

Daniel took the thin vole bone and dipped it in his own blood, then carried it to Magdalen's arm and mixed it with hers. Then he passed the bone over and she transferred some of her blood to his cut.

"And now we have to swear an oath."

"What should I say?"

"Say: 'I am your blood brother and will be your friend for life.'"

Magdalen repeated his words.

Using some rainwater which had collected in a bowl she rinsed her arm and wiped it dry with the hem of her dress. Suddenly she realised the sun had almost set and that she had to leave at once.

"I'll come back soon." She waited a moment before she set off in the hope that he would say goodbye, but he didn't.

She took her time going home and it took her longer than it had taken to get to Daniel's. Her arm was throbbing slightly, but it felt as if something else was different too. It must be because she and Daniel were blood brothers.

🐇 25th May 1669, near Thorney

Mathieu's horse was frisky when he set off and this matched his own feelings. He should have thought of asking Bastion before. Even though Bastion was a few years younger he was a level-headed, good man with whom he had been friends since they were boys. He would be discreet and would give sensible advice.

After five minutes the horse settled down and Mathieu took him at a slow trot so he could check on how the crops were doing. Nowadays he took it for granted that there were fields of oats and barley where once there had been water but occasionally – as happened today – he recalled how different it had been a decade ago.

He had only recently begun to be alert to the business side of things. Although his father had given him a basic idea of the financial arrangements underpinning the drainage, the whole focus of the work of the Huguenots in Thorney had been on the practical side of planning water courses, cutting channels, digging, banking, shoring up. Mathieu was certain of only two facts: that the Duke of Bedford and thirteen Adventurers had invested capital in the project in order to become owners of nearly one hundred thousand potentially productive acres, and that during the last few years, the Bedford Level Corporation was invested with the power to levy taxes on that land. But the numerous stories about loans, bonds, lots, debts and bankruptcies confused him. Never mind, he would learn more later. Knowing about sluices was what mattered now.

He reined in his horse and dismounted. At least a dozen larks must have been singing just there above the farm. He led his horse into the Le Pla's yard and found the stable empty which meant Bastion and his father were out, but he could hear voices inside the house.

He tied his horse to the rail and turned to see Madame Le Pla and Emily walking towards him.

They greeted him warmly.

"I hear you're going to be a sluice-keeper," said Madame.

"That's right. I start next week."

"Your father Samuel would have been proud of you, Mathieu. You deserve it."

"Thank you."

Emily said, "If you've come to see Bastion, he's gone over to the Cousteau's farm with my father to talk about pigs. They'll be at least an hour. Would you like some water?"

Mathieu drank the water and surveyed the sunny yard. There was always a feeling of order here, of good husbandry. Monsieur Le Pla had not been well recently so Bastion must be running things. If he married his Gedney girl they would surely make their home here.

"Will you have to move away for this new job?"

"No I won't. Not unless something goes wrong, and then I suppose I might be there all night. It's the White Hart Sluice."

"Oh! That's good."

They stood together by the wall, Mathieu unsure as to whether he should wait for Bastion or leave and return later.

"Please stay and wait," said Emily. "We could take a stroll towards Clough's Cross."

Why not? It would be a pleasant enough way to fill in the hour. He nodded his agreement and they set off along the pathway.

"It's a perfect morning, isn't it?" said Emily.

"It certainly is. I enjoyed riding over here."

Emily stretched out her hand and ran it along some tall grasses. "I wish you'd come here more often."

"Do you? Why?"

She plucked a handful of new leaves from a willow beside the path. "Because I like you, Mathieu."

What was she saying? What did she mean?

"Do *you* like *me*?" she asked.

"Of course I like you. I've known you for ever, haven't I?"

"Is that the only reason?"

"No. Of course not." He paused before he went on, "I like you because ... because you're kind, and you're friendly."

"Have you ever thought of marrying me?"

Mathieu stopped abruptly and looked at her.

"Have I ever thought of marrying you?"

"Well, have you?"

He looked across the fen to the flat horizon. "I don't think so."

Emily smiled, "Mathieu, I don't think you've thought of marrying me, either. But I wish you would."

Before he had time to be embarrassed she took his hand and said gently, "I'd make you a good wife, you know. Don't you agree?"

Mathieu felt the unfamiliar pressure of a small, warm hand around his. He liked the feeling.

"Emily, do you want to marry me?"

"Is that a proposal?"

"No. I'm not. I don't ... I can't just ...."

Emily watched him struggle to speak.

"Yes. It *is* a proposal. Will you marry me? Or do you need time to think?"

"No, I don't! Of course I'll marry you. I'd love to be your wife. I've wanted to be your wife for years."

Just as Mathieu was reeling from a mixture of delight and astonishment, Bastion and his father appeared from nowhere and slowed their horses to a walk.

As Monsieur Le Pla said, "Has something happened? You're as white as a sheet," Bastion asked, "Are you all right?"

Mathieu was lost for an answer and felt the blood surge to his face under the keen gaze of the two men.

Bastion rescued him by saying, "Come back to the house. We've something to celebrate – the very profitable sale of a boar."

"We'll catch you up in a minute," said Mathieu. As the two men cantered off Emily took both his hands in hers.

"We'll be very happy," she said.

"Of course we will."

He pulled her gently towards him. "How did I miss you? How on earth did I miss you?"

"You were looking straight through me as if I wasn't there, but it doesn't matter."

They made their slow way back arm in arm but Emily began to walk faster as they approached the farm.

"Why are you hurrying?" asked Mathieu.

"I can't wait to tell them!"

⤷ 28th May 1669, Thorney

Jacob liked being with his mother. She still played a central role in the kitchen and farm, but now that she had trouble with her sight some practical things were not so easy. Only last week she had placed a cloth too close to the fire and it had gone up in flames.

She took great pleasure in her grandchildren. Jacob and Alice's youngest, Benjamin, was only a year old, but Christian - a determined and enthusiastic boy - was already six. Helen, who was easy-going and undemanding, was nine, and Magdalen was fourteen. Or perhaps she was fifteen by now? Magdalen was the one she prayed for most and it was easier to talk about her with Jacob than with Jenne and Iain.

"She slipped through our fingers when she was little. First she slipped away from Jenne and Iain, and then from me and you. Somehow, we lost her. I'm not sure what will happen."

Jacob found himself trying to lessen her concern yet again. It was so difficult. He repeated what he always said.

"She'll grow up and settle down. She won't be like this for ever. She can't be, can she? No one behaves like she does when they are adults."

Jacob decided not to tell his mother how only two days ago Magdalen had assured Iain she had shut the hens up for the night when she had not, and a fox had taken four of them.

"I'm glad Samuel doesn't know. It would upset him. He believed everyone could be reached through a mixture of firmness and gentleness."

"I know he did. But think of Jenne. We couldn't reach her for many months, could we? But now she's well again, and happy."

Ann reflected on how Jenne described that bad time as being separated from the person she really was. She said it was as if she had lost herself but had no desire to find her way back. She had been very aware of her malaise and temper and the impact these had on her family, but her family no longer seemed to matter. Indeed, nothing had mattered. But time had healed her. Time and God.

Ann said, "Perhaps you're right. Perhaps Magdalen too will find herself again, but I always feel that she *is* being herself, and it's we who need to change and accept her."

"Come to the window, Mère. Come and see what's going on out there. I've been hearing a cuckoo."

He carried Ann's chair to the window and she sat and turned her face to the sun with her eyes closed. "It's so warm," she said, "And it's not yet June."

He leaned out of the window. "The fields are greening up well, aren't they? And look at those enormous clouds piling up in the east. There's a sort of haze in the west but it's clearing." He breathed in a long breath. "Can you smell that early summer smell?"

Ann kept her eyes shut.

"It's delicious. The sun is like a blessing."

He shut his own eyes and faced the sun. She was right. "Do you think the sun can heal?" he asked. "It feels so powerful."

"Yes. It's one of the ways God shows us His power."

As Mère became older she spoke more and more about God, and Jacob often found her in prayer.

"I've brought you a poem."

Ann opened her eyes.

"A poem? Good. It's time we had a change from the Psalms. I only like the cheerful ones and we're coming to the end of those now, aren't we? Please read it to me."

"It's called *Song on May Morning*.
Now the bright morning Star, Day's harbinger,
Comes dancing from the East, and leads with her
The flowery May, who from her green lap throws
The yellow cowslip, and the pale Primrose.
Hail bounteous May that doest inspire
Mirth and youth, and warm desire,
Woods and Groves, are of thy dressing,
Hill and Dale, doth boast thy blessing.
Thus we salute thee with our early song,
And welcome thee, and wish thee long.

"Thank you. It's lovely."

"I thought you'd like it."

They remained in silence for a minute until Mère asked him to read it again, so he read it once more and she enjoyed it again.

"Who wrote it?"

"Someone called John Milton. Alice's uncle showed it to me."

"I particularly like the idea of May having 'a green lap', don't you?"

"Yes, but my favourite lines are the first ones:
Now the bright morning Star, Day's harbinger,
Comes dancing from the East."

Jacob straightened up and looked outside again. A man was cantering along the bottom of Low Lode on a bay horse. He did not recognise the horse or the rider. Who could it be? While he watched the man slowed down because he appeared to have seen something. And then a small woman came into view on the wooden bridge and the man held his hand up to her. The woman stopped still, then walked towards him.

"What are you thinking about, Jacob? You've stopped talking so you must be deep in thought."

"I think we've got a visitor, but I've no idea who it is. He's talking to a … no, he's talking to Magdalen. I'm sure that's Magdalen. What on earth is she doing down there? And now he's got off his horse and is standing beside her. And now they're beginning to walk this way."

"I like visitors. Let's hope he's interesting."

"I think he might be. He's carrying several packs over his saddle."

"You'd better go out to greet him."

Magdalen had run off by the Low Lode to get away from lessons. When she heard her mother calling her name she climbed out of the window so no one would see her and raced off along the path and down to the fen, passing the new wind-engine. She had enjoyed watching this being constructed. Fen lighters had brought the materials and the men who were to build it, and gradually its insides had been put in place and then its cladding and sails, and now here it was, ready for the winter's high waters.

They couldn't do anything about her, could they? Why should she have to do what they wanted? It was much better to be outside by the wind-engine, or skating in winter, or doing things with Daniel than it was to sit indoors with the schoolmaster and Helen. Helen did everything she was supposed to do. Magdalen had wanted to shock her by telling her about the exchange of blood, but she had to avoid mentioning Daniel. She decided only to tell Helen she had cut her arm on purpose.

"Why?"

"To prove to myself that I'm brave. I bet you couldn't do it."

"I don't want to."

"Look, you can see where the knife point went."

Helen peered at Magdalen's arm doubtfully. "Didn't it hurt?"

"A little."

"I don't believe you. You must have just caught it on a branch or a nail."

Magdalen looked at her in disgust. "And don't say anything, or I'll do something you won't like."

As she watched Helen run off she suddenly recalled the rush of excitement she had felt as the sharp tip penetrated her skin. She had not been prepared for anything other than pain.

The incident with the hens led to more trouble than she had expected. She had agreed to shut the fowls into the roost after the evening meal but had forgotten, and the next morning the yard was covered in feathers. On this occasion her father had – unusually – shown his anger, so she was lying low for a day or two, but today it would have been impossible not to go outside because outside was so fresh and bright and green.

She had gone to see if Daniel was in his hut but he was not, so had come home the long way round in order to arrive back after the end of the lesson-time.

As she came up to the wooden bridge she heard horse's hooves and a jingle of harness. She waited to see who it was.

"Good morning," said a man she had never seen before, greeting her with his raised hand.

"Good morning."

"Do you live near here?"

She pointed. "Just along here."

"Then perhaps you can help me. Have you ever heard of a man called Iain Alleyn?"

Surprised, Magdalen took a step forward. "He's my father."

The horseman laughed and threw his head back in delight. "Your father?" he repeated. "Then I'm a lucky man."

He dismounted and led his horse towards Magdalen. "Please will you take me to him?"

She set off along the path with the stranger. His clothes were not like those of the men she knew, and he spoke differently.

"Where are you from?" she asked.

"That's not an easy question to answer. But today I've come from Boston. I arrived on a ship a few days ago and was expecting to make my way here by boat. But at the port they told me so much of the water had gone I'd do better on horseback, so I hired Nellie." He stroked the mare's mane affectionately. "I didn't believe them about the water, but they're right. I never thought such a thing would be possible."

"What thing?"

"All this," he waved his hand around him, "All this dry land. This all used to be rivers and channels and meers and lakes. You needed boats and bridges to get anywhere. But look at it now. I'm astonished."

They walked on.

"Why do you want to see my father?"

"Because he's a good man. You're very fortunate to be the daughter of a man like him, aren't you?"

Magdalen nodded.

"So, tell me about him. Is he a farmer? I always thought he would become a farmer if he stayed in the fens."

"Yes, but he's a healer too."

The man looked at her with interest.

"He heals people with herbs."

"You don't surprise me at all."

They walked on companionably.

"What's your name?"

"Magdalen."

"That's a lovely name. Have you got any brothers or sisters?"

"I've got a younger sister called Helen."

"But you came out by yourself today?"

She nodded. "I like being on my own."

"So, you're an adventurer." He patted Nellie again. "I like adventures too. Adventuring outside is more interesting than sitting down inside, isn't it?"

She nodded again.

"Do you want to see what I found when I went exploring?" He stopped and pulled a cloth from his pocket. He carefully unwrapped it and held out a handful of small shells.

Magdalen gasped. She had only seen a few shells before and these were nothing like them. These were blue-black, shiny and delicate. She could not imagine what sort of a place they might have come from.

"Go on, touch them."

She reached out her hand and picked one up. It was exquisite.

"Which one do you like best? That one?"

"Can I have it?"

"Take it. It's yours. It's a special shell, called a sewant. It's from the Indians."

"What are Indians?"

"You don't know about Indians?"

Magdalen shook her head.

"Do you know about America?"

"I've heard of it."

She held the shell tight in her palm and watched the man wrap up the remaining ones and put them back in his pocket. His hair flopped across his dark eyes. He caught her looking at him and laughed.

"Come on, let's get going again. How much further is it?"

"We're nearly there. Look, there's Uncle Jacob. He must have seen us coming."

Jacob came to greet them and the stranger smiled broadly and said, "Your niece Magdalen has been the perfect guide. I understand her father is Iain Alleyn."

"That's right."

"Well, I've travelled a long way to see him."

"You are welcome. Magdalen, please go and fetch your father. Sir, would you like to take your horse to the trough before tying her up?"

With her hand holding the sewant safe Magdalen ran into the house. At this time of day Père was sure to be in the kitchen making a potion or poultice. And there he was, measuring and mixing his leaves and roots.

Seeing him made her suddenly recall his recent anger and the fact that she had again missed lessons that morning, but the news of the visitor overrode her worry and she said, "Père, a man has come to see you. He's outside with Uncle Jacob."

Her father wiped his hands without looking up. "Who is it?"

"I don't know. But he's a real traveller. Look what he gave me." She held out the shell on the palm of her hand.

"So, perhaps he's come from a country across the sea."

"He has, he has," said Magdalen. "He arrived at Boston a few days ago. Hurry up and come and see him."

When Iain walked into the yard the man turned to him and extended his hand saying. "Alleyn, I'm pleased to see you again." They shook hands and regarded each other.

"You don't recognise me, and why should you? I'm Stuart Macpherson, and years ago you saved my life."

Magdalen watched her father frowning in his effort to recollect his connection to this man.

"You healed my chest when we were prisoners-of-war. You looked after me when we were living somewhere near here. We were shovelling mud and we were always, always wet and covered in mud."

"Yes! Of course! Now I remember." Iain held his hands to his face and lifted his head. "Macpherson. The boy with the sword wound to his chest." He held out his hand again and clasped Stuart's firmly. "So, you've come back."

They both began to laugh and look each other up and down.

"You're no longer a stripling, are you, Macpherson?"

"And it looks to me as if you're a man of substance!"

Jenne appeared out of the house and Iain introduced her, and then Alice appeared with the boys, and Ann with Helen.

"What a tribe!" said Stuart Macpherson. "What a thriving family!"

"You'll stay with us?" asked Iain.

"Thank you. I'd be delighted."

"We'll start preparing dinner," said Alice. "Come on girls, we've got plenty of work to do."

"I'll help," said Magdalen. "I'll build the fire up, shall I?"

As Jenne and Alice shooed the children into the house ahead of them they exchanged glances. What had brought about this change in Magdalen? Jenne crossed her fingers and held them up to Alice, and Alice laughed and nodded.

⏎ 30th May 1669, Thorney

Stuart became the centre of attention and caused the house to fill with conversation. Alice described it well. She said his arrival had moved everyone's usual mood up a key. When Helen asked her what she meant she had sung a simple tune and then sung it again but differently.

"It's the same tune, but higher, isn't it? And that's how we are now that Stuart's here. He's brought a bucketful of new energy and life and we are reacting to it."

And he was and they were.

He joined in with what everyone was doing. He went round the farm with Jacob and was impressed by its fertility. He searched for herbs with Iain on land whose dryness continued to amaze him. He admired Jenne's embroidery and Alice's pies. Ann told him about when she had first come to Thorney. Mathieu, once he had got over his initial embarrassment, took him off to meet Emily and see the sluice.

At first the children kept their distance from this stranger who laughed loudly and spoke with an odd accent, but he became their hero on the day when he took off his shirt and showed them the looping line of raised flesh across his chest and the glossy skin covering one side of his ribs.

Then he started to cart Benjamin around on his shoulders, was persuaded by Christian to play football, sat Helen in front of him on Nellie and cantered off to the Causeway with her shrieking with delight. And miraculously he brought out the best in Magdalen.

"How long will you stay?" she asked.

"A couple of weeks, I should think."

"Why not longer?"

"Because I need to go to London."

"Is that where your home is?"

"No. I haven't got a home."

"You must have."

"I haven't."

"Then this can be your home!"

Stuart shook his head.

"Won't you stay for a month? Please."

"I could do. It depends."

"So you might stay for a month?"

"Magdalen, I'm not promising anything."

"But you might?"

Stuart began to laugh. "Come on, I'm going to groom Nellie. I've been meaning to do it since Tuesday." He stood up and started to hum a tune which was running round in his head. "Oh, look what's landed beside me. A darner."

"A what? It's a dragonfly."

"In America they call them darners. That's short for devil's darning needles."

"Why?"

"They look a bit like big needles."

"I suppose they do. But why the Devil?"

"I've no idea, but you never know where or when the Devil's going to turn up, do you? There, it's gone already."

182

"What's that tune you keep humming?"

"I can't remember the words, but it starts off with '*I wish, I wish,*' and ends up with something about an apple tree. They were singing it in a tavern in Boston."

᥯ 1st June 1669, Thorney

The next day Stuart borrowed the herbal Jacob and Iain were compiling and took it to the shaded seat on the far side of the orchard.

In between looking at the drawings he kept lifting his eyes up to the view in front of him: young pear trees in the foreground, corn further off in the field, and then haziness caused by the heat. He tried to recall how it had looked before the draining was complete, but failed. The landscape looked as if it had always been like this. Flat green fields were separated from the vast sky by a thin, indistinct horizon.

He was familiar with horizons and even now as he admired Jacob's careful drawings and what he knew must be Iain's skill if only he could read, he wanted to go to and beyond the horizon in front of him. That was the trouble. However much he wanted a home or a family, he always found himself wanting to move on from where he was. Only this morning he had wondered whether there might be a possibility of staying at Thorney, of trying to create a new life for himself, but here he was a few hours later abandoning the idea as hopeless.

The illustrations made him realise he had no idea of how many different sorts of leaves there were. Some grew close to the ground, others from the stalk. Some were in pairs, some arranged alternately. Some were spiky, others rounded or with serrated edges. Jacob had observed them so carefully. He picked a leaf from a nearby plant and looked at it more closely than he had ever done before. It was quite beautiful.

He was yet again impressed by Iain's achievements, for not only had he learned which plant was which, but he was able to heal people with them.

Stuart was pleased he had come to Thorney for the visit was turning out to be much more enjoyable and interesting than he had expected. He had helped around the farm but, surprisingly, the most useful thing he had done was to calm Magdalen. How had she become so ill at ease with herself and others? On that first day he had sensed she was unhappy and wanted something other than what her life was giving her. Like him, she wanted to go beyond the horizon. But because she was a girl she would for ever be confined to these level fens unless she married someone who took her away. A husband was her only chance of escape.

He walked back to the house, replaced the herbal in a safe place and walked round to the stable humming, "*I wish, I wish but it's all in vain…* "

Every evening at dinner he told them about something else he had done since leaving Thorney. He explained how, after getting half way to Scotland he had decided against going on so found building work in York and then came south again to Boston where he was offered work on a ship. And since that time – about ten years ago – he had been a sailor.

They loved his stories. Although they had all been shown pictures of the sea, Ann and Iain were the only ones who had ever actually seen it. The strongest images in the minds of Stuart's listeners were the Israelites crossing the Red Sea, the wallowing whale swallowing Jonah, Jesus walking on the Sea of Galilee, Ann's memory of her crossing from Friesland and Iain's of the rocky coastline at Dunbar.

Stuart's descriptions made them realise that being at sea was so much more than they imagined. More loneliness and more companionship. More confinement and more freedom. More fear and more faith.

He told them about being missed by cannon balls, crossing the Equator, buying silk and brandy, seeing men ease their teeth from their rotting gums, gazing on porpoises and albatrosses, longing for the welcome call of Land-Ho! and watching St Elmo's fire falling from masts at night.

"What's St Elmo's Fire?" asked Jenne.

"It's a blue-white glow which covers a ship from its crow's nest to the hull with light. It's extraordinary – it's like a flame that doesn't burn."

"Like a will o' the wisp?" asked Magdalen.

"Yes," said Stuart, turning to Iain and nodding. "Yes, like a will o' the wisp, but more fiery and longer-lasting."

4th June 1669, Thorney

One night, days after he had distributed the last of his shells and sweetmeats to the children, he succumbed to their request to unpack one of his saddle-bags. So, when the meal was finished and cleared, he brought a bag in and began to untie it.

"This came from America," he said. "In 1664 I was on the *Elias*, one of four ships which sailed to claim New Amsterdam from the Dutch. Between us we had plenty of guns, but we did not need them."

He stopped undoing the bundle as he explained what had happened. "Their governor, Peg Leg, walked like this," Stuart broke off to stomp round the room. "One of his legs was made of silver.

"He expected the people to defend the land, but they did not want to fight. They were only tenants, so why should they risk their lives for a place which didn't belong to them? New Amsterdam was on an island called Lange Eylant, and it had a windmill – not like your wind-engines here – right by the sea. It had palisades too, and a fort."

He took out his knife and cut the last piece of twine round the bundle. "The town surrendered and became ours, and we renamed it New York after the Duke of York."

"Please open it, Uncle Stuart," pleaded Helen.

"Move back then. I need more room."

Everyone shifted back and created space on the floor between them and then, with a flick of his hand, he unrolled a thick, grey-black pelt. It rippled out from where he stood to where Magdalen was sitting cross-legged on the floor. It gave off a distinct, raw, foreign smell and it silenced them.

"It's beaver. Beaver from up along the North River. I got this one cheaply from a man in Boston last week but it's from America and it's just like the ones we used to buy. After New Amsterdam surrendered we had to stay there for months and we went upstream to a place called Beverwijck where the settlers met Indians. The Indians wanted muskets, knives and blankets and we wanted beaver pelts. Instead of money they used pelts and sewants, those shells I've shown you. A pelt was worth about ten guilders and four or five black sewants – they're more valuable than the white ones – were worth about one stiver. But the sewants were important for the Indians when there was a marriage or a funeral. If one tribe gave another one a string of sewants, it meant they wanted to be friends for ever."

"What will you do with this pelt?" asked Mathieu.

"I'll sell it to a hat maker. Just feel the quality."

Everyone touched the beaver skin and the children, cautious at first, dug their fingers into it and stroked and kneaded it as if it were still a living animal.

It had grown dark by then and was time to retire for the night. Benjamin was already asleep on Alice's lap.

Christian asked, "Will you tell us more about the Indians?"

"Not tonight."

In bed, Iain stretched out beside Jenne.

"He's done so much, hasn't he? He's been to Africa, to Spain and Italy, to America. He's seen things I'll never see, met people I'll never meet, fought in battles, survived storms, had experiences I can't imagine."

"That's his life, isn't it?"

Iain said nothing.

Jenne said, "That's how he's chosen, how he's choosing to live his life. It's what he's decided to do."

"Does anyone really decide what to do? Don't they just make their choice from what they know about? It's mostly luck, isn't it?"

"But what else could people do?"

"I'm thinking about my decision to stay here in Thorney with you. I had little idea then about what else there was in the world, but Stuart went off and found out."

"Do you regret staying here with me, with us?"

"Of course not. But listening to Stuart makes me think about what I haven't done and will never do."

"Do you want to go off and do what he does?"

"No, my sweet dearest, I don't. I certainly don't."

"Good," Jenne felt for his hand and squeezed it. "I don't know what I'd do if you went away."

Just as he thought she was dropping off to sleep she said, "I can't believe how gentle and happy Magdalen has become."

"No. It surprises me too, but I'm thanking my lucky stars for it."

"Iain, it's God you should thank. Do you think she's feeling a little like I did when you arrived?"

Iain said, "She's not as mature as you were then. I think she finds it easier to talk to Stuart because he's new, so she can be her true self with him."

"Her true self. That's it. That's what I want – for her to be her true self, the self she was before I made everything go wrong."

"You didn't make things go wrong. Don't say that. You were ill, you couldn't help it."

"Could Stuart help her to recover herself?"

"I don't know. It's possible."

They stopped speaking, and soon Iain knew by the even-ness of her breathing that she was asleep. He withdrew his arm from around her and turned on to his stomach.

His mind was unquiet. It was full of blizzards, shanties, whippings, camels, flying fish, decks too hot to stand on, turbans, compasses, foreign words and back-breaking work in desperate conditions. The two hours of stories had been exhilarating but when Stuart had unrolled that beaver-skin it was as if he had not only furs but the whole world in his saddle-bag.

And here was he, Iain Alleyn, in a small village in the fens, living the same life day after day with the same people. They sowed, protected, harvested and sold or used their crops. They looked after their animals, slaughtered and sold or ate them. Every now and then they built a new stable, or barn or house. They went to church. They made love, had children and brought them up. They cared for the sick and buried the dead. They went through the same seasons and the same rituals year after year.

Was that enough?

Did the fact that he had stayed put in this place he had once despised mean he had made the best of what life presented, or that he was weak or even a coward? If Stuart had changed from a timid youth into a confident, worldly adult could he too have grown and developed more had he not limited himself to these fenlands which were even now still not completely under control?

Shouldn't there be more to life than merely keep going? Wasn't Stuart right to have decided to go off and find new worlds?

Iain turned on to his back again, annoyed that he had allowed himself to become unsettled. Stuart had turned up with his smiles and his stories and his sewants and had somehow destroyed his peace of mind. He was little better than a mountebank and it was time he went on this way.

Iain turned on his side and put his arm over Jenne's hip. Yes. The family had shown Stuart warm hospitality for ten days, but now it was time for him to move on.

ᴄ⊱ 5th June 1669, Thorney

When Iain went into the kitchen the next morning an argument was taking place. Magdalen was back to her usual behaviour, shouting and sulking. It turned out that Jenne had noticed a red patch on her arm and wanted to look at it but Magdalen had refused to let her.

"Let me see," said Iain, "I won't touch it."

"No."

"Does it hurt?"

Magdalen looked sullenly at the floor, one hand over her upper arm.

Iain picked up his cup and plate and sat down to eat. He would ask her again later. The important issue today was to get Stuart to leave, or at least begin to think about leaving, but as soon as Stuart came into the room bidding everyone good morning Iain suddenly felt ashamed of his desire to be rid of him. Stuart was good-natured and warm-hearted whereas he, Iain, was being negative and uncivil. Of course the man could stay longer if he wanted to.

"You're very quiet, Magdalen," remarked Stuart. "Have you eaten yet?"

"I don't want anything."

After a few minutes Iain saw Jenne beckon Stuart outside on to the step. They stood together for a moment, spoke briefly, and then came back in.

"Does anyone know how to arm-wrestle?" asked Stuart.

The children shook their heads.

"It's a game where you have to try to push the other person's arm to the table. I'll show you when I've finished my food."

Within minutes the table edge was cleared, sleeves were rolled up and Iain was feigning a struggle with Christian.

"My turn next!" said Helen.

He let himself be beaten again and said, "And now with our left arms."

When it was Magdalen's turn Stuart pushed her arm to the table in a single smooth movement.

"That's not fair!"

"I know. It's no fun unless you do it with someone of about your own strength. But what's that on your arm?" He had hold of her elbow in a firm grip and was able to inspect a small greenish lump surrounded by an area of red, hot skin. "Your father should have a look at this, shouldn't he?"

It was nasty. The skin had not healed and the flesh was oozing pus. Magdalen refused to tell them how she had come by the wound and silenced Helen with a ferocious glare.

Within an hour Iain had boiled some seeds and roots of mullein, soaked a cloth in the liquid and bound it round her arm. Magdalen went rushing off as soon as it was securely tied.

Stuart turned to Jenne, "She certainly knows her own mind, doesn't she?"

"Thank you for your help. You seem to calm her down."

"Has she always been like this?" asked Stuart.

"No. When she was little she was happy but …. "

Suddenly Jenne stopped speaking and buried her face in her hands. Iain comforted her and said, "She can be so difficult at times. Sometimes we feel as if we might lose her completely."

Stuart watched Jenne screwing the cloth up in her hands. "I'll do whatever I can to help. Believe me, whatever I can."

"You'll stay as long as you like, won't you?" said Iain. How could he even have thought of asking him to go?

Magdalen was feeling guilty because she had not been to see Daniel since Stuart's arrival. So, on this lovely June morning she was already making her way to his den. And there he was, on the other side of the wooden bridge, looking even taller than he did only two weeks ago. He had never come to meet her before and she was pleased.

"How did you know I was coming?"

"I just guessed."

As they started walking back to the hut she only just stopped herself from skipping.

"I've got so much to tell you. A man called Stuart is staying with us. He used to work on the dykes with my father when they were prisoners. But when he was set free he went off and became a sailor, and he's been all over the world. He's seen waterspouts, snakes, black men, whales – I can't remember all the things – and last night he showed us the skin of a beaver."

Daniel did not respond to what she said but asked about the bandage, so she explained how her cut had not healed up.

"Mine's fine," said Daniel, showing her a neat scab.

When they reached the hut Magdalen felt up her sleeve for the shell she had hidden.

"Oh no. I can't find it. I brought you a special shell – it's called a sewant – but I can't find it." She searched in her other sleeve and in the other folds of her dress but it was gone. "I must have dropped it. It could be anywhere."

In a bored voice Daniel asked, "Why would I have wanted a shell?"

Suddenly in that instant she saw she could not please him, would never be able to please him. She had kept coming to him for all these months – all these years – because she needed to escape. He had become important to her and so she wanted him to like her, but now she saw that even though they were blood brothers he would never like her as much as she liked him.

She hung her head down so he would not see her face but he softened slightly and put his hand on her shoulder. He had not touched her since they were much younger and had climbed and played together.

"Perhaps you'll find it on the way home. Anyway, I've another idea. We could exchange secrets instead of things."

"I haven't got any secrets."

"Yes you have. No one knows you come here, do they?"

No, they didn't.

"And I bet you have other secrets. Think about it while I make you some of my tea."

Tea? He had never offered her tea before.

She sat outside the hut and thought not about secrets but about Stuart. If only he would ride up now and take her away.

Daniel brewed up a pot of water on the fire and poured it over some tea in his only cup. He smiled at her. "You'll like this."

She drank it slowly, he was right – she liked it. She passed the cup back so he could have some and relaxed into the midday's warmth.

"Have you thought of any secrets?"

"No."

"Well, answer me this. What's the worst thing you've ever done?"

She was mean to Helen and Christian, rude to her parents and the other adults, indeed to everyone; she lied; she did not do as she should do; she sometimes stole; she avoided lessons. There was so much.

"But what's the worst thing?"

"I don't know."

"Then I'll tell you my worst thing." He looked at her expectantly. "I left my mother to die. I knew she would die and I left her all alone."

"How did she die?"

"She coughed her heart out."

Magdalen shivered at the thought of it. What Daniel had done was bad, very bad, but wasn't her worst thing worse? She did not want to confess and quickly tried to make something up, but her head felt muddled and she couldn't.

"You've got to tell me yours now."

Magdalen took a deep breath. "I tried to poison my sister when she was a baby."

"Who have you told about that except me?"

"No one."

"Then it's a secret, isn't it?"

She nodded miserably.

"What did you do?"

"I put a berry in her mouth. I thought it was poisonous."

"But she didn't die?"

"No, but on the exact same day my mother had a falling fit."

"She must be a witch."

"No she's not. She's just ill sometimes."

Magdalen thought back to when her mother had fallen to the floor, her mouth dribbling, her legs kicking. Everyone had told her that Mère was ill and would recover, and she did, so what Daniel said was horrible and untrue.

"Or perhaps you're a witch."

Magdalen began to cry, and Daniel moved towards her and put his arm around her.

She leaned into him and felt his bony shoulder against hers, his thigh next to her thigh, his hand holding her hand. It was a new feeling and she wanted it to last. Yes, perhaps things would be all right. Today, for the first time, he had come to meet her, had made her tea and was comforting her. Perhaps it didn't matter that he was sometimes unkind. She stopped herself from thinking about the time a few years ago when she had taken him to see a nest of pale greenish snipe eggs and he had stamped on them, and about when he had cut the back legs off a frog and made it swim. But he had never been very unkind to *her*. She relaxed against him in the warm sunshine. Nothing else mattered. Even her arm had stopped hurting.

"When do you have to go home?"

"Soon, but not yet."

As she closed her eyes Iain's tune ran quietly through her mind.

ᕗ Mid-morning, 6th June 1669, Thorney

Stuart was studying a picture on the wall. "Who's that?"

"My father."

"It's good."

"I did it from memory, about a year after he died."

When asked if there were any more drawings Jacob fetched a sheaf of them. There were sketches of everyone: Ann, Samuel, Mathieu, Iain, Jenne, Magdalen, Helen, Alice, Christian and Benjamin. Stuart picked up two of Magdalen and studied them. He noticed she was happy in one when she was small, but not in the next when she was slightly older. The gap between them couldn't have been more than a year or two.

"What about since then? Have you any more recent ones of her?"

"Every time I try to draw her she runs off."

Ann came to the doorway.

"Come in, Mère. We're only looking at my drawings."

Ann sat in her usual place by the window. "I wish I could still see them properly. Have you shown Stuart your self-portrait?"

Jacob opened a second sheaf and pulled out a large sheet. There he was, aged about twenty, with his hair half over one of his eyes, his left hand at his chin.

"It's a good likeness. The cheek here, your eyebrows, and your expression. You should do another now you're older."

"I haven't got time. Mathieu has already asked me to do one of him and Emily, and at present I'm keen to do more landscapes." He put the portrait away. "Would you like to see some of my early ones of round Thorney?"

From the back of the second sheaf he brought out some smaller sheets.

Stuart was intrigued. "That's how I remember it. Yes, that's exactly what it was like. All that water. It's extraordinary. There was so much more water than land, wasn't there? I didn't think it'd ever be brought under control."

"Well, we've still not managed to do it entirely."

"I know. Mathieu's been telling me about it."

Jacob turned over another sheet.

"Do you remember Morton's Leam?"

"I'm afraid not. All these dykes look the same to me."

He pulled out more. "And this is the house before we built on the extra part when Alice and I married. And here's one of the Abbey Church but the proportions aren't quite right so I'm about to do another."

"You're so lucky to have a record of your lives and your world," said Stuart.

"I suppose I am."

"He's very fortunate," said Ann. "We all are. I'm hoping that either Christian or Benjamin will enjoy drawing too. You were only about seven or eight when you started, weren't you?"

"I used to draw on my slate when I was supposed to be doing lessons. But I must have been about ten when I did my first serious drawing."

"What was it?"

"It was an owl. A dead owl."

Afternoon, 6th June 1669, Thorney

Later, Iain asked Stuart to do him a favour. He had been asked to send someone over to near Whittlesey to help dig out a bog oak but he had no one spare to send. Stuart volunteered at once. Apparently several men were working on it already and it was expected to take a few days to shift. A friend of Iain's had offered Stuart a bed to save him travelling each day.

"Of course I'll go, but I'd like to go round the farm with you for an hour or so before setting off."

As they rode out along French Drove Stuart made a wide gesture, "You're a lucky man. All this is yours."

"I don't own it all. It's only mine from here," Iain pointed to the Abbey Church and swung his arm round to the south, "To about there."

"I don't own anything apart from my sea-trunk which I've left at Boston and the things in my saddle-bags. And although I've cared about a few women I haven't got a family. I don't have a wife, or any children – at least none who call me father – and I sometimes feel bad because I don't even know what's happened to my parents or brothers or sisters."

"And I don't know what's happened to mine."

"But you've created something. You've made this land dry, you grow food, you breed animals. You've done what the people did in that town in America, in Beverwijck. They built houses, worked, went to church and traded. The things you buy and sell are different to what they bought and sold, but basically you've made your own wealth as they did. And did I tell you they were Dutch, not English? America's got people from everywhere.

"And I bet those sheep are yours, aren't they?"

Iain nodded.

"That's what I mean – you have things which belong to you: sheep, cattle, land, a family, friends." Stuart paused as a darner zoomed diagonally across the path. "In my life I come across the same people from time to time, but my home on a ship – my neighbourhood, if you like – only lasts for a few weeks or months. You're on solid ground, you have a real base. I'd give my eye teeth for a family and a home like yours. Do you realise there are *ten* of you? And everything seems so good. In your life you've done so much that's good."

"But so have you in your world. You're a good sailor, a hard worker."

"Perhaps I am, but I've done bad things too. I didn't tell everything when the women and children were there. When I've been drunk – and I've been drunk too often – I've fought and injured men. I put a tapster's eye out once. And I've persuaded half-willing girls to be willing for no better reason than that I wanted them. So when I look at your life I think about the bad choices I've made."

Stuart gazed across the green meadow into the distance. "But it's too late to change things now."

"No it's not. You're still young."

"I don't know any other way to live."

The horses swished their tails and lowered their heads every now and again to pull at the grass.

"My life isn't perfect, you know. Over the years there have been difficulties and disagreements. Jenne was very ill after she had Helen, and you've seen what Magdalen can be like. But I believe people can change. You have to think of what it is you want from life and then work out how to achieve it."

"I don't know what I want. I was more or less content before coming here – I like going to sea and I like being free. But you're making me see what I've missed. You're doing so much with your life, and I'm doing nothing with mine."

Iain looked at Stuart again. He was hardly recognisable as the man who, only the previous evening, had enthralled a roomful of people with his stories, his bold gestures and that almost magical unrolling of the beaver skin. Now, with the spirit and spark drained out of him, he looked vulnerable and older than his years.

In the stillness of the hot, early afternoon Iain dismounted to pick some mayweed and spiky mellilot.

Should he invite Stuart to stay with them at Thorney? Is that what Samuel would have done?

As they rode on he thought again about the fragility of a man's well-being, even of his whole life.

Stuart made his horse walk a little faster and said, "I'll pack a few things and be off at once. I want to reach Whittlesey well before it gets dark so I can at least give them a couple of hours of digging this evening."

"We'll expect you back in a few days."

Evening, 6th June 1669, Thorney

Early that evening, when Iain was putting the mellilot into bunches ready to be hung up and dried he became aware of someone shouting. He hurried to the door and saw Mathieu tying up his horse up while Magdalen screamed at him.

"You don't know anything about me! You can't order me around!"

Mathieu's face was hard and determined. "Perhaps not, but I can tell your father what I found you doing."

In her frenzy Magdalen caught her foot and tripped and Mathieu grabbed her by her wrist.

"Let me go, let me go!"

"Come with me, Magdalen. Stop struggling."

Mathieu hauled her towards Iain.

"Tell him to let me go! Make him let me go!"

Iain looked at them in astonishment. "What on earth's the matter? Mathieu, what are you doing?"

Suddenly Mathieu gave a yell of pain. "You bitch!" He put his hand to his mouth as Magdalen ran off sobbing.

"You little cow!" he said as he nursed his bitten hand. "You can go to the Devil!"

"Don't you dare," began Iain, "Don't you dare speak to my daughter like that. What in God's name were you doing?"

"I found her with a boy, I think it was that Ridman boy. They were … they were … on the ground outside some hovel. I don't know exactly what was happening, but the boy was on top of Magdalen and her skirts were all rucked up."

Iain stared at him in disbelief and asked, "So why are you treating her as if, as if …"

"She's just a dirty little … She wasn't fighting him off, you know."

Iain's voice rose sharply "What are you saying about Magdalen?" He was spitting with fury and could hardly get his words out. "Are you telling me she's a whore? For God's sake Mathieu, she's only a child. Have you no pity?"

He sat down at the table, put his head in his hands and felt his heart's fast beat.

Mathieu said, "You ought to… "

"Don't you tell me what to do. Get away from me, will you?"

There was a pause before Mathieu spoke again. "Do you want me to fetch Jenne?"

"No I don't." Iain got to his feet, his mind already filling up with images of Magdalen being pushed over and held down, her legs forced apart. He hit his hand on the doorway as he hurried through to where he knew Jenne was doing her embroidery with Ann.

He entered the room feeling as if he had been punched in the stomach.

"What's wrong, Iain? What on earth's the matter?"

After he told them he sat down and closed his eyes. Jenne ran to him at once and wept quietly into his shoulder.

"I feel sick and weak," he said. "Poor, poor Magdalen."

He clung on to Jenne for what seemed minutes, his mind in turmoil, aware that the room and the whole house was silent. His head was full of a boy using his strength and will to silence and overcome Magdalen. How, *how* could he have done this? He pulled away from Jenne to say, "I don't know what I should do."

Ann spoke slowly. "Don't do anything. There's no need to do anything straight away, and you can't until she tells you what happened. What matters is to look after dear Magdalen."

"But she's run away," moaned Jenne. "She could be any-where."

"She won't have gone far. She'll come back soon," said Iain. "It's that boy I'm thinking about. If I don't find him now he'll just disappear."

"Never mind about him," said Jenne, "Mère's right. Magdalen is the one who matters."

"I'm determined to find the boy who raped her." The unfa-miliar word, spoken for the first time, hung in the air.

He felt as if he had been beaten all over his head, neck, back, legs. And then he remembered Mathieu and his hurt increased still further. How could Mathieu have treated Magdalen like that? How could he have thought of her like that?

When he and Jenne left the room Ann knelt and mouthed a quiet prayer. *O Seigneur, Dieu tout puissant éternel et plein de grand bénignité.* She prayed for Magdalen, for Jenne and Iain, for the whole family, for those who had suffered and for those who were still suffering. She prayed for Samuel's soul. She prayed that they should receive God's guidance.

Magdalen was hiding in the barn. She had crawled under a heap of straw. Gradually she recovered and her heart slowed down, her sobbing ceased. How had she done what she had done? She had let Daniel touch her all over. She had let him see the secret parts of her body. She had let him…

Two girls who lived along the Causeway said that some women liked it when a man did that thing to them, but she hadn't. It had hurt and she was still hurting. And it was the worst thing she had ever done – worse than trying to poison Helen, because Helen had not been harmed and she herself had only been little at the time.

And Uncle Mathieu had seen her doing it, had actually seen her doing it. When she was lying there with Daniel she had heard the clink of a bridle and had opened her eyes and there was her strict uncle looking down on them from his horse. Daniel had sprinted away in seconds and she, feeling dazed, had got to her feet and not even questioned Uncle Mathieu's instruction to follow him home.

She would never be able to look at him again. Or at her mother and father. Or at anyone. It was awful to think of her grandmother knowing about it. And what would Stuart think? She began to cry again. The barn door opened and she froze as someone came in.

"Magdalen?" called Alice's voice, quite gently. "Are you there?"

Alice lifted up some sacking, climbed up the ladder to the loft and even checked in the place where the hens roosted.

Magdalen willed herself not to make a sound or a movement until the door banged shut again.

An hour later she heard her mother calling. She stayed in her hiding place, torn between surrendering and holding out. She could not stay in the barn for ever but where else could she go? Not to Daniel, for why would she want to be with him again and in any case he would be far away by now. And how could he be her blood brother and friend for life if he had done this thing with her and then run away?

"Magdalen! Please come back."

She realised she would have to come out so, as dusk passed and the dry heat made her desperate for a drink, she emerged.

When she crossed the yard Christian tore off to tell his mother. Then he raced back to say, "Everyone's been looking for you."

Then Jenne came hurrying out of the house and hugged her and Magdalen found herself hugging her back.

"Come inside, my dearest."

Jenne poured her a drink of cool, cool water. When she put the cup down Helen and Christian were standing on the other side of the table staring at her.

"Where were you?" asked Helen. "And why were you hiding?"

"You're bleeding," said Christian. "There's blood on your gown."

"Children, go outside please. Leave Magdalen alone. She's not well."

She sat holding her mother's hand.

"I want to lie down." She slowly raised her head but could not meet her mother's eyes. "Mère, I want to die."

She did not resist when she was gently urged to her feet, held and rocked. She had fought off embraces for years, but now she did not. She let herself be taken to her bed and soothed.

"Père will bring you something to make you sleep. You'll feel better after a sleep."

*

While all this was happening Stuart was riding south towards the Nene. When he reached it he shared the ferry with the ferryman, a woman carrying a piglet and Nellie whose dislike of being on the boat threatened to upset it. Almost all the waterways ran directly across his route. Once past across Morton's Leam he was uncertain of where Bassenhally Farm lay, so decided to ask the next person he met. He rode on as the sun began to set in a pink-striped sky.

After a while he made out a group of men to the east and turned his horse's head towards them. As he neared them he realised he had by chance found the right place for they were occupied with a tree trunk half-in and half-out of the ground. A man's arm could have reached across the width of the end which was sticking out but the widest part was still under the earth and the still-buried long length of it must have been at least eight or nine yards. Two boys were standing on top of the trunk trying to push each other off, while four men were digging deeply under it.

Stuart dismounted and looked round for something to tie Nellie to. Finding neither a post nor a tree nor even a bush nearby he called one of the boys to hold his horse and went over to the men. He introduced himself and was immediately given a spade and told where to dig. They were trying to free the trunk so they could haul it out from its bed where, in winter, it diverted the run-off from the field from the course it was supposed to take. The deeper they dug the more the earth became mud.

He could tell by the men's glances, especially those he noticed between two who appeared to be brothers, that they did not think he would amount to much. He was a stranger who came from somewhere they did not know, had a horse better than any they could afford and for some reason was willing to work without pay.

It was good to dig after the days of relaxing. Stuart lifted the spade, dug it in as close to the tree as possible and scraped out the wet earth. After half an hour he saw he had hardly made any difference so took off his doublet, registered briefly that the other man on his side of the trunk was doing no better, and continued. However hard they worked it was clear progress would be slow. After another half hour he stood up to stretch his back. The task would surely take at least a week.

He surveyed the land around them. There were reeds, rushes and crops but not a tree in sight – not even a small one let alone anything similar to this dead giant. He walked round to the uncovered end and prodded it with his spade. It felt and sounded more like stone than wood. What was it doing here?

He started again to excavate the soil while the boys took turns in keeping an eye on his horse and barrowing the mud out of the way. Even though he was not even up to his knees in it he was reminded of his banking days by the scrabble of the spades, the alternate stooping and stretching and the dank smell in the dark space under the tree-trunk. He felt some of what he had felt fifteen years earlier, but now he had food in his belly, was healthy and was free. And that arrogant supervisor was not there criticising him or behaving as if he owned the land himself. He recalled, from all those years ago, Iain telling him not to challenge Mathieu Deschamps because no good could come of it, and now Iain had married his sister. There was no telling how things might turn out, was there?

It was becoming too dark to see what they were doing, so the men and boys set off along the bank to Whittlesey, and Iain followed behind on Nellie. He was looking forward to a meal, to ale and to bed.

✒ 7th June 1669, in the fens

The next day they walked to work through a thin mist which did not lift until an hour after dawn. Then it revealed acres of yellow corn, herons on the sides of dykes, swallowtail butterflies waiting for warmth.

They set to at a steady pace and Stuart found himself silently humming the songs sailors sing on board as they haul together.

He was sure these fenmen would never sing, for they hardly even spoke and seemed to be bowed by their lives.

But they had noticed he did not complain once about his hands or his back or the task and was as good at digging as they were and so, when it was time to rest and eat, one of the brothers asked where he was from. He told them he was a sailor.

"Where have you sailed to?"

"Africa. Spain. Italy. America."

"America?"

"Yes. I was there a few years ago and I stayed there for twelve months."

"Did they try to kill you?"

"Who?"

"The people who live there."

"Plenty of people live there – Dutchmen, Swedes, Germans, the French, the English, Indians."

"That's who I mean. The Indians. I've heard about them."

The man in charge picked up his spade and urged the little group back to work. "Come on. Let's get on with it."

They worked on through the day until evening and agreed with each other that on the following day they would be able to loosen the trunk slightly from the bog. Then it would be a question of levering it with poles, attaching chains and harnessing horses to it. As they ate their meal in the farmhouse that evening Stuart was asked more about America.

So he told them about sailing up the North River which Henry Hudson had explored on his ship the *Half Moon* over fifty years earlier. How they'd waited in New York until the thaw came, until the big floes of ice came noisily down the river grating and riding up on each other past ice still being carried inland on the tides from the frozen sea.

"How could the river flow in two directions at once?"

"It does that here too," said a man called Peter.

"Not any more," said another. "Not since the drainage."

He told them about mountains, islands, beaches, waterfalls, sandbanks, cliffs. About how their boat was dragged off route by gales and whirlpools. About Fort Orange where, when the English were sighted, bells were rung to summon everyone to safety.

"It sounds the very opposite to the fens."

"It is, and there aren't any mosquitoes either."

"So no one's ill with the Bailiff of the Marshes?"

"No."

"How wide was this river you were on compared to Vermuyden's Drain?"

"Many, many times wider."

"Ten times wider?" asked one of the boys who was listening in.

Stuart thought for a moment. "More than fifty times wider. Near the sea, perhaps a hundred times wider. And over thirty fathoms deep in places."

The group fell silent.

"I wish I could see it," said the other boy.

9th June 1669, Thorney

Iain had never felt such rage. The more he imagined what must have happened the more determined he became to find the boy. He found himself wondering whether Magdalen had been screaming as she was dragged to the ground, or had she been terrified into silence? Had the boy had a knife or had he held his hand over her mouth? How must she have felt as he pulled at her clothes, as he stuck himself into her? He must have been more like an animal than a human being. She was so young, too young to know about rape, too young to know its consequences.

As soon as she had confirmed that it was indeed Daniel Ridman he sank his grief in sending Jacob out to find him and in going to see the hovel himself. While looking around the place where this damned thing had happened his eye was caught by a dark object on the ground. It was a small shell. He was sure it was one Magdalen had got from Stuart. Grimly, he told himself that she might even have stolen it from him. He picked it up and put it in his pocket.

Two days later, after a fruitless day spent looking for Ridman, Ann said, "I know this is a terrible situation, Iain, but why not abandon this search? You're wasting energy that you could be spending on something positive."

"He's wrecked Magdalen's life, all our lives. He's committed the most foul crime and I want him punished."

"Do not let your hatred destroy you. If you continue like this he will make you a victim too."

"I can't live with this."

"Let Magdalen be at the centre of your thoughts as she is of Jenne's. For the first time in years she could turn to you, so make sure you are facing her."

"Any father would feel as I do."

"Have you forgotten what happened when you were in Daniel Ridman's position?"

"Of course not, but I was absolutely innocent and he is absolutely guilty."

In the silence which followed he felt tension in his neck and his back. His stomach tautened and he found himself staring unseeingly ahead. This angered him further because he needed to be robust to deal with all this and had no wish to argue with his mother-in-law. And then Mathieu came into his mind again and he struggled to push his words away. He feared he would feel as desperate as this for ever, playing in his mind the picture of Magdalen being pawed and violated over and over again.

But then he saw Samuel looking out at him from his frame on the wall. Had *he* felt like this? Had he wanted revenge and punishment? Surely he had. But with Mark Le Pla he had at least been willing to explore why he, Iain, had done what he was accused of doing.

"How can you be so sure this boy is guilty?" asked Ann.

"I swear by God's truth he was not with Magdalen because she had a falling fit. He must have met her by chance and persuaded or forced her to go with him. He did what he did quite deliberately."

Immediately he felt his anger re-surfacing. Who cared why Ridman had done this? Surely the action spoke for itself?

He looked at the portrait of Samuel again. Over the recent years when faced with difficult decisions he had often asked himself, 'What would Samuel do?' So, what would Samuel do in these circumstances?

He went out into the garden. It was a warm evening and he made himself walk down to the wooden seat to sit and think.

Samuel would be slower to condemn than he was. He would

be feeling grief rather than anger. He would be praying. He would be ready to understand and to forgive. He would be as fair as it was possible for any man to be.

Would he be trying to find Ridman? Possibly not. Probably not. His attention would be on his daughter, his wife and God.

But surely it would be wrong to let Ridman get away with rape? If he wasn't stopped he could do it again. That boy, that boy whose foot he had tried to heal and whom he had taken into his own home had repaid him by raping his daughter. *By raping his daughter*. He had ruined her future in one afternoon. There was no question: he had to be punished.

☙ 10th June 1669, Thorney

Late the following day he went quietly to Magdalen's room. She was asleep and Jenne was sitting beside her.

"That syrup you gave her has settled her. I'll give her some more when she wakes."

"Has she told you anything else?"

"No. Other than that she wants to die, that this is the worst day of her life."

"It is."

"No. It's bad, very bad, but it's not as bad as I thought. Mère says that although something fearful has happened to Magdalen she is safe in her home with us, she is healthy and she is young. Iain, I'm beginning to feel hope about her for the first time in years."

If Jenne was right, wasn't it still the case that it was the worst day of *his* life? Or had it been worse when Jenne had lost her spirit completely? He sat down and put his head in his hands and sighed. Such comparisons were pointless.

"Shall I call the doctor?" asked Iain.

"What can the doctor do?"

"He can tell us what has happened. I want to know exactly what happened."

"We should wait," said Jenne. "Perhaps she will tell us herself."

But while they were waiting Ridman would be getting further and further away, feeling more and more pleased with himself and perhaps even boasting. When he was far enough from Thorney he could even be joking about what he had done to a naïve French girl in the fens.

"Be patient, Iain. I believe the experience has changed her. I think she is coming back to us." She reached out her hand to his and continued, "When I was so distant after Helen's birth the doctor could not help me and nor could anyone else. But I came back when God wanted me to come back. We must trust He will help Magdalen to do the same."

Iain stood up and walked over to the bed so he could look down on Magdalen. Without the usual fight in her she looked so young, much younger than fourteen.

Perhaps he should sleep on it. Yes, that was what Samuel would have done. He would take his time before deciding how to act.

ᚕ 11th June 1669, Thorney

On Friday Stuart arrived back long after the evening meal. He came into the house in his usual cheerful way having had a good ride and wanting to tell everyone about how the huge oak had finally been hauled out from its bog.

But something was wrong. The children had been put to bed, the big room was empty and the only person around was Mathieu.

Mathieu made him sit down and told him what had been going on. Magdalen had been found rolling on the ground with a boy, both of them half undressed. It was clear the worst had happened.

"My God," groaned Stuart. "Oh, my God."

"Iain should never have brought that boy into this house," said Mathieu. "It was a bad mistake. He was well aware of what Ridman's father was like, what sort of a man that boy would become. People like that should be kept out, not invited in." He explained how and why, Ridman had been brought to the Deschamps when he was a child.

"But do you think there's a connection between him being here years ago and being with Magdalen today?"

"I don't know. But Iain makes poor decisions sometimes. I

know you admire him – and so do I, of course – but he takes too long over things. It's clear he wants Ridman dead but he can't even organise a proper search for him. If I were in his position I'd act at once, but he lets time pass until it's too late."

Stuart was silent for a few moments before asking, "How's Magdalen?"

"Jenne says she's shocked and miserable." Mathieu rose from the table and bade Stuart goodnight because the next day he had to be up before dawn. As he left the room he called back, "And why does all this have to happen just as we're making preparations for my wedding?"

Stuart sat on the doorstep in the nearly dark night.

Magdalen, dear, difficult Magdalen had been raped by some wretched boy. Even if she did not become pregnant her whole life would change. How could she hope to find happiness after this? Her chances of marriage had probably been ruined and she would never explore more of the world. The incident had severed her future like a knife.

And what must Iain and Jenne be going through?

He thought of his conversation with Iain in which he had admitted his feelings of envy and regret. Although it had taken place only a few days ago it felt as if it had happened much earlier. Suddenly, he recalled telling Iain about his adventures with women. What had he said, exactly? Something about 'making them more willing'? What on earth had Iain, a family man through and through, thought of him for saying that? At least he had not lain with any girl against her will. Or had he? He could not deny that he had sometimes taken advantage of girls, but did that make him a bad person? Most men he knew did the same, but at this minute on this doorstep the fact seemed irrelevant. The thought that kept coming into his head now was that he, Stuart, was no better than the boy who had been with Magdalen.

Staying at Thorney longer was out of the question for it was clear that Iain and Mathieu, indeed all the family once they knew what sort of a man he was, would want him gone. So he would leave tomorrow.

As he stood up Iain and Jenne came into the kitchen.

"I'm so sorry," he said with embarrassment. "Mathieu told me."

Iain nodded his thanks. "She's asleep now. She's refusing to tell us what happened."

"Perhaps that's just as well."

It was a relief that Iain chose to be polite, but would it be best to tell them now or tomorrow that he would be leaving?

When Jenne let out a big sigh he realised his decision would have no meaning for them for of course they were thinking only of Magdalen.

Before he slept he tried to remember all the girls he had been with. He had enjoyed making love to women but could remember a few he had had to persuade. He struggled again to remember exactly what it was he had said to Iain, and whether it had sounded boastful. It was a pity to end his visit in such a way. He had been so warmly welcomed and had found his stay so agreeable.

Suddenly, the words of the tune came back to him.

I wish, I wish but it's all in vain
I wish I was but a maid again.
A maid again I shall never be
Till apples grow on the orange tree.

12th June 1669, Thorney

Jenne and Iain were still awake in the small hours. Though it had taken them a long time to voice the impossible possibility that Magdalen might be pregnant, one of their deepest fears was that this experience would have scarred her so badly it would cause even more disturbed and difficult behaviour. The thought of this – especially if she were to have a baby – was almost unbearable and too painful to admit to each other.

Iain began to think about juleps and decoctions which could soothe her and rest her, but within half an hour he was scouring his memory for plants such as pennyroyal which he knew could provoke a miscarriage. And if he obtained them, would he – could he – deliberately administer them to his own daughter?

And if he did, would he tell Jenne what he was doing? It was appalling and shameful to even be considering such things, but here he was doing it. Worse, once having thought of it, he was both unable and unwilling to abandon the idea.

He was also anxious about how his family would now be perceived in Thorney. People were generally tolerant of Magdalen's demeanour but he had always attributed that to the established good standing of the Deschamps household. It was a relief that at least everyone would believe she had been raped, for although rape was horrifying there was less shame attached to an unmarried girl who was raped than to one who lay with a man because she wanted to. His anger flared up again as he recalled Mathieu's words, 'She wasn't fighting him off, you know.'

"I still wish we knew exactly what happened," said Iain.

"And I'm not sure that I do. It would be hard for her to tell us and hard for us to hear it."

Iain said, "But it might help if she could talk to someone. Otherwise, it will stay closed up in her for ever." He thought back to when Jenne had been at her lowest. There had been occasions over the years when she had tried to explain to him what she had been going through, and though what she said had not lessened her experience he believed it had helped him understand.

But when he tried to imagine Magdalen telling them about the rape he could not imagine what she would say and quickly realised they would all end up weeping.

At least Magdalen had been passive since her struggle to get away from Mathieu. What on earth had Mathieu been hoping to achieve by hanging on to her as if she was a criminal? Another flush of anger went through him as he thought of Mathieu treating her like a cutpurse. How could he have considered she was anything but a victim? He wondered for a moment about Emily. Did she have any idea how dogmatic Mathieu could be?

But that didn't matter now. Instead of getting angry again he should be racking his brains about what to do. They couldn't just carry on as before, could they? They had to do *something*, but the only thing he could think of doing was almost – but not totally – unbearable. Was it a sin to help your own daughter lose a child which resulted from rape? Was he capable of such an action? Jenne was sleeping now and he wished Samuel were there although he knew he would never, ever share such terrible thoughts with either him or Jenne.

There was not one person in the world he could share them with. He found himself more alone than he had ever been.

⚘ Morning, 13th June 1669, Thorney

The next morning Magdalen said she had slept badly but she willingly ate and drank everything that was put in front of her while Jenne and Iain watched her in near silence.

After a while Iain asked yet again, "Will you tell us what happened?"

She shook her head and said, "Am I allowed to get up?"

As Jenne asked whether she felt ready to, Iain was marvelling that Magdalen had sought permission – something she had not done for years.

"I'd like to see Mamie."

"She can come in here. You don't have to get up."

"But I'd like to go to her room."

"Of course you may."

So Magdalen got out of bed, dressed and went through to her grandmother. She moved slowly because she was sore.

"Come in, Magdalen. Come and sit over here."

She sat down without looking at or speaking to her grand-mother.

"Thank you for coming to me. Come here whenever you want. We can just sit together."

They sat without speaking half-listening to the sounds in the house and yard: Jacob calling out for Christian, the squawking of chickens as they were fed; a horse and cart going past, Helen's laughter, the ticking of a clock. It felt better in Mamie's room. Mamie would not ask questions.

But before long Magdalen was curled up in her chair weeping.

"Come here, ma petite."

She did not want to go to Mamie like a child so she pulled her overskirt to her face and began to cry more and more. She could not stop herself from saying, "I'm so bad. I'm so, so bad."

"Of course you're not."

"Yes I am! You don't know! You don't know how bad I am. I didn't know this would happen. I didn't mean it to happen. But it has, and now, and now I don't know what to do." Her voice rose in a crescendo. "I don't want to go on living. I wish I was dead."

"Ma petite, do not wish you were dead. You are young and you will be all right."

"I can't ever be all right, not after this. I was bad before, and now I'm even worse because I'm dirty."

In her distress she was rocking herself backwards and forwards, crying and crying.

"I've spoiled things for everyone. Everyone wants me dead."

Ann rose and went to stand by her. She pulled Magdalen's head to her thigh and stroked her hair.

"No they don't, ma petite. They want you to be happy."

"I'll never be happy."

Ann went on stroking her hair, and gradually she ceased sobbing and her breath calmed down.

"That's better. That's better."

Magdalen heard her grandmother saying the familiar phrases under her breath. *"O Seigneur, Dieu tout puissant éternel et plein de grand bénignité…."*

There was a knock and Jacob put his head round the door.

"Excuse me, Mère," he said quietly, "But Stuart would like to say goodbye."

Magdalen, her face wet and blotchy, looked up at Jacob and said, "Where's he going? He can't be going away yet?"

"He's just told us he's off this afternoon."

"But why?" asked Magdalen.

Ann said, "Please tell him I'll come and find him in an hour or so."

She sat down again on her seat by the window.

Magdalen said bitterly, "So he's leaving too."

"What do you mean?"

"Everyone who matters leaves, don't they? When I was little Papi went, and then Daniel, my only friend, left – though now I never want to see him again – and this time it's Stuart. No one stays, do they?"

"I do. So do your mother and father. Many more people are here than have gone."

Mamie was right, she supposed, but it felt as if the people who had gone mattered more than the people who stayed.

Her grandmother asked, "Would you like to come with me to say goodbye to Stuart?"

Is that what she wanted? She recalled him as good as promising to stay for a month, but here he was leaving before three weeks were up. She wasn't sure if she felt anger or disappointment.

"Think about it. You needn't decide at once."

Magdalen stood up and went to the window. On the far side of the yard she could see Stuart carrying his saddle bags out to the stable ready for his departure. Christian was at his heels lugging a smaller bag.

She leaned out further and heard Helen calling. "Uncle Stuart, can I plait a ribbon into Nellie's mane?"

He answered in his distinctive voice, "Of course you can. Thank you. Nellie and I would like that."

When she turned back into the room her grandmother was watching her.

"Yes. I would like to see him. I wish he wasn't going and I don't want to say goodbye, but I'd like to see him."

"Then I'll tell him, for I'm sure he'll want to see you."

ᘓ Early afternoon, 13th June 1669, Thorney

Magdalen found the most comfortable place to sit was on the soft armchair which used to be her grandfather's and which was her favourite place of retreat when things were difficult. The room was cool and dark, and when Stuart came she saw his body outlined against the light but could not see his face. Only when he drew up a chair next to her could she see his expression. It puzzled her at first. What was he thinking? But within moments she was blaming herself for being slow. It was clear he knew how bad and dirty she was.

"Hallo, Magdalen."

What could she say? Now she thought about it, it was obvious that someone would have told him what had happened, so of course he wouldn't want to see her and would try to leave as soon as possible. He had only come to see her out of politeness.

She put her hands to her face and began to cry. She felt Stuart reach out his hand to comfort her but she shrugged him off. If she said nothing he would go quickly and that would be for the best.

But he didn't go. He stayed beside her until her sobs quietened down, until her shoulders stopped shaking, until she was merely sniffing.

"Why don't you go now? I know you don't want to be here."

"Of course I want to be here," he said. "I want to see you, and your grandmother said you wanted to see me."

She sniffed again.

"But now you're telling me to go away?"

She said nothing.

"I'd like to stay with you, but I'll go if you want me to."

So they sat there and Stuart reached out his hand again to hers, held it for a moment and let go.

"I know why you're leaving," she announced.

There was a pause. He was probably trying to think of something to say which would not make her feel worse.

"I need to get on with my life. I need to find another ship and earn some money."

"Why won't you tell me the truth?"

She heard him hesitate before he said, "It is the truth." His hesitation proved he was lying.

"It's not the whole truth, is it? You don't want to tell me the real reason because you think it'll hurt me, but I know it anyway."

"What do you mean?"

"You know I'm bad, don't you? Even though I haven't told you about the bad things I've done, I know you know I've done them."

"Magdalen, I've no idea what you're talking about."

Outside, Helen's voice called to her mother to come and help her with the plait in Nellie's mane.

"What I know is that you have had a terrible experience.

213

You've had a fearful shock, and it will take time to recover but you will recover. You will be all right."

"I can't be all right after what I've done."

"But you haven't done anything!"

"Yes I have."

"Magdalen, that boy hurt you."

"It was my fault."

"It can't have been."

But it was and there was nothing for it but to spell out to him the contact she had had with Daniel, her continuing willingness to visit him and the whole story from giving him that special stone all those years ago to exchanging objects and then secrets, to becoming blood brothers and so to what happened a few days ago. Was it really so recent?

Stuart heard her out without interrupting, then asked, "Why did you like being with him?"

"At first I was sorry for him because he was lame – he told me he was born lame. And I felt better with him and away from the family, and it's the same when I'm with you."

"But your family love you, Magdalen. Why won't you let them love you? Why do you run away from them?"

"They're only pretending they like me. They really only want Helen, Christian and Benjamin. I'm just a nuisance."

"Your mother and father and grandmother and everybody want you to be part of the family and to be happy."

"I'm happy when I'm with you, and now you're going away, so I'll be sad again."

"That's a pity."

"I'm used to it."

Magdalen fell into silence. The sun had moved and was shining into her eyes, so she shut them and felt the warmth on her eyelids. "I *wish* you weren't leaving."

They sat in silence a little longer until she opened her eyes again. "I've thought of another line for that song you can't remember." Quietly and breathily she sang,

> *"I wish, I wish but it's all in vain,*
> *I wish that you would come back again,*

but you won't, will you?"

Because Stuart looked away it was clear he meant he would never return and there was no point in asking any more.

"You won't tell my parents or anyone a word of what I've told you, will you?"

Yet another pause. He clearly didn't want to promise her anything. The best he could manage was, "Not if you don't want me to. But why don't you want them to know?"

How could he not understand? "Don't you see how angry they would be?"

"Magdalen, they wouldn't be angry. They want to help you. They love you and want to help you. No one is angry with a girl or a woman when this happens."

"Uncle Mathieu was. He raised his whip to me." Stuart did not understand at all. It was too difficult. It was better to say nothing. But there was one question she wanted to ask and as they sat there she tried to find the courage to voice it. It was so, so hard. It was the hardest question in the world.

Stuart announced, "I'm going to have to go."

"Don't."

"I can't stay longer."

"You don't really need to find a ship. Please stay here."

Again, she felt him pause before replying, "No. I can't. This is your home and I don't belong here. I have to make my own way."

"But everybody likes you being here."

Stuart remained silent and in that moment she dared to ask her question.

"Will I have a baby?"

Why did he not answer? Surely he knew if she would or not?

"I don't know. It depends."

"What on?"

He hesitated yet again.

"Why won't you tell me?"

"Magdalen, I can't talk to you about this. You should be asking your mother, not me."

"I can't. I couldn't. She would be furious."

Why was he putting his head in his hands? Why was it so hard to get an answer from him?

"She and your father would be very upset with me if I talked to you about it. It's very private. I can't do it." He lifted his head. "Believe me, your parents will not be angry if you ask them. They're hoping you will talk to them more. They will listen and help you."

He stood up.

"You're going."

"Yes."

He bent down to reach her hands, lifted them in his and kissed them.

"Make the best of your life. Don't push your family away." He put his hand to her cheek. "Goodbye, Magdalen."

By the time he reached the door she was in tears again. Soon she heard the horse's hooves on the path and voices calling. She imagined him giving the children a last swing and hug. Now he would be shaking hands and giving his thanks. Now he would be mounting Nellie and admiring the braided ribbon. She waited expectantly for the sound of trotting, but realised from the fading voices that he must be going along the grassy track in the other direction.

She curled up on the chair, easing herself to the most comfortable position. Was she brave enough to ask that difficult question of her mother? Perhaps. Perhaps she might be. Exhausted, she shut her eyes and slept.

Late afternoon, 17th June 1669, near Thorney

Iain hardly gave Stuart a thought. He assumed he was leaving suddenly because he felt in the family's way at such a sad, difficult time. It was considerate of him, but he was soon forgotten for there was too much else to do and think about. As well as worrying about Magdalen he was still furious with Mathieu, and the house was full of neighbours – mostly well-wishers but also some who were merely inquisitive. After the Reverend Danois had paid a long and prayerful visit he escaped outside.

As he searched for the herbs which would soothe Magdalen his mind kept going back to the picture he could not get out of his head: Daniel Ridman pressing Magdalen down on to the ground and pulling her shift up. Thinking about it made his heart race. Before an hour was up he realised he was looking for tansy and pennyroyal rather than borage and camomile. He was no longer shocked by what he had in mind and deliberately put behind him the fact that any woman found using such plants for the purpose he was considering would be condemned and tried as a witch.

☙ Early evening, 17th June 1669, in the fens

As Stuart settled into his journey north he went over and over his time in Thorney and his farewell to Magdalen. What a miserable, sad story.

When he first started talking to Magdalen he had feared Iain might march in and throw him out because of what he had said about his history with women. Magdalen did not know this, of course, and for some reason he could not fathom she had been blaming herself for what had happened. She was quite convinced he was leaving because she was bad and he had had no idea what she been talking about. But then it had all come pouring out.

The question he was churning over as he rode along the fen droves was whether he should have told Iain what Magdalen had told him in confidence.

After he had come out of the house when he had said goodbye to her his horse had been ready and he had stuck to his plan of leaving immediately. But, once alone on the road he had begun to worry about his disloyalty to Iain, the man to whom he owed his life. Miles further on, just before he reached Spalding, he reined Nellie in and started off back to Thorney. Of course he should have told Iain, for it was only right that a father should know what happened to his daughter. It had been wrong to ride off without telling him. How had he done it? He reasoned that if he were in the same position as Iain he would definitely want to know.

But within half an hour he found himself slowing down on the straight track. How could he ignore the trust Magdalen had put in him? Poor girl. She had been so pathetic, so listless. His horse came to a halt and shook her bridle. He, Stuart, was the only person Magdalen had confided in and he was considering betraying her. He let Nellie munch the lush grass as he looked across Cowbit Wash.

Now that he was thinking about bringing Magdalen's pregnancy to an early end Iain kept on seeing clumps of tansy. Its big yellow flowers and strong green fronds seemed to present themselves to him every day as if drawing attention to themselves and what they were capable of. If – and only if, for he had not made any decision – he were to attempt to abort Magdalen's baby, it would have to be done in a way which could not be detected. He would have to prepare something for Magdalen to eat or drink which neither she nor anyone else would be aware of. This meant it would have to have a bland taste and texture and be capable of being mixed in with something else.

Tansy tea was both easy to prepare and likely to be effective. Only last year he had used a weak concoction to ease headaches and he had heard of it being mixed with honey to treat toothache. But the strength of tea he was now envisaging would be extremely dangerous. If several cups of it were to be drunk for a few consecutive days it would almost certainly lead to the loss of a child. But it might do worse for it could harm the mother and, if the pregnancy were by any chance to continue, the baby.

He needed time to think about this carefully. If only he did not have to decide such an important thing on his own. Every day that passed was a day lost, but this was not something to ask God about. Or was it? He had been praying for days that Magdalen would not be pregnant but could not bring himself to pray for the child to die.

Late evening, 17th June 1669, in the fens

The fens were beginning to weigh Stuart down. He wanted to get on to Boston and abroad. He couldn't continue to stand in the middle of nowhere under a clouded sky wondering what to do.

And what good would telling Iain do? Wouldn't it make him feel even worse? Wouldn't it make him think about Magdalen differently? That she was, in some sense, to blame? After all, that was what she herself said and certainly her story complicated matters. Surely it was better for Iain and Jenne to go on believing that she was Ridman's innocent victim?

Anyway, given what he had said to Iain about women, would Iain even believe what he said? He would be bound to think that he, Stuart, was trying to justify his own past actions by as good as proving to him how girls could be as unchaste as boys.

The more he thought about it the more he came to believe he was right not to tell Iain. Yes. He would stick to his original decision. He tugged at the reins, turned Nellie round and set off at a trot back up the road towards Spalding .

He regretted he had not been able to help Magdalen. She had been hoping he would do so, but he could never have answered those questions. When she had asked if she would have a baby and then what it would depend on, what could he have done but back away?

It had been hard to walk out of that room knowing she wanted him and needed him to stay, but the worst thing of all was when she sang that little verse. When he heard her thin voice he had not been able to look at her.

He urged Nellie to a canter. With luck he would be able to make up the two hours he had lost.

⚘ 18th June 1669, Boston

The following evening he was in a tavern in Boston, having been taken on by *Berschermer*, a ship which had just come from Leiden and was bound for Massachusetts. He had already taken his chest aboard and claimed his tiny space.

He called for another drink. The place was filling up with the crew of a ship which had landed only a couple of hours earlier and he gestured to several men to share his bench. He wanted some company but was determined not to spend all of the small profit the beaver pelt had earned him that afternoon. He had hardly made any money on it but had no desire to go to London now. What he needed was to get away as soon as possible.

A young man standing nearby started to down his drink too fast, and he remembered how he too used to drink like that. It didn't look as if he would remain on his feet for long.

Magdalen had loved Stuart's attention, his stories and his treasures. Perhaps she had even loved him with a child's love. And what he had felt was affection for the daughter of his friend made stronger because he seemed, quite by chance, to be the only person she would accept warmth from.

The men on his bench were discussing the problems with the outfalls. The young one who had been drinking fast was leaning against the end of the next table, had pushed up his sleeve and was now engrossed in picking at a scab.

"Quit doing that," said Stuart, "Or there'll be blood all down your arm and over the table."

The youth stopped at once. He looked across the tavern and then down at the table. Unlike his companions he seemed disinclined to talk. Stuart hoped there would be some music later. That would cheer things up.

"Sit down with us, will you? You'll fall over if you don't."

The men shunted along, causing the young man to be directly opposite Stuart. This was a pity, for everyone but him seemed to willing to make conversation. However, after a while he got up from the table and another man shifted sideways to take his place, and before long someone else pulled out a fiddle and soon everyone was thumping the table and singing.

Oh I thought I heard the Ol' Man say
Leave her, Johnny, leave her!
Tomorrow you will get your pay
And it's time for us to leave her!

At last it was time to go back to the ship. Gradually, the men got up and made their way to the door still in full voice.

The work was hard and the voyage was long
Leave her, Johnny, leave her!
The sea was high and the wind was strong
And it's time for us to leave her!

"Where's the boy?" called the man who had been sitting opposite Stuart.

"I'm over here."

"Come on, we're going."

Stuart watched the lad get up from a corner and make his way out after his companions. He was swaying and someone called out, "Daniel Ridman, I wager you won't reach the ship on your own two legs!"

Daniel Ridman. Stuart's head was a little fuddled, but not too fuddled to remember that name immediately. He got up quickly and went outside. The cool, quiet air sobered him at once.

What should he do? Indeed, what could he do? This was no place to grab the boy or find an officer to arrest him. No one would take any notice anyway because he himself was half-drunk, and if he caused a hullabaloo he might well find it was him who spent the night in a cell and then missed his ship.

Stuart followed Daniel as he limped his lopsided way along the quay. What exactly was he guilty of? If Magdalen herself did not think it was rape, surely no one else would. He recalled his own life as a young sailor, his own story. Did he want to be the cause of this young man, not so different from how he had once been, being sent to prison for years?

Daniel swayed his way to the edge of the hard and steadied himself against a bollard before stepping forward and peeing into the water. The other men had gone on ahead and there was no one else around.

No one would know. No one would ask any questions about a drunk man falling into the water and drowning for it often happened. Stuart thought of what Mathieu had said about Daniel, 'It's clear he wants Ridman dead.' All it would take was one little push.

As Daniel moved away from the bollard he stumbled over a rope and Stuart found himself stepping forward instinctively. But the boy recovered himself and set off along the quay. Stuart continued to follow him until he reached his ship's gangplank. He pulled himself up it slowly and unsteadily.

The strains of the song reached him again:

The sails is furled and our work is done
Leave her, Johnny, leave her!
And now ashore we'll have our fun
And it's time for us to leave her!

He turned and walked back to his own ship, *Berschermer*, where he slept an undisturbed sleep.

The next morning he rose in the dark and climbed up to the deck. The port was quiet, the water still. The air was full of smells: sisal, tar, urine, a spice he couldn't identify, sawn timber, oil, rotting fruit, dung. He noticed a big rat running along some rigging and a single rowing boat making its careful way between ships' hulls. Heaps of wooden boxes were waiting to be lifted and loaded; a man was coiling rope; several caged cockerels were starting to crow. As daylight came more men emerged from below decks and several women hurried away down gangplanks.

Now on his own territory again Stuart felt the pleasure of anticipation. For a minute he thought about Magdalen and the Deschamps. He remembered Daniel Ridman again and was relieved he had not pushed him. Did he really want to be responsible for killing a young man? No. It was best to let the boy move on and away from trouble. Anyway, there was no chance of finding him now for the quayside was already filling up.

When he had first gone to sea the great majority of passengers on ships going to Massachusetts had been Puritans. They had risked leaving home to escape persecution, but he had met some coming back after a year or two out there, complaining they had suffered discrimination from the very people they had gone to join. Those on this voyage were more likely to be seeking riches and, inconveniently, were the sort who would panic rather than pray if a storm arose. Religious passengers were nearly always the best ones, even if they sang too many hymns.

Only two hours until high tide. Then the Boston Stump would diminish with every mile as they left it behind and sailed for America.

☙ 23rd June 1669, Thorney

After a week Magdalen's spirits seemed to rise. She refused to be seen by a doctor but had more colour and was in less discomfort. Helen and Christian were told to keep out of her way, but Benjamin was too young to understand and liked to follow her around. Jenne held her breath as she watched him tug on Magdalen's gown or take up something she had put down. But Magdalen did not shout at him or even complain as she would have done in the past; she just moved or lifted him out of her way.

She spent most of her time with her grandmother. They would sit and talk a little about who had visited, or what Benjamin had done, but often they sat in silence.

"Are you bored, ma petite?"

"I don't really know. I'm just here with you."

"That's good, but we should find you something to do now you're recovering. I was hoping you might like to read to me. Jacob often does so, but at present he's too busy."

"I haven't read anything for a long time."

"That doesn't matter."

Magdalen fetched the Bible and a pile of papers from the window ledge. She searched for the two texts her grandmother wanted. One was Psalm 121 and one was a poem.

"Read the psalm first, please."

Magdalen read it out carefully.

"Thank you. Isn't it beautiful? It's one of my favourites. And now the poem. It's a long one but I only like the first verse so you needn't read it all."

Magdalen took the sheet of paper.

"Give me my scallop-shell of quiet,
My staff of faith to walk upon,
My scrip of joy, immortal diet,
My bottle of salvation,
My gown of glory, hope's true gage,
And thus I'll make my pilgrimage.

"Stuart gave me a scallop-shell but I liked the sewants best," said Magdalen. "I wonder if Stuart's heard the poem. He won't have read it because he can't read. Isn't that strange?"

"Most people can't read."

"But he's so clever! He doesn't know everything though. I asked him … I asked him … I asked him a question and he couldn't answer it."

Her grandmother asked, "What was the question?"

Magdalen did not reply.

"Was it something important?"

She nodded.

"Then why don't you ask me?"

She did not know what to do.

"Ask me, ma petite."

Magdalen returned the poem to the window-ledge and stood with her back to the room, her hands over her face.

"Can't you ask me?"

"No."

"Then I'll ask the question for you. It's 'Am I going to have a baby?'"

Magdalen said nothing.

Her grandmother spoke slowly. "The answer is that you might do, but no one can say yet. You won't know until you see if your courses stop or not. If they stop, it usually means you are pregnant. If they do not, it usually means you are not pregnant. But many things can happen between being with a man and having a baby."

Magdalen began to fret. "I don't want to be pregnant."

"Don't cry. Whatever happens you're going to be all right. We're all looking after you, and if you have a baby we will help you to look after it. But it would be a good idea to see a doctor."

"Why should I?" she said indignantly. "It isn't me who wants to see him, it's everyone else who wants him to look at me and I don't want to be looked at."

"He will make sure you are healing properly. You don't want to go on hurting, do you?"

Magdalen took her hands from her face and raised her head. "If I say yes, will you be there?"

"Of course. Can I tell your mother you'll see him?"

"All right."

"Good girl. Things will get better, you'll see."

24th June 1669, Thorney

Emily insisted that Mathieu made a full apology. He had made a wrong, a completely wrong assumption and Iain had every right to be angry.

"I can't believe you pulled her and pushed her and then said what you said."

"Emily, I've lived with Magdalen for her entire life. She's behaved in an appalling way since she was a little girl. She hates her sister and Jacob's boys, and she'll probably hate any children we have. She's surly and dangerous as well as being rude. I've seen her throw things at the wall, even at her mother."

"But that doesn't mean she would choose to … to lie down and … and be with that boy."

"I told you that when I saw her she certainly wasn't trying to get away."

"But you don't know what was happening. You only saw them for a split second."

"It was longer than that. It was several minutes at least."

"Several minutes?" repeated Emily vehemently, "Then why didn't you *do* something? Don't tell me you sat on your horse watching them."

"Of course I didn't."

"So what did you do?"

"Ridman ran off and I told Magdalen to follow me home at once or …."

"Or what?"

"Oh, I don't know. You can't expect me to remember every single word – and look," he held out his hand, "You can still see where she bit me. There's no denying it – she's wild."

"It was only yesterday." Emily huffed with annoyance. "You *can't* have been there for minutes."

"Well, it seemed like minutes."

"Mathieu, you can't really be sure what happened so it was wrong of you to say – even to think – that Magdalen had any choice in what was happening. She may be difficult, but she's not wicked. She would never have given herself to that boy willingly." Emily folded her arms firmly. "You must apologise to Iain at once."

Mathieu flared up at her. "Don't you start telling me what to do. Don't forget we're talking about my niece, not yours."

"I know." Emily put her hand on his shoulder and said in a quieter voice, "But I was hoping our marriage would pull our families closer together, not divide them."

Later that day Mathieu sought Iain out and found him examining the farm accounts. With some embarrassment, he apologised.

Iain made no sign that he accepted the apology and continued to look at the papers in front of him. Then he said, "Tell me what you saw."

Mathieu hesitated.

"Go on. Tell me. I want to know."

"They were on the ground. Ridman was half on, half off her. Her shift seemed to be open at the front and I could see her thighs, and he ... he was ...."

"He was what?"

"I think he was pushing ... pushing himself ....You know what I mean."

"Was she crying ?"

"She was quiet. And she was still, very still. When they saw me he was off like lightening but I was surprised how slowly she got to her feet."

"She was shocked and hurt, wasn't she? But that didn't occur to you, did it?"

"I couldn't tell, I didn't know quite what was going on."

"But that didn't stop you treating her like some ... like some loose little whore," said Iain bitterly. "For God's sake Mathieu, you're supposed to be – you are – her *uncle*."

He put his elbows on the table and held his head in his hands. After a minute he recovered himself and lent back in the chair, looking at Mathieu.

"Let me give you some advice. Think about things more carefully before you act or speak. I tell you this not just because of what's happened with you and Magdalen, but because I wish your marriage to be happy."

☙ July and August 1669, Thorney

It was a question of waiting. Magdalen had not yet started her courses and so could not tell if she had missed them. Her mother had said she would know whether or not she was pregnant in two months' time, though even then it might not be absolutely certain.

It was the very end of June, so she would have to wait through the thirty-one days of July and then through the next thirty-one days of August. Sixty-two days of not knowing. Sixty-two long days.

How did anyone know when their courses would first start? Nowadays she hardly saw the girls who used to be her friends, but she remembered a conversation a group of them had had a couple of years ago. One was sure you had courses on your fifteenth birthday and that they carried on every month until you were old. Another said they started when you first went courting, and another did not believe there were such things at all. Magdalen distinctly recalled her saying, "If it was true, then eventually you'd bleed to death, wouldn't you?"

But there was something else to think about. Punishment. It was obvious that God would punish her for having done the thing she had done with Daniel. Every prayer she had ever heard asked for the forgiveness of sins, and she began to worry more about sins. Was her sin worse than killing? It could be. Of course she might not get her punishment until she was dead but she doubted God would wait that long or else people who did wrong might think they could get away with things. On the other hand, perhaps it was worse to know your punishment was waiting for you and dread it all through your life.

No. She was sure He'd be planning something for her now. In fact, not knowing for sixty-two days felt like a punishment – as it did when the doctor had pushed his shaking fingers right inside her – but she knew she deserved worse.

She decided she should pray each morning and evening to ask for forgiveness. So twice a day she said the prayer she had composed: *Dear Lord, Please forgive me for what I did wrong. Please don't let me be pregnant. I promise I will not do that thing again. Please forgive me. Amen.*

One night it occurred to her that God's punishment might be to make her pregnant, but when she woke in the morning she decided He would not choose something so obviously connected with her sin. Her punishment would be something else. She had an idea of what it would be but tried to push it away whenever she thought about it which was very often. During these weeks of waiting she was thinking much more about her punishment than whether or not she would have a baby.

"Magdalen, why don't you let me teach you to embroider? I think you'd enjoy it."

"I couldn't do it. I'd get it wrong."

"It looks difficult at first, but it's not. Look, here's something I did for you. You could do a simple one like this."

And there was the word *Magdalen* and the date of her birth surrounded by a ring of celandines. She hadn't seen it for years, and suddenly found herself looking at it properly and liking it.

"When did you do it?"

"When you were little."

There were two more framed samplers on the walls, one with a prayer and berries, and one with a line from a psalm in a circle round an apple tree. Perhaps she could do something for Benjamin.

"I'd rather write words than sew them."

"You needn't do words. You could do a picture. Flowers, a fish, birds. Anything. You could make any picture you want and do a little bit every day."

Perhaps embroidering might make time pass more quickly – though was that what she wanted? Increasingly she was not sure what she wanted. While the expectation of her punishment had changed from being a sharp, frequent jab to an ever-present ache the other question was changing from 'Am I pregnant or not?' to 'What would it be like to have a baby?' They weren't the same thing at all. She needed time to think about both of these but of course every day through the sixty-two (though now it was only fifty-one) also meant she was a day nearer her punishment, so it was just as well if time passed slowly.

Another change taking place was that life was getting smaller. She was used to running outside and racing away from lessons down to the fen, but now she was living almost as if she was an invalid. Although it was fine weather she hardly went out of doors. Helen preferred to spend time with friends but Christian often approached Magdalen. She tolerated him but was annoyed by his constant scratching and took it upon herself to ensure he took every dose of every concoction which Iain prepared in the hope of ridding him of worms. She liked to carry Benjamin around and talk to any adult except Mathieu whom she refused to go near. For the first time she did the jobs she was asked to do without coercion, and was content to read to her grandmother. It felt to her as if although she was moving and seeing less she was thinking more.

Forty-eight days till the end of August. Forty-four. Forty. How strange to be waiting for blood like this. Somehow every day without it made its appearance both less and more likely. Each day made her world smaller, made her focus more on herself and her body.

"Do come outside for a little walk, ma petite," begged her grandmother. "You're all cooped up." So they walked down to the wind-engine and looked along the cut. A huge heron lifted itself up and flapped heavily across the fen.

They took a different way back to the Causeway and greeted a man they knew on the way. He was pleasant enough, but would he have shunned her if she was pregnant? If that happened she decided there and then she would stay at home for ever and would never go out. She didn't care if she had no friends.

Just as she was thinking this Mamie suddenly announced, "You should see your friends again. You need more than the family."

Thirty-six days. She had got through one half of the time and was still not certain if the fact that there was no blood was good or bad. If she had a baby, she would have a whole new person to think about and a purpose in her life. If she didn't, she would be left after all this time and all this upset with nothing. Except the punishment, of course, which there was still no sign of.

Iain was racked with indecision. He counted almost each hour of each day and prayed repeatedly that Magdalen's courses would come but swung between resolving to bring about a miscarriage and feeling himself go hot with guilt at even having thought of it. The idea of her having a bastard son by Ridman caused him anguish. He kept on running her life through his mind and identifying all the times when he might have intervened or done or not done something which would have stopped things from turning out the way they had.

"Don't go on grieving about the past," pleaded Jenne. "It may be that there is no baby, that it does not exist at all. But even if there is you can't deny she is much better than she was, and we should be nourishing her new spirit."

"I can't help it. I can't stop blaming myself and hating Ridman. I'll never accept his child as my grandchild."

He had given up wondering what Samuel would do in the situation, for Samuel was dead and gone. It was up to him.

◌✿ 3rd August 1669, Thorney

Time was running out and one day he woke up determined to reach a resolution for he couldn't go on changing his mind from one day to the next, one hour to the next. In struggling to decide he deliberately brought to mind once again the image of Magdalen and Daniel which caused him most pain, and by midday it had sent him out to gather pungent bunches of tansy.

It felt good to be getting on with something practical and down-to-earth after all that indecision, and as he cut the plants and pushed them into his bag he began to calculate what proportion of the tansy heads he should use to each pint of water, and how he would persuade Magdalen to drink it. Should he make her take two cups a day, or just one? Should he be giving it now, or should he wait until they were sure she was pregnant and so reduce the risk to Magdalen herself? And for how many consecutive days should he administer it? The fear that he could poison her with too great a quantity or strength of the herb ran like an undercurrent beneath the surface of his thoughts.

But it was the only course of action open to him. It felt better to prepare for the worst and assume she was pregnant than to go on hoping and praying that she was not. He kept telling himself that to induce the baby at this early stage was far kinder than leaving the pregnancy to take its course. For the first time he realised how uncaring he must have appeared in the past to those women who had been desperate to end their pregnancies but whom he had refused to help. And, quite separately, he suddenly remembered the time Jenne had lost her second baby. All those years ago it would have seemed impossible that either of them would ever forget it, but the pain had gradually faded and now he hardly ever thought of it. It had been terrible for them both, but life had gone on, hadn't it?

He just had to believe that what he was doing was for the best. For Magdalen's best and for the whole family's best. He was fairly confident that, given her recent more settled state, she would accept any herbal potion he offered if he explained why she should take it. This meant inventing a lie but the lie would mean that she and they would soon be through with all this.

After getting her to take the tansy tea he would have to wait a few days before he knew if it had worked, but he would be the only person who was waiting and he would just have to bear it. The hardest part, the very worst part of all, would be when she actually lost the baby, but the experience would be no different from what he and Jenne – and indeed many others – had gone through. It was bad but they would all survive it.

He arrived home, shook the bag out over a basin full of water and started to wash the tansy. The current of conscience inside him kept surfacing and asking, But what if Magdalen becomes ill? Or what if the baby lives and is damaged? He shoved the tansy round the basin fiercely, slopping water on to the floor.

"Why are you cross, Uncle Iain?"

Without Iain noticing, Christian had come up close to watch what he was doing.

"I'm not cross. I'm busy."

"You look cross." Christian climbed on a box to get a closer look. "What's that plant?"

"Tansy."

"What's it for?"

At that moment Alice and Helen came into the house from the yard carrying baskets of vegetables from the garden.

"Christian, come and help shell the peas."

"I love peas!" He jumped down from the box, took a handful of peapods and began to shell and eat them at once.

ᘓ 15th August 1669, Thorney

"She told me today she wants to embroider a wind-engine! Jacob is going to draw one for her," said Jenne.

"What difference can embroidery make?" asked Iain bitterly. "The fact is that if she does not have her courses in the next ten days we can be almost certain she is pregnant. We will know our daughter Magdalen is going to give birth to the child of an evil man."

Jenne answered slowly. "And if that happens we will do our best to ensure he or she is also the child of a girl who is capable of growing beyond her past."

She leaned forward and stroked Iain as he sat bent over the table holding his head in his hands. "Don't give up," she said. "Keep faith."

He raised his head slowly and then stood up. "Jacob and I are going to that meeting at Monsieur Frouchart's about the complaints. We'll be back late."

He kissed Jenne, left the room and went to the stables. He felt terrible hiding his plans from Jenne.

Jacob was already saddling up. He smiled at Iain. "I've got good news," he said.

"Just a minute. Keep it for when we're on our way." Iain lifted his saddle down from where it hung against the wall. His head was full of his plans.

If only he could tell Jenne about them, but he couldn't tell her he was going to do something wicked in order to achieve good. And even if he were to manage to do so, it would be impossible to admit there was also a small possibility of error whose effect might be unthinkably serious. He hurriedly tugged the picture of Magdalen and Daniel back into the front of his mind to bolster himself.

He reached up for the bridle. And Jacob said he had good news. What could it be? Not another baby, surely? There was nothing Jacob could say that would please him on this miserable afternoon, but he needed something – anything – to make him stop thinking about what he was intending to do.

Soon they were both on horseback and walking along the track. It was already autumn, already colder. The land looked heavy under a sky ready to rain.

"You know my painting of the Abbey Church?" said Jacob.

"The one you did recently?"

"Yes. Well, someone wants to buy it."

Iain looked at Jacob with interest. "Who?"

"A minister who was visiting from London saw me at my easel in the churchyard. He spoke to me about it and yesterday I received a letter saying he'd like to buy the painting and he'd also like one of Crowland Abbey."

"Well done! I hope you agreed on a good price."

"He's offered me more than I would ever dare ask."

"You're a lucky man, but you deserve it."

They rode on as the clouds rolled lower across the fenland.

"Do you believe people get what they deserve in life?" asked Iain.

"Why do you ask?"

"Because, on the whole, I don't think they do."

"You've got Ridman in mind, haven't you?"

"Yes."

"Isn't he an exception?" asked Jacob.

"I'm also thinking about your parents. They did – and your mother is still doing – their best. Throughout their lives they could not have done more. But nevertheless some things went wrong, and they didn't deserve that."

Jacob knew Iain was thinking of his own problems too but did not say so.

They slackened the reins and let the horses walk at their own steady pace while they proceeded in single file along a ditch-edge. Iain was very tempted to tell Jacob everything. But would Jacob understand, or would telling him cause him to risk losing the only chance he had of making things better?

When they were level again Jacob said, "I know what you need."

"What?"

"One of your own medicines."

Iain smiled and considered various herbs. "Viper's bugloss. That's what I'd prescribe myself if it were summer." He recalled the distinctive prickly stalk and leaves, the blue-violet flowers. As well as giving comfort to the heart it was supposed to protect anyone who took it against the poison of serpents. "Daniel Ridman was a viper. If only Magdalen could have taken some bugloss before he poisoned her."

"Iain, if you go on thinking like that you'll drive yourself mad."

The Frouchart's farm came into sight behind a few bare trees. Other riders were approaching from the east.

No. He couldn't tell Jacob. Although he was close to him this was something he had to do on his own. There was no getting away from it, what he was planning was a sin. He had been tempted to commit a sin and he was going to do it.

"You must concentrate on the future," said Jacob. "You must keep faith that things will be well."

"I pray you never have such troubles." Iain spurred his horse to a trot in a sudden moment of energy, turned round and called, "And to think I thought you were about to tell me Alice was pregnant again!"

"She is! I've been putting off telling you, but she is!"

As soon as Iain had congratulated Jacob he felt bad again. Two babies were to be born, one to a man who was almost his brother and one to his daughter. What sort of a man was he if he wanted his daughter's to die?

They continued to ride side by side as the rain began to fall.

And how had it never occurred to him throughout these desperate months to treat himself with herbs?

16th August 1669, Thorney

The next morning after another night of anxiety, he rose early and went to the Abbey churchyard. He made his way through the long wet grass to the place where his and Jenne's second child was buried. The carved words on the wooden cross were faint but he could read

Isaac
Born 15th December 1659, Died 15th December 1659

Isaac had been born too soon and too small. He and Jenne, despite having each other and being surrounded by goodwill and love, had taken many, many months to recover from his death.

Faced with the grave he found himself unable to conjure up the picture of Magdalen being pulled to the ground by Daniel. Instead, he recalled his own steps and Jenne's weeping as he carried the child's coffin to this exact place where he was standing. It had been one of the very worst days of their lives, and one which he had often said he would wish on no one.

But here he was, wishing it on his own daughter. He thought

of the crock of yellow tansy he had boiled up and left steeped in water with honey. It had been in the kitchen for two days and today he was due to reduce it slightly and make it into tea. He planned to give a cupful to Magdalen before she went to bed this very night. Yesterday he had been telling himself with some satisfaction that in twenty-four hours it would have begun to work to expel the unborn child if indeed there was one.

He and Jenne were separated from their son by death. Samuel was separated from his family by death, he was separated from his brother by death and from his parents by distance. No one had chosen such separations and deaths, but now he, Iain Alleyn, was planning to end a life, to separate his daughter from her child, and he and Jenne from their grandchild.

He made himself consider again the risk to which he would also be subjecting Magdalen and gradually he felt his resolve weakening, his whole body giving in. He went round to the front of the Abbey Church and in through the door. He found a seat and put his head in his hands. He wanted to pray but could not. His hands were shaking and he ached for peace of mind.

After a few minutes a voice said, "Bonjour, Monsieur," and Iain opened his eyes to see the pastor. He stood up and shook hands, but turned away when Ezekiel Danois looked him in the eyes because he felt so full of guilt.

"Monsieur Alleyn, I am sorry to see you troubled. Come and pray with me for a few minutes."

Iain did not resist as he followed the pastor to the front of the church and listened as the French prayers were chanted quietly. He felt unable to do anything but stand in silence and join in the final Amen.

"Would you like to sit and talk with me?"

"No thank you. I'm needed at home."

"Then I shall pray for you and bless you and your family. I know you are doing your best during this time of so much difficulty, but the scriptures can always help us." The two men walked back to the west door but just before they reached it the pastor said, "May I advise you to read the First Epistle of Peter? I find that in times of suffering it always encourages steadfastness and helps one to persevere."

He picked up an English Bible, handed it to Iain and walked back down the nave. Iain did not know the New Testament well but leafed through the pages until he found the First Epistle of Peter. He began to read but was in no state to take it in, so let his eye run down the page. A particular sentence in Chapter 5 jumped out at him:

Be sober, be vigilant; because your adversary the devil, as a roaring lion, walketh about, seeking whom he may devour.

He returned home immediately, took the crock of tansy liquid into the yard and began to tip it away. When it was nearly all gone he had second thoughts and pulled the crock towards him so it poured more slowly. He stopped when there was a little left in the bottom and transferred it into a cup which he took into the barn and pushed to the very back of the shelf. He knew himself well enough to know he might change his mind yet again. Then he came out again and washed the crock thoroughly.

"Uncle Iain, why did you tip that stuff away?"

"Christian! Where did you come from? You nearly made me jump out of my skin."

"Why did you throw it away?"

Iain picked up the crock to take it back inside. "I decided I didn't need it."

Christian waited until he was sure his uncle was well out of the way, then went into the barn and searched until he found the cup of liquid.

It tasted sweet and he drank all of it there and then.

☙ Five months later, December 1669, Thorney

By Christmas Magdalen was big. Her belly stuck out from her thin body and grew bigger each month. The baby was expected in February.

As soon as the sixty-two days had passed and it became known her courses had not appeared everyone except her father and Mathieu had cautiously started to say they wanted her to have a baby even though they had not said that earlier. All in all, although Magdalen began to notice unfamiliar changes in her body it was much better to know than not know. Somehow life began to feel more settled. She passed whole days without arguing, sulking or running out. She smiled more. She even began to hope that perhaps she was not going to be punished after all.

And here she was embroidering the sails of a wind-engine which Jacob had drawn for her. Christian was particularly interested in seeing it grow and she never complained about him watching her sew now because several months ago he had suddenly, by some small miracle, stopped wriggling and scratching at the back of his breeches.

At first she talked with Mère about patterns, stitches and threads, but gradually their conversation ranged further. They would speak of a neighbour, perhaps, or Magdalen might ask something about her grandfather. From time to time her father would appear at the door. She knew why he never stayed long but her grandmother assured her he would accept the baby when it came and she just had to be patient.

Jenne noticed a change in Iain and it gladdened her. He was eating and sleeping more now, and was better tempered. For some reason he was less negative about Magdalen and was starting to resume interest in his work. Jenne discussed these things with her mother and together they thanked God.

Winter had come suddenly and frozen everything hard, and it was made clear to Magdalen that she could not go out sliding and skating.

"It's not worth the risk," said Jenne to Emily and Mathieu. "She could fall and lose the baby."

Emily agreed, "Yes, it would be dangerous," and Mathieu nodded.

But later, when he was alone with Emily, Mathieu said, "It would solve a lot of problems if Magdalen lost the baby."

"Don't say that."

"She'd get over it and neither her future nor ours would be spoiled."

"Mathieu, how can you think such a thing?"

"Because any sensible person would."

"What if it were your – our – daughter?"

"No child of ours would ever be in that position, would she? But if she were, I'd say the same. How could such a child or its parents be happy? It would be far better if it were not born."

Emily stared at him. "That's a wicked, wicked thing to say."

"Hasn't it occurred to you that Iain might be thinking the same thing?"

"Mathieu, how could you? Iain tries to make people well. He would never, never cause harm to anyone – least of all his own daughter. Anyone can see he's worried sick about her."

1670

13th January 1670, Thorney

Even though Magdalen had come to want the baby it was disappointing to have to miss going out on the frozen fens. Last year she had been one of the two best girl skaters in Thorney and now Helen was using her skates and Christian was using Helen's. All the children in the village spent every minute they could out of doors. Just as she had done last year they only went to their homes when they wanted a meal or because it became too dark.

"They are so lucky to be out there while I'm stuck inside." Magdalen heard the clock ticking and Alice humming in the other room as she pulled the red thread through the fabric.

"I remember feeling left out like that when I was young," said Mère.

"Why couldn't you go out?"

"I was ill. I had just had my first fit."

"Tell me again about the falling sickness."

So Mère told her as she had told her and Helen before how she sometimes fell and jerked her limbs about. "No one knows why it happens, and I hate it when it does, but it's only happened six or seven times in my whole life so I try not to think about it. Anyway, the time I'm telling you about was during the Sunday service in the Abbey Church and I was made to stay in bed for weeks, or it seemed like weeks. Once I'd recovered I was very upset because Mathieu had promised to skate with me to Whittlesey Meer and he and Piere Roo went without me."

This was astonishing. "Uncle Mathieu and Monsieur Roo skated all that way?"

"Yes. And our parents wouldn't have allowed it, so we swore Jacob to secrecy!"

Could it be that Mère had done things she was not allowed to do? Magdalen put the end of a white silk in her mouth to wet it before threading it through the brass needle. It had never occurred to her that her mother would or could have been disobedient.

"Did you do anything else like that?"

"Jacob and I often went down to the fen when we weren't supposed to. That was after we had Bou-Bou."

"Bou-Bou?"

"The owl. Surely I've told you about the owl?"

Perhaps she had heard the story, but if so she had forgotten it. So her mother told her again, and finished with the last line she always used, "And then, sadly, one day we went into the barn and found him dead."

They sewed on in silence and Magdalen thought again about the falling sickness. She had a particular image of her mother's mouth open and drooling, calling out with sounds she had never heard before.

"I was frightened that time I saw you have a fit."

"It's always frightening for me too. Some people thought it happened because I had done something wrong and had the Devil in me."

Magdalen stopped stitching.

"I used to rack my brain for what I'd done. At first I thought I hadn't done anything bad, but then I thought perhaps I had done something without realising it, so I spent hours going over every detail to discover what it was."

"And what was it?"

"Nothing! I was only about your age, thirteen or fourteen, I think. Of course I hadn't done anything wrong at all. Only a very few children ever do bad things."

But Magdalen knew that she was one of those few and she lay awake that night going over all the bad things she had done. And now she was certain of what God was going to do: He would strike her with a fit of the falling sickness. It was a terrible punishment and it was as obvious a punishment as making her pregnant. She had been imagining different things: Benjamin having an accident or the house catching fire or that other awful thing she tried not to think about.

How different she was from her mother. Mère had been so good and she was so bad. Since finding out she was pregnant she had almost given up praying, but now she was angry at herself for letting things slide. Now she knew what was coming she would clearly have to pray harder. God might even decide to send a fit *and* make the other thing happen.

Dear Lord, Please forgive me for what I did wrong. I am very sorry I did something so bad. Please, please don't let me have falling fits. I promise I will never, ever do that thing again. I promise I will be good from now on. Please forgive me. Amen.

⟡ Morning, 14th January 1670, Thorney

The next day she made herself say the whole prayer through every time she saw her mother, even if it meant saying it three times in a row.

In less than twenty four hours her life had changed from being better than it had been for years to being bad again.

She buried herself in her sewing for she found that creating each stitch and gradually seeing the picture fill out with colour soothed her, but her fear made her go back into herself and she withdrew from Jenne.

When asked, "What is it, Magdalen? Is something the matter?" she shook her head and said nothing.

"Something's changed," said her grandmother. "Please tell me what it is."

"No."

"Are you worried about the birth?"

"No."

Magdalen had given almost no thought to the birth at all although she had a picture in her mind of the baby curled up inside her. It would come slithering out in a rush the way kittens or lambs did, covered in a thick wet skin. This might hurt, but pain was something she knew about. Pain could be dealt with there and then, not like a baby who would be there for ever or fits which she would suffer from all her life.

As the size of her stomach and breasts increased her life reduced further. It was shrinking to what she could see through the window frame, to the same few psalms she read aloud to her grandmother, to the tiny embroidery stitches she had learned. It sometimes seemed as if it might close down altogether and all that would be left of her would be a heap of clothes in the chair, but even that would be better than having fits which made you roll on the floor and gurgle.

❧ Evening, 14th January 1670, Thorney

She had refused the meal and was staring out of the window. They would be talking about her but she didn't care. Benjamin came running in and, suspecting they had sent him in the hope he might cheer her up, she sent him back so curtly that he cried.

She started to say her prayer, but what was the point? You only had to look around and see that praying didn't work. Even Grandmère said God did not always answer prayers.

Crying didn't help either. When she had felt as bad as this before she had run off to Daniel or to Stuart, but who was there to go to now? She was back to the bare, bald fact that she had known for ever: she was on her own.

She thought of the last two times she had seen Daniel. She thought of how she had lost the precious sewant, how he had made her tea. Their exchange of secrets, their exchange of blood. The knife with the broken blade. The cut.

The cut. It had felt so good. How could she have forgotten? Of course, that was the answer.

She waited until the meal was over then crept into the kitchen, surprising Alice who was still putting things away.

"Magdalen! Let me get you something to eat. Look, there's plenty of meat left over."

"May I have an apple? That's all I want."

"Choose one from the bowl. Not that one, it's got bad bits."

"I don't mind, I'll cut them out."

She took an apple and a knife back to where she had been

sitting. She would do it at night when she was in bed. Even thinking about it made her feel better.

So, when the house was quiet except for the murmur of conversation, she took the knife and held it against the top of her thigh. She had made sure this blade was clean but no one would know a cut was there whether it healed or not. It was too dark to see but she held the flat sides either side of the tip like a quill and pushed it gently to her knowing it was making a little dip in the warm skin. Then she put her other hand around the handle and pushed harder so the point went in. She felt immediate energy. She wound a cloth round her thigh and lay awake enjoying the sense of excitement until this gradually lessened and allowed her to get the best sleep she had had for a week.

24th January 1670, Thorney

She was tempted to do the same ten days later. She had promised herself not to do it again but it was hard to ignore the instant lift of spirits it gave. Surely once more wouldn't matter?

When her mother noticed Magdalen's bloodied nightdress she told her the baby would be born within hours, even though it was not expected until February. But it did not arrive, causing Jenne to become sick with worry and Iain to struggle once more against the temptation to hope that the baby might be lost. When this increased pressure within the household reached Magdalen she found herself wanting to make another cut. She told herself they were just nicks, just slight punctures made with the end of the blade.

One Monday things were too much to bear and she could not wait until night so went into the barn and settled herself on a pile of straw. She pulled her skirt up almost to her waist and saw for the first time in clear daylight what she had not seen in darkness – two red marks surrounded by a bluish bruise which spread across her left thigh. Holding the knife in her hand she hesitated. Where was the best place? Should she do it on the other leg?

At that moment the door opened and Jacob came in with a couple of spades. He dropped them as soon as he saw Magdalen.

"What on earth are you doing? Put that knife down."

He hurried over to her and she tugged her skirt down but he put his hand on hers and said gently, "Tell me. You must tell me what you have done."

She lifted her gown and showed him the cuts.

She was surprised to see him relax a little before he said, "Oh Magdalen, I thought… I thought you …."

What had he thought?

"Why did you do this?"

He wouldn't understand.

"How can you have done that, hurt yourself on purpose?"

"I don't know."

"You shouldn't do it."

She began to cry quietly and let herself be comforted by her favourite uncle, the uncle who liked her most.

He took her back into the house and to the future she was dreading.

⟶ 10th February 1670, Thorney

Then two weeks later, while the family were in church for Mathieu and Emily's wedding, Magdalen's travail began. She started to feel uncomfortable in the middle of the pastor's sermon.

"I want to sit down," she whispered to her grandmother, "My stomach is hurting as if I'd eaten something bad."

So Jenne took her home and called the birthing woman and by the time the service was over and everyone was home again she had just been given her tiny, new son.

"Dear child," Mamie said, "He looks just like Samuel."

But Magdalen was trying to tug the shawl off him.

"What are you doing?" asked Jenne. "Leave him as he is. He needs the shawl on."

"I want to see his feet. Please, please let me see his feet."

When they were uncovered she held each of them in turn and studied them.

"They're all right," she said. "They're how they should be, aren't they?"

"Of course they are. He's perfect. But what's the matter, ma petite? What on earth's the matter?"

Choked by tears Magdalen managed to say, "I thought he might be born lame."

"But why?"

"Because he … *he* … was lame."

"Oh, my poor darling," said Jenne. "To think you've been worrying about that through all these months."

They wrapped him up snugly again and Jenne rocked him.

"I'm glad he's born," said Magdalen, "Do you think Père will like him too?"

"I think he will. Yes. I'm certain he will."

Iain was in the middle of the wedding party trying to hide his feelings. He ought to have been sharing in the day's quiet celebrations with Mathieu and Emily and the two families, but he felt terrible. He had not yet brought himself to see the baby for he could not prevent himself from thinking that his intention, his appalling intention, had been to kill it. How could he go and see it while he felt such guilt? He also felt profound sadness for Magdalen, for Jenne and for himself. He was praying too that the last nine bad months would not send Jenne into another dark tunnel as she started on the task of caring for the baby which Magdalen would be unable to look after properly. He felt as if life had renewed its assault on him but he was not allowed to fight back.

Where had those steady years gone? Could such peaceful and productive times come again? He looked at Ann smiling at her new daughter-in-law. She was happy. They were both happy. When would his own optimism and energy return?

His friend Mark Le Pla approached. "Mes félicitations!" he said, extending his hand. Iain took it in bewilderment. He and Mark had already congratulated each other on the marriage of a Deschamps son to a Le Pla daughter, a marriage which pleased Ann and would have pleased Samuel because it bolstered both the Huguenot heritage and the long-standing friendship between their families.

"Your first grandson. May he bring you much joy."

When Iain made no response Monsieur Le Pla put his arm round his shoulder and steered him to a quiet corner. "No one would have chosen to become a grandfather under the circumstances you have had to endure. But do not forget God has sent this child to your family – indeed, from today he is also part of *my* family. Iain, I believe we should accept him with thanks."

He hadn't thought of it like that. He had thought of the baby as Daniel Ridman's rather than God's. Mark was an experienced and wise man whom Samuel had admired greatly. He was usually right and today Iain could not deny he was right again. The child was part of both their families.

"We should love him."

Iain knew this was true. He also felt himself stuck: he was reluctant to celebrate the birth himself yet reluctant to impose his negativity on the celebrations of others.

"If we love him others will do so too, won't they?"

Did he want to remain locked into and by his hopeless attitude? Surely he could do better than this?

"Thank you, Mark."

"C'est bien."

ᜂ 11th February 1670, Thorney

When Magdalen woke the following morning it took her a moment to remember that her baby had been born and was sleeping next to her in his crib. She leaned over to see him.

There lay her tiny child whose body had been growing in hers for months and for whom she now had to care. He amazed her. She got out of bed and picked him up. He was warm and pink and wonderful. She had never held anything so special and important. She loved him and repeated his name over and over again. She took him to the window and had to scratch the patterns of frost off the glass with her fingernail before she could see outside. The day was just emerging from darkness and snow still lay on the ground. She told the baby that this was his home and she pointed out the path which led to the fen, but he stayed asleep.

Later, her father came to see her.

He entered the room slowly and found her with the child in her arms. With his eyes he asked if he could hold him and she handed him over carefully. He gazed into the baby's face and then placed his finger under the little hand and lifted it.

"Look, he's holding on to me."

It was the first time Magdalen had seen her father weep and it made her feel both older and younger than him. She wanted to comfort him.

The baby kept his eyes shut and Iain said, "I like him."

When he waved his small, soft arm he looked up at Magdalen and smiled. Then he pouted his mouth into an O and poked out the tip of his tiny tongue.

"God is rewarding you. This boy is your reward."

"What for? Why would God reward me?"

"For the difficulties you have been through."

Magdalen started to reply but Iain interrupted her saying, "Let's think about him, not about us. He's the one who matters most." He passed him back. "And he's yours, isn't he? He'll always be yours."

"I'm going to call him Stuart because I liked Stuart. He was kind to me and I'll always remember him."

"Stuart Macpherson would be very pleased," said Iain leaning forward to stroke the baby. "And he's a Deschamps, isn't he?"

"So he'll be Stuart Deschamps."

As Iain stood there he felt an urge to give thanks to God for this child he had nearly missed and for forgiveness for the terrible thing he had planned and all but prayed for. So he knelt by the cot and said the Lord's Prayer as his mother had said it

Oor Father in Heiven hallowt be Thy Name,
Thy will be dune on the Yird as in Heiven

Magdalen stood with the baby, looking down at her father's bowed head and shoulders and listening to the unfamiliar words. Could it be possible that this little Stuart was a reward?

Forgie us the wrangs we hae wrocht,
as we hae forgien the wrangs we hae dree'd,
An say-us-na sairlie but sauf us frae the ill-ane.

No. It wasn't possible. It couldn't possibly be possible. Papa was wrong. There had been many times in her life when Magdalen had disagreed with him but this was the first time she knew him to be totally wrong. She had often wanted to prove to him that he was wrong but now that she was right, and right about something important, she found herself in a position where she could not speak the truth. But instead of feeling satisfaction at his being wrong, she felt rather as if something had been lost.

Iain stood up slowly. "I have a small present for the baby." He took his leather pouch from his pocket, felt inside it and brought out a blue-black stone.

"Papa! It's the sewant I lost! Where did you find it?"

"On the grass somewhere."

"But where?"

"I'm not sure now. Down by Jackwater, I think."

Magdalen let him place it in the cupped palm of her hand and tipped it gently from side to side. "I'll keep it safe for him until he's older."

᥊ Spring and summer 1670

Life settled down as spring approached. At first people were amazed how after having gone through such a terrible experience Magdalen seemed to begin to thrive. She was not predictable, and there were times when she reverted to yelling and answering back but gradually the bad days became less frequent. She and the baby fell into a steady routine which Benjamin, in particular, liked to be part of. He was usually tender with Stuart but would poke him from time to time and thus earn a fierce slap from Magdalen. The embroidered wind-engine was hung on the wall, and when Ester called to the house after a gap of over a year the two girls renewed their friendship. Iain and Jenne's spirits rose as the tension from the recent months fell away. Iain completed his herbal and it was talked about throughout the village.

Alice positively blossomed in her third pregnancy, and Jacob painted whenever his responsibilities on the farm allowed him to. He was doing sketches – he had already done two – of the stone crosses built to mark the extent of the land formerly owned by Thorney Abbey.

As soon as Christian and Helen had finished their lessons they went out searching for the first nests and the first frogspawn of the year. Mathieu moved to the Le Pla's farm where he and Emily began to adjust to life together. Ann, every day and twice a day, gave thanks for the restoration of her family's well-being and prayed that Magdalen's still fitful progress would eventually win through.

The farms round Thorney followed their well-established routines. The lodes, leams and rivers continued to flow but became more and more difficult to navigate. Wind-engines continued to be built even as an increasing number of complaints about them were lodged by farmers whose lands were flooded by their neighbours' engines.

A line like a thin rope continued to mark where the land met the sky.

PART III

1673

❧ Three years later, 1673

As time went on Magdalen's fear of the threat of falling sickness began to reduce though she continued to recite the prayer she had said throughout most of her pregnancy, especially the words: *Please, please don't let me have falling fits. I promise I will never, ever do that thing again.* If she kept her promise she would be safe, and it was only occasionally that she remembered the sickness might be there waiting to get her as Daniel had got her, when she was momentarily off her guard.

And although she could no longer recall Stuart Macpherson's face she had not forgotten him. She told her son of how Stuart had appeared from nowhere and became the best thing in her life for a few weeks until she had him, her own precious boy. As he grew she began to tell him all that the sailor Stuart had told her. She described becalming, making soundings, crossing the Equator. And she whispered into his ear that she loved him, she loved them both.

She was determined her son's life would not be limited to Thorney. She wanted him to be a sailor. She wanted him to explore.

And her own world was getting larger again. Through becoming a mother she learned far more than any schoolmaster could have taught her, and gradually she became increasingly able to thrive and grow. The family felt her to be a different daughter, sister and cousin than she had been before. Only Ann, while acknowledging that her grand-daughter's behaviour had changed, considered her to be the very same person she had always been.

When Jenne commented that she was herself again, Ann replied, "She's always been herself. All the way through. She's never been anyone else."

Magdalen began to visit Ester up on the Causeway, and came to know more people outside the family. Few avoided her. As well as looking after Stuart she could usually be relied on to do her share of the work around the house and farm and she agreed to take the decoction of fennel which Iain prepared to calm her.

Even before Stuart could speak she encouraged him to make his own tracks across both land and sea. She made him listen to accounts of where visitors had been and when merchants passed through she took him to find out what they were carrying, where they had brought the goods from and where they were taking them. She was determined that by the time he was six she would have succeeded in making him want to live his life anywhere but in the fens.

"I can't leave here," she told him, "But you can and you must."

᧒ Late 1673

When the thaw came the rivers and channels were sluggish with sediment instead of running free. By early April river levels were alarmingly similar to those usual in winter and the dyke-reeves organised rotas of watchers to patrol the most vulnerable banks.

Mathieu worked like a Trojan late into each night and thanked God that he and the Le Plas lived at Thorney. Even being ten feet higher than the surrounding fen meant they would always be safe. Emily and their young son Samuel were out of danger and so were all the others back in the old house.

Trouble came to Spalding first. It had been noted how the fen-lands to the south were sinking below the silt lands the rivers had to cross to reach the Wash. This meant that when heavy rains came the water could not be discharged to the north and so flowed backwards, and when the tides pushed in they could not get out again. One windy night the pressure collapsed a bank thus allowing the river it contained to empty itself on to pasture land.

At dawn grazing cows were found to have been swept off their feet and dumped half a furlong away. After the farmers had driven the remaining cattle on to the few dry slopes they hurried to see what had become of their new wheat. Acres of green tips were waving gently under a yard's depth of displaced dykewater. Sacks of corn and coleseed grown on land reclaimed a score of years earlier by Vermuyden's men sat as uselessly as sodden drunkards.

Crowland was the next to be drowned, and then, closer to home, parts of the north bank of Morton's Leam broke. The church bells rang out as people pulled children upstairs and climbed on to rooftops while boys led horses out of stables and gawped at the quantities of water gushing over the brinks.

As geese and ducks settled on the new lakes and lagoons some of those who were not marooned headed for Thorney where they were looked after by strangers. In the homes of their hosts the women comforted their children feeling simultaneously grateful and anxious and the men hurried back to the river to build cradges and shore up the gaping gaps.

The levels returned to normal within weeks but by then two skeletons had been found washed out of the dyke-walls and people started to speak of ghosts.

And then it was Wisbech's turn. Because of the way the land lay it was almost possible to plot where the next breach would occur but despite this few people were properly prepared and they waded through the waist-high water in their houses not knowing whether to curse or pray.

1674

Only a year after these drownings the west side of the great bank at Swavesey in the South Level was destroyed by floods. As a result ten labourers were set by the Bedford Level Corporation to cut and dig in the drain to repair it. After settling to their work a group of men approached shouting at them to stop work immediately, threatening that if they were not gone within the hour they would return, put up a gallows and hang both the bankers and their masters. The reason for their objection was their belief that if the banks were mended to prevent the excess water escaping it would flow back into the town and drown everyone.

The Corporation labourers, though shaken, were not interrupted again that day but someone took the trouble to obtain a warrant from the authorities to ensure they had permission to carry on. On Thursday they came back soon after dawn and continued working but a couple of hours later the Swavesey men returned in full force. They rushed forward and wrestled the barrows from the workers' hands, broke them and threw them in the river. When the warrant was read out they shouted it down saying they could get another from their own court which would be more lawful. They angrily accused the labourers of felony because they had stolen earth belonging to Swavesey.

"We haven't forgotten the gallows!" they yelled.

When Mr Pierson, the man in charge, told his men to carry on digging one of the Swavesey men forcibly grabbed a spade from a worker. Wielding the tool like a weapon he swore to kill anyone who dared to dig.

"If you do," he spat, "We'll kill you and fill the drain with your bodies."

The workers drew back but Mr Pierson ordered them to get hold of the remaining barrows and charge at the Swavesey men. They managed to shove one of them into the river and flung clods of earth at him as he tried to swim while his fellow townsmen continued to shout and yell.

Their leader swore that even if the workers brought ten thousand more with them, his men would attack them. He announced, "We would rather die on dry land than let you mend these banks. If the water can't escape, we'll be drowned."

Then the others vowed that if the labourers did not leave and take away every single thing they had brought with them, the men of Swavesey would make a bonfire of them and their houses.

Subpoenas were issued to those who had trespassed, requiring them to appear at Westminster on 3rd November.

News of these disasters and disturbances was passed throughout the fens from fowler to fisherman, from fisherman to boatman, from boatman to fowler.

One evening in December when Iain and Jenne were sitting by the fire Jenne said, "I've been thinking about something Père used to say when we were growing up. He said drainage could teach us about life."

"What did he mean?"

"That sometimes you have to check on what a family is doing just as you must check how the drainage is progressing. He said a family is like land which could be ruined so you must protect it and keep it in good repair."

"We try to do that," said Iain slowly. "But things happen which are too difficult. Take what's been happening in the fens. Most of what's gone wrong has been caused by the drainage but neither Vermuyden nor your father could have imagined that peat would shrink or that breaches would lead to more floods and to fights. Other engineers might have done it differently but that doesn't mean they would have done it better.

"And that's how it is with us, isn't it? Who could have known you would be ill or that Magdalen would have been as she was?"

"But we did our best, didn't we?" asked Jenne "You always, always do your best."

Iain gazed into the fire.

Jenne continued, "If Alice had been as I was how would she and Jacob have managed? What might Mathieu have done if his daughter suffered what Magdalen suffered? No one on this earth could have done more than you did.

"And some things turn out differently to what might be expected. Look at Magdalen. She's as she is now *because of* what went wrong. All I want for her now is that she finds a husband."

Iain said gently, "Just accept today as it is. Samuel was right in wanting to address what needed to be done, but sometimes it is also right to accept things as they are, even if they are not what we would choose. The boy is well and Magdalen is usually content, so we should be too. This life we have is enough."

They sat in silence watching the smoke.

"Iain, sometimes you are full of sadness."

"Yes."

"You weren't sad when I met you."

"I hadn't lived much life then."

"Have I made you unhappy?"

Iain took her hand. "Of course not. You know you make me happy, but sadness is part of life."

He got to his feet and held out his hand.

"Come to bed, my sweet Jenne. It's late."

1692

Seven years later, 1692

Marie was Jacob and Alice's third child. Brought up in a houseful of Deschamps cousins she became particularly close to Stuart who was only a matter of months older than her. When she was ten she began to have falling fits. They were usually over quickly, but they made her feel exhausted. The whole family rallied round and helped her recover, and Stuart was always impatient for her to be up and about again.

He liked to repeat to Marie the stories his mother told him and get her to illustrate them. Sometimes her idea of what he wanted drawn – such as an iceberg or a beaver – was quite different to his and they would appeal to Magdalen for the truth, and she would look at the sketches and say yes, this is how it should be or no, it is not like that. All of them knew Magdalen had not seen the things she was describing but what mattered was the way in which the stories held the three of them together.

When Stuart grew up and went away Marie thought about him for months but then accepted his absence and continued working and living in the house and farm with her mother and all the family. She was close to her aunt Magdalen and they would often sit in near silence, the one embroidering and the other drawing. Marie shared her father's liking for portraits, but she also became interested in birds and would take a stool down to the fen in summer and sit until a moorhen or grebe grew used to her and came close. "If I have a fit, I have a fit," she would say. "I would prefer to fall on the grass than on the road."

As she neared her twentieth birthday she became worried because few men approached her and none had asked for her hand in marriage. When she talked about this to Magdalen, Magdalen declared she had promised God she herself would never marry or lie with a man.

"But God wants people to marry," protested Marie, "And He blesses couples with children."

"In the end everyone has to live their lives on their own. And children are neither blessings nor curses. They are just what they are: flesh and blood formed from a particular act between a man and a woman – any man and any woman. They are neither rewards or punishments. They are just themselves."

After such conversations Marie would end up feeling distressed and go running to her mother for warmth and comfort, wondering if what they said about Magdalen was true – that she was not a real Deschamps.

One day when she was about twenty three she had a bad bout of the falling sickness. It was the worst sort of fit because it happened in public on the Causeway. Amongst those who stopped to help were some who stood and stared. She was taken home and put to bed and as she regained consciousness in the middle of the night she heard a steady, regular banging which she at first thought was her heart insisting that she stay alive. But then she realised it came from outside as if someone were beating on a door to be let in. She called out in fear and woke her aunt Helen who was asleep in a chair by the bedside. Marie asked her what the noise was but Helen said she could not hear anything and the disturbance must be in Marie's still fitful mind.

The next day was Sunday and when the family had gone to the Abbey Church Marie made herself get out of bed and go outside. She was sure the sound had been real and that she would find some sign of it. She looked round the yard and there, up above eye-level, was a newly-killed owl nailed by its wings to the barn door. Its head drooped, its claws hung loose. She stood weeping in the wet yard knowing someone had done this as a warning to keep the Devil inside her and away from them.

On his return her father Jacob knew what to do. He took her cold hand, led her back to bed and brought her pen, ink and paper. Then he un-nailed the owl, smoothed its torn feathers, and placed it close to her on a table.

When she was ready, she began to draw.

1696

⌖ Four years later, 1696

Stuart Deschamps was on a ship heading up the Hudson from New York to Albany. Seven bells of the last dog watch had just been struck and he was lying on his bunk smoking and wondering whether he should stay in America this time.

He had first gone to sea when he was fourteen. Because of his mother's encouragement he had been eager for his first voyage but had spent most of it cold, ill and homesick. When he arrived home in Thorney she turned him round and packed him off back to Lynne immediately, and since then he had stayed away. That was the last time he saw Marie.

His mother refused to say anything about his real father but Marie had told him he was a bad man who had left years ago. However, he always wondered about a man called Stuart whom he was named after although his mother insisted he had never been her husband and was not his father.

So here he was on his tenth or twelfth voyage, heading due north and thinking about the Dutch girl he had met a year ago. He tugged at the blue-black shell on a cord round his neck as he wondered whether she would be someone's else's sweetheart by now. And if not, did he want to marry her? And would she want to marry him?

After a short sleep he went on deck again. Green mountains shimmered in the clear sunlight. The Hudson stretched out smoothly all round the ship like ice. This was a place where water was water and land was land, where men could thrive without having to dry the ground first.

Yes, America was a better to live in than the fens. Whatever happened, he would stay.

1713

Samuel Deschamps was employed by the Bedford Level Corporation as his father Mathieu had been. He was the keeper at Denver Sluice, the most important sluice in the fens. Built years ago by men working for his grandfather, it was designed to control out-going river water and in-coming sea water but turned out to be a barrier to vessels because frequently it had to be closed. Such closures led not only to the flooding from inland water unable to escape but also to the tiresome unloading of ships and transfer of cargoes.

Samuel considered Denver Sluice as his inheritance and hoped to work there for the rest of his life. Despite the difficulties he was proud of his family's continuing involvement in maintaining a vital part of the drainage scheme.

1713 was a bad year. A wild winter was followed by vicious blows which roughened the surface of each dyke, wash and river. Every door of every hut and house admitted fine earth. Anyone using a sail, pole or oar swore as they struggled to keep their boats from being blown off course. Farmers waited for weeks to sow their seed if they did not want to see it whipped away by the wind.

And when the blows ceased they were replaced by rain so savage it appeared not to fall but to be driven into the ground.

For more than twenty-four hours Samuel watched the water levels intently, noting the slightest changes in height, the strength of the flow, the colour of the sky. He made his way to the south side and gazed out to where the Old Ouse was already leaking across the fields. Such spreading reduced pressure on the sluice but also ruined young crops, causing farmers as well as navigators to complain to the Corporation.

There was nothing more he could do but he had to stay and watch. Time and time again he inspected every beam, gate and pier and at each inspection he gave thanks to those who had built the structures so well. He studied the water carefully. Sometimes it was thick and viscous, sometimes loose and fluid, sometimes waxy. There were even more types of water than there were of wind.

But one evening, when he had just come inside to shelter from a gale, there was a tremendous roaring. He had never heard anything like it and thought at first it must be thunder. But the noise increased and changed, and he ran outside and saw the sluice gates had been forced off by the incoming tide and the timber posts and stone columns were being washed away. The water racing upstream was throwing up great chunks of masonry. This would cause vessels moored on the southern side to be wrecked, men drowned and acres inundated.

He was filled with sorrow. His grandfather and father had devoted so much of their lives to the fens and now their work was being destroyed before his very eyes. Would it all have to be done again?

GLOSSARY

Banker	A labourer whose job was to dig out watercourses and create firm banks of mud
Chain	A length of chain 22 yards long, used for measuring
Cloot	A dam which prevents water running backwards
Clough	A sluice with doors which, when open, enables water to escape from inside or, when shut, be kept outside
Colza	Coleseed, a brassica
Cradge	A temporary bank
Croome	To clean out culverts and drains
Drove	A wide pathway
Dydle	To cleanse a length of waterway by hauling out weed and silt
Dyke reeve	An officer appointed to ensure the good maintenance of dykes
Haar	Thick mist
Haffing	Clearing out grass and weed from waterways
Hassocking	Clearing turves off land in preparation for cultivation
Gad	A pole used for measuring length
Glaive	A long handled fork for catching eels
Grig	A long basket for catching eels
Leam	A thin watercourse
Lode	A fen drain
Meer	A mere or lake
Rodding	Clearing sediment and reeds from waterways
Quant	A long pole used for propelling boats
Sasse	A sluice designed to keep tidal water from flowing upstream
Turves	Sections of peat dug for fuel
Washes	Areas of land onto which excess water overflows

THE THORNEY SOCIETY

The Thorney Society is a registered charity (no. 298235) which works to educate people about the history and geography of the parish of Thorney in northwest Cambridgeshire. It operates Thorney Heritage Museum which welcomes visitors from all over the world, and issues a newsletter for members.

If you have any enquiries about the history, buildings or families of Thorney, please contact the Society's secretary at:

Thorney Heritage Museum
The Tankyard, Station Road, Thorney, Peterborough PE6 0SE

www.thorney-museum.org.uk

OTHER NOVELS BY TESSA WEST
www.tessawest.co.uk

The Estuary

RAF officers Susan and Mark and a young ferryman, Robert, steer their different ways through work, friendships, families and aloneness. Susan is trying to focus on her career, while Mark's priority is Susan. The death of Susan's father throws the couple's romantic and family relationships into different perspectives as Robert ploughs on across the river, questioning his feelings about his absent family and his ability to be independent.

On January 31st 1953 the disastrous East Coast floods change the shape of the estuary overnight. The ensuing devastation brings new challenges, new opportunities, new decisions.

The Reed Flute

After long, separate journeys, an Iraqi grandfather and his granddaughter arrive in England. They live with a relation in Great Yarmouth but find their new circumstances confusing and uncertain, causing the girl to take drastic action. In Norwich a widower is trying to build himself a new life, and his bird watching and oboe playing become routes to unexpected meetings and events.

The Reed Flute vividly depicts a winter journey upstream along the bank of the Yare in which the three main characters are nourished as much by the slow river and the subtle beauty of Broadland as by memory, hope and faith.